Loretta's

and other stories

Earlyworks Press Fiction

Loretta's Parrot
and other stories

Earlyworks Press Fiction

ISBN 978-1-906451-14-1

Published by Earlyworks Press
Creative Media Centre
45 Robertson St, Hastings
Sussex TN34 1HL

Printed by the MPG Books Group in the UK

Cover Art

Artist and illustrator Catherine Edmunds has provided the cover art for a number of Earlyworks Press and Circaidy Gregory Press publications, including her own poetry collection, *wormwood, earth and honey*. Her illustrations – featuring exploding dogs, baboons in electric chairs, quills inserted into veins, and rotting toads – can be seen in Daniel Abelman's *ALLAKAZZAM!* (BeWrite Books), *Night Falls on Everyone* (Readme Publishing) and the shortly to be released *Anomalous Appetites* (Editor John Irvine). She is also in demand as a portrait artist, as she resists the temptation to make her sitters' heads explode or melt.

www.earlyworkspress.co.uk

Contents

Loretta's Parrot

by

Ronnie Nixon

Loretta Banks woke with a stinker of a hangover. She crawled out of bed still wearing yesterday's clothes.

The events of previous evening slowly came back to her: the pub after work . . . the guy who sat at the table uninvited . . . the guy chatting her up . . . Julie and Colin leaving after three or four drinks . . . the guy walking her back at closing time . . . inviting him up for a drink . . . the crude drunken pass . . .

What the hell happened after that?

Blank.

Loretta went into the kitchen, put on the kettle and snapped up the blind – her hand shot up to shade her eyes from the unexpected glare, it must have been snowing most of the night. She made a mug of strong coffee and padded through to the front room. When she opened the door an icy blast of air met her. One of the bay windows was wide open.

So was Bukowski's cage.

*

In a tenement flat – less than a mile away as the parrot flies – James Crilley was woken by a high-pitched squawking sound followed by a sharp, rapid tapping noise. He rolled onto his side and listened. Nothing. He rolled back. The squawking and the tapping resumed more clearly:

Rat-a-tat-tat . . . '*Stick 'em up!*' Rat-a-tat-tat . . . '*Goddamit!*' Rat-a-tat-tat . . . '*Stick 'em right up in the air buddy!*' Rat-a-tat-tat…

James got out of bed, went over to the window and very slowly parted the curtains. On the window ledge was a stunning multicoloured bird, dusted with snow, framed by a pale blue winter sky.

'I said stick 'em up, wiseguy!' Rat-a-tat-tat . . . *'God save Armenia!'* Rat-a-tat-tat . . . *'Get your goddam thumb outta your goddam asshole!'* Rat-a-tat-tat . . .

James stood there transfixed, scratching his balls and staring at the parrot.

*

'Something wrong Loretta?' said Julie when Loretta arrived almost an hour late at the bookshop. 'You look awful.'

'Jeez, Julie. I've got the mother and father of a hangover. That guy in the pub last night was a real jerk. He walked me home. I stupidly asked him up for a drink, thought he was okay at first. Then he started slobbering all over me, grabbed my tits without a how d'ya do! I must've told him to beat it. That's the last I remember. Next thing I'm waking up still dressed, go into the front room – the dirty sonofabitch has let Bukowski out! Look Julie, if it's okay, can I have the rest of today off? I've gotta go look for the parrot.'

'Christ, Loretta! Are you off your bloody head? When you said you were going straight home once you'd finished your drink I didn't think you were going to take that arsehole with you!' Julie could see Loretta was near to tears. 'Look, on you go. If Evans comes in I'll tell him you got the curse that bad I had to send you home.'

'Thanks Julie. You're a doll.'

'Never mind that. Get out of here before the wee bugger appears.'

Loretta walked back to the flat via the park.

She loved Glasgow. The crazy hotchpotch of buildings and architectural styles; the different atmosphere of the tenements; the sudden breathtaking views of countryside; the straightforward friendliness of the people; the dinky "Clockwork Orange" subway system. After New York the scale of the place delighted her. But by the time she got home all it was giving her was a severe pain in her neck from scanning every tree and building that she'd passed. She went straight to the computer and printed off dozens of posters: LOST PARROT – £50 REWARD; there was a picture of Bukowski and a contact phone number. She went around the west end and the city centre taping them onto lampposts and bus shelters.

*

James very carefully opened the window. The parrot hopped onto the back of his hand and gave it a sharp peck that drew blood. With the bird still balanced on his bleeding hand, he lowered himself gently onto the edge of his bed.

'My, you're a handsome fellow. What's your name?'

'What's your name! What'syourname! Bukowski! Bukowski! The boy stood on the burning deck – Asshole! . . . Could murder a goddam drink! . . . Bukowski's a fucking genius!'

'Well, Bukowski, pleased to meet you. I'm James. I'll get you something to drink.'

James shut the window, made sure his bedroom door was properly closed, and, so as not to disturb Bobby, his flatmate, who was watching morning television, tiptoed through the hall to the kitchen. He got a saucer from the pile of unwashed crockery in the sink, gave it a wipe on his t-shirt, poured in some water and carried it through to the desk in the corner of his bedroom. 'There you go Bukowski.' James sat on his bed sucking his parrot wound, watching Bukowski's head bobbing up and down as he drank.

The parrot finished the water.

'Flames rolled on, he would not go – Cocksucker! . . . Horse's ass! Horse's ass! Could eat a goddam horse's ass!'

James tiptoed back to the kitchen.

*

'Still no sign of Bukowski?' Julie asked, shuddering slightly: the mere thought of feathered things flying anywhere near her, particularly indoors, was enough to make her flesh creep.

'Nope. Been three days now. Nuthin. Christ, Julie, I really miss that bird. What with the weather and all he's probably stone dead by now' – Loretta put on a silly English voice – 'deceased . . . an ex-parrot . . . gone to join the bleedin' choir invisible . . . Shit! It's not funny. Oh Julie!' Loretta put her head on Julie's shoulder and bawled.

'C'mon, Loretta,' said Julie, putting a comforting arm around her and patting her back. 'You never know, maybe someone's taken him in.' She fished a crumpled handkerchief out of her skirt pocket and stuffed it in Loretta's hand.

Loretta wiped her eyes and blew her nose loudly.

A bemused customer, who had been standing at the counter for quite some time, staring at his shoes, eventually plucked up the courage to speak. 'Excuse me ladies, sorry to interrupt, but do you happen to have a copy of *Mockingbird Wish Me Luck,* by Charles Bukowski? Can't see it on the shelf.'

Loretta fled to the toilet.

*

A few days after Bukowski's arrival James was walking up Byres Road when his eye caught sight of a familiar looking image lying in the gutter beside a bus shelter. He bent down, picked up a battered, slightly soggy poster and smoothed it out on the side of the shelter. There was no mistaking the picture on it. Bukowski. He stuffed the poster into his jacket pocket.

He realized now who the parrot was referring to when he said: '*Loretta loves Bukowski! Nuts, Loretta! Gimme my goddam nuts you gorgeous slut!*'

He walked back home, very slowly.

James' flatmate, Bobby, had been staying with him since he got discharged from the psychiatric hospital where they'd met five years ago. The two men got on remarkably well. For instance, Bobby never commented on the fact that James hardly ever ate in the flat, never sat in the living room or watched TV, and could often go for weeks on end without speaking. Nor did he say anything about the loud, sometimes violent conversations James conducted with himself in his bedroom.

On the other hand, James never questioned the fact that every so often Bobby would – be it for an hour, or a day, or a week – suddenly stop being Bobby Ewen, the monosyllabic couch potato, and become Father Patrick O'Malley, the garrulous man of the cloth.

Bobby came out of the kitchen and almost collided with James in the hall.

'Ah. Er . . . James, my son. I know you rarely eat in the house, but do you know where my grub's disappearing to?'

'Yes. Sorry, Bobby, I've been taking it. I'll buy you more.'

'Y'know James, theft is a sin, a venial one perhaps, but a sin nonetheless. And you should address me as Father O'Malley, my name's not Bobby,' said Bobby smiling indulgently and making the sign of the cross before continuing, 'Are you eating the stuff raw, my son? My recent inventory of kitchen supplies suggests that two sausages, a rasher of bacon, half a hamburger, a chicken drumstick and a bunch of grapes have gone the way of the five loaves and the two wee fishes. But alas, I seem to have missed the multitudes passing through and scoffing them. What's going on James?'

'I've got a bird Bob – sorry, Father O'Malley.'

'You've got a bird! Congratulations my boy! If you're thinking of tying the knot give us a shout. Ah, God forgive me, I've always admired big lassies with healthy appetites. Do you take my rations round to her place and cook them there, then?'

'No. He's in my room.'

'*He's* . . . ? Did you say, *he*? You mean, *she's* in your room.'

'No. I mean, he. He's a parrot, called Bukowski. Sorry about the grub.'

'You've got a parrot in your room! And there was me thinking you were just talking to yourself in a particularly strange voice. God bless you and your flighty friend. My old mate Saint Francis would've been very proud of you.'

'Thank you, Father.'

'Might I see the feathered wonder?'

'Sure. Have you any sausages left?'

*

'Been getting weirdo calls on my mobile these last few days, Julie. Whoever it is hangs up when I answer, and if I don't they never leave a message. Tried ringing it back, but no dice, never answers. Getting a bit spooky.'

The shop door opened.

'Look busy,' said Julie. 'There's Evans just come in.'

'Let's go get bombed after work,' whispered Loretta.

'You're on,' said Julie.

They were on their third drink when Loretta's mobile went off. She looked at the number. 'It's that creepy caller again, Julie.'

'Just switch it off. Report it to the phone company, they can maybe block it.'

'I'm gonna give the bastard a mouthful first.' Loretta pressed accept. 'Listen, asshole! Stick your goddamn mobile where the sun don't shine you creepy sonofa – '

A voice broke in.

'Er . . . would you be Bukowski's owner? And is your name Loretta?'

' . . . Oh my God! Yes! I'm Bukowski's owner! You found the poster. You've got him? You've got Bukowski? Is he okay . . . *please*, tell me he's okay?'

'Yes. Bukowski's very well.'

'Oh, thank God. What d'you want? Why haven't you answered before? If it's more money you want I'll give it you . . . Just let me have my bird back. How the hell – Sorry! Didn't mean to be rude. Don't hang up! How do you know my name? I didn't put a name on the poster.'

'Bukowski talks about you a lot. Look, I want you to get your parrot back but I've grown very fond of him. To tell you the truth, I need him.'

'I can appreciate that you've got to like Bukowski, but what do you mean, you need him?'

'It's hard to explain. I just do.'

'Are you telling me I can't have him back? C'mon . . . what's your name by the way?'

'James.'

'Look James, I love that bird. Please give him back. I'll give you enough money to buy your own parrot.'

'It's not that simple. In fact, I want to buy him off you.'

'He's not for sale, James.'

'He's not yours to sell at the moment,' James pointed out.

'He is mine! You've parrotnapped him!'

'I did not. He landed on my window ledge and hopped into my room.'

'Jeez, I don't believe this.'

'Give me your address and I'll send you a thousand pounds. I've got the money.'

'A grand! Are you nuts? I don't want the money. I want Bukowski!'

'I'd let you visit him.'

'Godsakes! I'm in the middle of a parrot custody battle with some guy I've never even clapped eyes on!'

'I'll give you a thousand and you can come and see him any time you want.'

'Listen James, we've got to meet and talk this through, it's no good over the phone.'

'Er . . . okay. What's your address? I'll come and see you tomorrow.'

'I'm not trying to be awkward, but I live on my own. I'd feel happier if we met at my work.' Loretta told him the name and address of the bookshop.

'That's fine. How will I know which one you are?'

'I'll be wearing a name badge that says Loretta on it. I'm usually working on the ground floor. If you can make it for around midday I can take my break then. By the way – '

Loretta's phone went dead.

The next morning they were sorting through a batch of paperbacks. 'Do you think he'll show up?' asked Julie.

'Dunno, took him a week to talk on his phone. He's gotta be a total screwball. He'll probably show up six months from now, look me over and walk out of the store without a word.'

'He's obviously got money. Maybe he's an eccentric millionaire,' said Julie with a wild gleam in her eyes. 'He might look like Tom Cruise . . . fall madly in love with you – love at first sight! He'll take you away to a castle in the highlands and you, him and Bukowski will live happily ever after.'

'Yeah? Only thing is I'm not into smarmy midgets. On the other hand, if he looks like Brad Pitt I'll let him ravish me on the store floor in front of Evans and the customers. Anyway, it's a safe bet this guy's an ugly asshole with no life. I mean, he said he needs Bukowski. What's that all about? The guy's bananas.'

'You sure about going for lunch with him, Loretta? Might be safer staying in the store, talk to him here.'

'What happens if it ends up in a shouting match? Or more likely, me attacking him? Na, be better if we discuss this somewhere neutral. I'll be all right. There was a mad molester on the loose when I was at Columbia. They ran self-defence courses for the female students. It was the only class I came top of.'

Later that morning, after replacing some books, Loretta checked her watch for the third time. Evans came over to her. 'Miss Banks, if you stop staring at the door for a minute you'll observe that there are two customers waiting to pay at your cash point.'

'Oh! Sorry, Mr Evans. Not with it this morning.' She scurried over and dealt with the customers. She looked at her watch again: 11.58.

Just after twelve a man came in and stood in the middle of the shop. Loretta glared at him. He was about early-thirties, average height, quite good-looking in a dishevelled sort of way. His eyes met Loretta's, which, by now, were boring into him. He went up to the counter, checked her name badge. He put his hand out. 'Hello. I'm James.'

She stared at his hand and eventually shook it. 'Lemme get my coat.'

They went to a pub near the bookshop where the staff knew her and Julie well. James went to the bar to order the drinks and Loretta found them a table.

'Okay James,' Loretta said as soon as he sat down. 'What's the deal? Do I get Bukowski back or not?'

'Are you a fan of Charles Bukowski? He's one of my favourite writers.'

'Yeah, he's brilliant! Well, some of his stuff is amazing, some of it is just mad alcohol fuelled misogynistic ravings. He's best when – ' Loretta stopped dead: she couldn't believe it; she felt a hot flush rising to her cheeks. She was beginning to feel strangely disorientated by this guy. 'Just wait a god damn minute, James. We're not here to talk about Bukowski. I mean, we are, but not – '

'That's fine then,' James broke in, 'we won't talk about him. Do you like Kelman's stuff? *The Busconductor Hines* is – '

Loretta broke in this time, 'Very good, James. Nice one.' He was really beginning to piss her off now. Her voice went up an octave. 'Now let's talk about getting the *parrot* Bukowski, returned to his rightful owner. And that's me pal!' she yelled.

Davie the barman stopped serving. The pub went silent. Customers turned round to look.

'You okay, Loretta?' Davie shouted over.

'Yeah, yeah. I'm all right, Davie.'

'Sorry, I didn't mean to upset you,' James said. 'There are reasons I need to keep Bukowski. Please take the money. I'll double it if you want. And I told you before you can come and visit him anytime you like.'

'Screw the money,' Loretta said keeping her voice to a vicious whisper. 'I want the bird back. You must be a reasonable guy to go to the trouble of contacting me, why can't you be a really reasonable guy and return what's rightly mine. Get yourself another parrot, you can obviously afford to buy a whole goddamn jungle full of them.'

'Actually, it's debatable that anyone can *own* a living creature,' James said evenly. 'You can buy them, but that doesn't mean you own them. Think back to your country. The people that bought slaves thought they owned them too. Were they right?'

'Jesus H. Christ! You are one exasperating son of a bitch, James.'

'I'm only trying to be fair. Bukowski decided to leave your house and come and live in mine. I didn't force him.'

Loretta, with a supreme effort of will, managed not to scream. She said through clenched teeth, 'Bukowski was thrown outta the window of my house by a drunken lecherous asshole. He did not go of his own free will! What's so important that you need him? He's just a parrot.'

'Don't ask me why, it's too hard to explain. But my life's been changed since he arrived, and if he leaves . . . ' James shrugged his shoulders.

Something was bothering Loretta, she could swear she'd seen his face somewhere before. 'What is it you do, James? What was your life like before Bukowski arrived?'

'To use a phrase from your country, I'm in recovery. And it's all down to Bukowski.'

'Recovery from what?'

'I've been unwell. Now I'm getting better.'

'I'm sure I've seen your face someplace before. You ever stayed in New York?'

'No. Never.'

'This is nuts. Watch my coat James, I have to go to the ladies.'

When Loretta returned James, and her coat, had gone.

'The lousy bastard. The dirty. Rotten. Lousy bastard!'

Davie the barman came over with her coat. 'That bloke you were with said sorry, he had to leave urgently. You okay, hen?'

'Yeah. I'm okay, Davie. Thanks.'

Loretta walked back to the bookshop. She put her hand in the pocket of her coat and felt something bulky. It was an envelope containing twenty £100 notes.

Two weeks passed. She heard nothing more from James. She'd tried phoning him, but his number was unobtainable.

*

One Sunday night Loretta got round to sorting out a trunk load of stuff she'd eventually had shipped over from the States. She came across a book that had been a present from a boyfriend when she was in her final year at high school. The minute she saw the title a loud bell went off in her head. Her stomach did a backflip. She knew what she was going to find when she opened it: there it was, on the inside back cover of the book, a photograph of James. He looked in his mid-twenties, fresh faced, quite good-looking in a dishevelled sort of way. There was a short blurb underneath the photograph:

James Crilley was born and brought up in one of the roughest housing schemes in the east end of Glasgow. His best selling debut novel 'God Has Just Left The Building*' is a searing indictment of the injustices and brutality endemic to that part of the city. The author works and lives in Glasgow.*

She flicked to the front of the book and looked at the print history: it was published eight years ago. She went to the computer, fired in his name and that of the publisher. It was listed: she clicked on it. There was the same picture and blurb, with the added information that since the book was published it had won a major literary award; James had been listed, the following year, as one of the UK's top twenty young writers. The film rights to the novel had been purchased by a major Hollywood studio for a very large, but undisclosed, sum. There was no other information. Loretta opened a bottle of wine and composed an e-mail to his publishers:

I have read and very much admired 'God Has Just Left The Building' by James Crilley. I am a student on the Creative Writing Course at Columbia University in New York. I'm doing a project on Scottish

writers and would very much like to include Mr Crilley in it. Can you advise me of any other published work by him? I am in Glasgow at the moment and would be very grateful if you could supply me with an address or a contact number so I can get in touch with Mr Crilley.
Regards,
Loretta Banks

Two days later Loretta received a reply from the publishers:

Dear Ms Banks
We received your e-mail regarding James Crilley. Mr Crilley, to our regret, has produced no other work since his first novel was published. As it was at the time reported in the press, I am not betraying any confidences when I tell you that Mr Crilley had a breakdown a year or so after the publication of his book, resulting in him spending a period in hospital. We have tried, unsuccessfully, to get in touch with him in the past but we no longer have any contact with him, nor know of his current whereabouts. Sorry that we cannot be of any more help.
Good luck with your project.

Loretta picked up *God Has Just Left The Building* and looked again at the photograph. She remembered when she'd originally read the book how she had often flicked to the back cover – particularly after she'd read an insightful or moving passage – and studied the author's picture. Unlike most books, where she'd have been hard put to remember anything much about it a week later, this was one of those novels that stayed with her a long time after reading it.

She sat down in her armchair, intending to glance through a few pages. It was four-thirty in the morning when she read the last sentence. Her eyes closed, the book fell into her lap. She dreamt of herself, James and Bukowski on a golden sun-drenched beach in the middle of a burned out, derelict housing estate in the east end of Glasgow.

*

James lay back on his bed – Bukowski perched contentedly on his forehead – and reflected on how his life had changed with the bird's arrival. He realized he felt protective and caring towards something for the first time in many years. He found the bird's chatter made him laugh – another sensation he had not experienced in a long time. It slowly dawned on him: the voices that used to routinely torment his head, if not entirely gone, were taking a lot of time off – almost as if Bukowski had taken them over by some weird osmosis. And he had started to write again. This, however, did not stop him occasionally feeling guilty for depriving the attractive American girl in the bookshop of Bukowski. When this happened he couldn't continue writing. He racked his brains for a solution. The money, he knew, did not compensate her for the loss of the parrot. He often thought of going to see her, try and reason with her again. In fact he had gone to the bookshop on several occasions, glanced in the window, got cold feet and walked on by.

*

Loretta decided to use some of the money – blood money she called it – to try and trace James. She got out the Yellow Pages and looked under Detective Agencies.

The next day she was ushered into an office on the top floor of a dilapidated tenement several blocks away from her work. The girl stopped chewing her gum long enough to announce, 'Here's your twelve-thirty, Mr McDowell.'

'Thank you, Sharon.'

McDowell gestured to Loretta, 'Take a seat Miss Banks.' He was a large, balding man in his early fifties with a good-humoured florid face and a nose that looked like it would glow in the dark. Loretta smelled mint, garlic and the faint aroma of whisky wafting over from his desk. She thought about saying she'd made a mistake and leaving, but, despite appearances, there was something reassuring about McDowell.

She sat down.

'Miss Banks. What can I do for you?'

She told him that she wanted to trace a missing person. McDowell listened carefully, took a few notes.

'So, Miss Banks, you want me to trace a Mr James Crilley. You're fairly certain he stays in Glasgow, but is not listed in the phone book. You have also tried to trace him through his publisher, but they have had no contact with him for several years since he suffered a breakdown. Can you give me a description of Mr Crilley?'

Loretta produced the novel and pointed to the photograph on the back cover.

'That's the guy about eight or nine years ago. He looks much the same now.'

'So you've seen him recently?'

'Yeah. I saw him a couple of weeks ago.'

McDowell picked the book up off his desk. 'Och. I remember this! Got it out of the library ages ago – cracking good read. May I ask why you want to trace Mr Crilley? Errant boyfriend? Libel? Slander? Owes you money . . . ?'

'He stole my parrot . . . well, no, that's unfair. My parrot escaped and he has it. But he won't return it.'

'Hmm, a parrot. I see . . .' McDowell scratched his head and squinted up at the ceiling. 'If you met him recently and you know he's got your parrot, how come you don't know where he lives? And how did you discover he had your bird in the first place?'

Loretta explained about the poster, the long delay before James talked to her on the phone, the abortive meeting and the money.

'Two grand!' McDowell whistled softly. 'So it's the parrot you want to retrieve, if I can trace Mr Crilley. And if I do find him, do you think he's going to have a sudden change of mind and simply hand the parrot over?'

'You try and find him Mr McDowell – I'll handle it from there,' Loretta said with a look that left him in no doubt that she would do just that.

A few days later she got a call from McDowell. He had tried all the usual channels without success. Advised her that he could keep looking, but thought that she'd be wasting her money. He would send his bill.

*

A couple of months passed. Winter was melting into spring. Loretta had more or less given up on finding James or getting Bukowski back. She even thought of buying another parrot, but that smacked of giving in to James and somehow betraying Bukowski. She hadn't given up all hope.

Loretta and Julie finished a long hard day in the bookshop.

Julie was going to meet her boyfriend for a drink. 'Sure you don't want to come for one, Loretta?'

'Na, on you go Julie, my feet are killing me. I'm going to go home and lie in a hot bath with a glass of wine.'

'Okay, see you tomorrow.'

'Night, Julie.'

Loretta's mobile went off just as she was about to go into the subway station.

'Hello. Miss Banks?'

'Yeah. Who's this?'

'It's Mr McDowell. I've got some information about Mr Crilley.'

'You've what! That's great Mr McDowell. D'you want to give me . . . hang on I'll get a – '

McDowell interrupted. 'Miss Banks, I think we should arrange a meeting at my office.'

'How's that? Can't you just give me his address over the phone?'

'I didn't say I had his address. Look, come to my office tomorrow. I need to talk to you.'

'What's up, is he the mad axe murderer or something?' Loretta laughed nervously when McDowell did not immediately reply. 'Are you in your office just now Mr McDowell?'

'As a matter of fact I am.'

'I've just finished work. Thursday's a late night. I'm only a few blocks away. I could come up and see you?'

'I've got a better idea, do you know the Horseshoe Bar?'

'Yeah, I'm five minutes walk from it.'

'I'll be there before you, Miss Banks.'

When Loretta got into the Horseshoe McDowell was already propping up the bar, draining a pint of Guinness. He ordered another for himself and a drink for Loretta. They found a table.

'So what's the news, Mr McDowell?'

'I bumped into an old acquaintance of mine this afternoon, used to be a nurse in a high security mental hospital, retired now. We somehow got onto the subject of Crilley's book. Turns out he was a patient when my friend worked there. Got to know each other very well. Crilley was eventually released under supervision. Have you any idea what he did to get locked up?'

'Never really thought about it. All the publisher said was that he had some sort of breakdown. Not exactly unknown amongst writers,' Loretta said giving McDowell a quizzical look. 'What did he do? He's not dangerous?'

'That's why I wanted to talk to you. Hard to say. But he's certainly capable of being extremely unstable. And there's his background.' McDowell downed half his pint of Guinness in one gulp before continuing, 'Does this ring any bells? The father was a work-shy, dope smoking, chronic alcoholic prone to sudden violence. The mother was a nervous wreck with a Valium dependency. The eldest brother, a vicious psychopath, was locked up for armed robbery and attempted murder. The sister, once a runner-up in a Miss Scotland beauty competition, made a fortune pimping high-class call girls to businessmen, media people and assorted celebrities visiting Glasgow and Edinburgh. The youngest brother was a crack and heroin addict dying of Aids.'

'Sure. They're all characters out of *God Has Just Left The Building.*'

'They are – given a few minor embellishments, and one hell of a lot of toning down – James Crilley's real family, Miss Banks.'

'Jesus. They must have gone nuts when they read his book?'

'Not exactly. His father was dead by then. His younger brother – the Aids junkie in the book – was actually one of his older brothers in real life. He sawed his dad's head off with a rusty bread knife when he came home one night, found his mother beaten senseless on the kitchen floor, and his father lying in a drunken stupor across the kitchen table. James came down for his cornflakes in the morning, slid in a pool of congealing blood and inadvertently booted his old man's head across the kitchen floor. The brother managed to OD on some dodgy heroin while he was on remand in Barlinnie. The other brother, the eldest one, who was indeed a vicious psychopath doing time for armed robbery and attempted murder, was found later the same year hanging from a shower rail in the jail; nothing was proved, but they didn't think it was suicide. The mother is still alive. Doesn't know whether it's Christmas day or Pancake Tuesday. And the sister is now a tax exile in the Isle of Man. James was actually the youngest in the family and was half way through his third year in secondary school when all this happened. He was only fifteen. Taken into care. Wrote his book about ten years later.' McDowell swallowed the last of his Guinness, 'Fancy another drink, Miss Banks?'

'Christ. Make it a double.'

McDowell returned and put the drinks on the table. 'What concerns me, Miss Banks, is that you might find out Crilley's whereabouts, and you can't tell what his reaction would be if you provoked him. Look, he gave you the money, why don't you just forget about the parrot?'

Loretta ignored the question. 'You still haven't told me what Crilley did to get put away?'

McDowell raised an eyebrow and shook his head. 'He was apprehended on the roof of the City Chambers, dressed in combat gear, waving a machine gun about, and yelling at the rapidly gathering crowd below that he was going to save the planet from the forces of evil.'

Loretta stared at McDowell. 'Had he joined some sort of army or something?'

'Nope. The voices told him what to do.'

'How'd they get him down off the roof of the City Chambers if he had a goddamn machine gun with him?'

'He was very, very lucky. The police SWAT team that were despatched to remove him from the roof – by whatever means possible – realized what they were dealing with when they told him over the loudhailer to drop his weapon and put his hands on his head. He shouted back that he needed his hands free and more batteries for his machine gun if he was going to save the planet. The marksman that was just about to shoot him, saw through his telescopic sight that he was removing a couple of triple-A batteries from, what was on closer inspection, a toy machine gun. He was jailed then sectioned. Was in for three years. My pal, the nurse, and Crilley left the place about the same time.'

'And you don't know his address? Your pal couldn't find that out?'

McDowall slammed his drink on the table and glowered at her. 'For heaven sakes, lassie! You're not still determined to get your damn parrot back after all I've told you? And no, I wouldn't ask my pal to find out where he lived, even if he could! You're messing with a certified nutter. Just let the matter drop, will you?'

'I don't believe Crilley is dangerous. And I still want my parrot back,' Loretta said with that determined look McDowell was getting used to. 'How much do I owe you for your time, Mr McDowell?'

'God! You're a stubborn . . . ' McDowell shook his head in defeat. 'Get me a pint of Guinness and a large Bell's, and we'll call it quits.'

Loretta brought the drinks over. 'Thanks, McDowell. You're a good guy,' she said and left the pub.

*

They were just finishing their morning break.

'For God's sake, Loretta, forget about the sodding parrot,' said Julie. 'McDowell's right. There's probably no chance of getting him back now. Anyway, better get a move on. Evans is in one of his "I-Am-God-Almighty" moods this morning. I'll buy you a curry after work, how does that sound?'

Loretta banged down her cup and opened her mouth. Julie gave her a warning stare. She shook her head and sighed deeply. 'Yeah, curry sounds good, Julie.'

She was in the middle of serving a customer when something made her glance over at the door. She couldn't believe her eyes. James was standing outside the shop, tugging at his chin with his thumb and forefinger and staring down at the pavement. She froze for a split second, then – to the customer's utter amazement – vaulted over the counter yelling at the top of her voice, 'James! James! Stay right there James!' She raced through the shop dodging bemused customers – suddenly Evans leapt into her path and held up his hand like a traffic policeman – without hesitation Loretta lowered her head and delivered a shoulder charge any American footballer would have been proud of – Evans went flying backwards into a display of books that had taken most of the previous day to set up. James, looking up from the pavement, saw a demented Loretta just about to reach the door. He started running down the street, weaving in and out of the crowds. Loretta shot through the doorway and sprinted after him. James glanced over his shoulder – she was gaining on him – he turned just in time to see a large, grey haired woman in a bulky ankle length overcoat stepping out of Marks and Spencers – they crashed to the ground in a writhing heap. Loretta arrived and immediately dived on top of them. The woman was screaming blue murder, frantically trying to get out from under them. Two passing policemen waded in and broke up what they took to be the vicious mugging of a defenceless old lady.

*

'So let me get this right,' said the desk sergeant. 'You, Miss Banks, were chasing this gentleman, Mr Crilley, down the street because he stole your parrot a couple of months ago?'

'That's correct, officer,' Loretta said, giving James a murderous look.

He turned to James. 'And you, sir, were trying to escape this lady's hostile advances.' He pointed to Loretta with his pen. 'When you collided with Miss MacPherson here?'

'That's right, sergeant.'

'And you, Miss MacPherson – nice to see you back again by the way – had half of Marks and Sparks spring collection up your jumper when Mr Crilley and Miss Banks landed on top of you?'

Miss MacPherson, without the overcoat, the stolen goods and the grey wig, was a tall, skinny, surly blonde woman in her late thirties. She glared defiantly at James and Loretta and then at the desk sergeant.

'Ah'm sayin nuthin withoot a lawyer.'

'Okay Willie,' the sergeant said to one of the constables, 'take Miss Weightwatcher of the year to the interview room and book her.' He fixed his gaze on Loretta and James. 'You two could either be charged with breach of the peace or given an award for a citizen's arrest. But, under the circumstances, I'll let you both get on your way. We'll be in touch if we need you. And Miss Banks . . . '

'Yes officer?'

'If you assault Mr Crilley once you're out of here, you will be sharing a cell with Miss MacPherson before you can say *Who's a pretty Polly!* Got that?'

'Yes sergeant.'

When they got out of the police station they were both shaken. James said, 'Don't know about you, but I could do with a drink.'

Loretta, tight-lipped, gave him a threatening look. 'Is Bukowski okay?'

'He's fine, he's doing great. I was about to come into the shop and talk to you about him when you . . . Anyway, I'm not thinking, you must have to get back to your work. We could maybe have that drink some other time?'

Work! Loretta had entirely forgotten about her work – the image of Evans spread-eagled amongst the wrecked display in the shop came vividly back to her. She started giggling, then laughing loudly. James stared at her, wondering if she'd flipped. She eventually drew a breath and said, 'Oh no you don't, buster! You're not going to disappear this time. For one thing, I know your address, heard you telling the cop, and for two, I almost certainly don't have a job anymore. You can take me for that drink, then you're going to take me back to your place to see good old Bukowski.'

James grinned widely and said, 'Actually I've got a favour to ask you, I'll tell you about it in the pub.'

'Can't wait to hear what that could be,' Loretta said. She suddenly thought about Julie in the shop, imagining James doing all sorts of horrible things to her. Without meaning to she said out loud, 'She probably thinks I'm floating face down in the Clyde by now.'

'Sorry?' said a baffled James, 'What was that?'

'Nothing. Nothing James, I was just talking to myself. Listen, we need to go back to the shop first, get my things, see my friend Julie, and tell my boss to jam his job up his skinny ass before he has the chance to fire me.'

'No problem. I'd like to see that.'

James hailed a passing taxi.

Evans had been taken to hospital – a broken collarbone – but not before he'd given Julie strict instructions to dismiss Loretta when she returned.

'Loretta!' Julie screamed with relief when Loretta walked into the shop. They threw their arms round each other and hugged. Julie stepped back, a furious look on her face. She put one hand on her hip, wagged her finger at Loretta with the other and said, 'You! Miss Banks. Are fired!' She burst out laughing. 'And I, Miss Banks, have just resigned! Only Evans doesn't know it yet. I'll take great pleasure in telling the odious wee nyaff in person when he gets back from the hospital. You are okay, Loretta?' Julie glared over at James who was leaning against one of the cash points with his arms folded, looking highly amused.

'Yeah, I'm great.' She squeezed Julie's arm. 'Honest, Julie, he's fine, there's nothing to worry about. I'm going for a drink with him and then he's taking me to see Bukowski. I'll call you later.'

Julie didn't look convinced. She walked over to James, poked him hard in the chest with her index finger, leaned over and whispered in his ear, in her finest Glaswegian, 'Mess her aboot again, pal, and you're fucking deid – got it!?'

James quickly unfolded his arms, stood up straight and nodded his head several times.

'Hope youse two are going to behave yourselves,' joked Davie the barman as he passed Loretta their drinks.

'No worries Davie, we won't frighten the customers this time.' Loretta took the drinks over to the table. 'Right James, I'm dying to know. What's this favour you're going to ask me?'

James told her he had written the first two chapters of a new novel and had been in touch with his publishers. Needless to say the publishers were delighted. Not only that, the well known movie director who had persuaded the Hollywood studio to option *God Has Just Left The Building* all those years ago, had got the go-ahead, at last, to make the movie, and he wanted James to go over to Hollywood for a few months to collaborate on the screenplay. The favour was to take back Bukowski and, if it was alright with her, let him visit the bird now and again when he returned. They had one more drink to celebrate the arrangement before heading off to get Bukowksi.

*

At the same time as James and Loretta were having their drinks in the pub, Bobby, James' flatmate, was having another one of his Father O'Malley moments. He clearly heard the voice of a Franciscan friar speaking to him: the monk was reciting the special prayer to the animals *The Blessing of Pets*. Father O'Malley was so moved by the simple beauty of this sacrament that he decided the notoriously profane Bukowski would benefit no end from a bit of the same.

It is customary to conduct *The Blessing of Pets* outdoors; as the prayer is offered, the pet is usually gently sprinkled with holy water. He got Bukowski into his cage and took him down to the backcourt. All was going well until Father O'Malley got to the sprinkly bit:

. . . You called forth the fish in the sea, birds in the air and animals on the land. You inspired St. Francis to call all of them his brothers and sisters. We ask you to bless this . . .

He opened Bukowski's cage and tipped half a mug of freezing cold tap water over his head.

As he watched the outraged parrot sail over the roof of the tenement opposite, Father O'Malley heard the distant strains of Bukowski's voice float down to him one last time:

'Goddam asshole!'

Peter's Testimony

by

Elisabeth Weir

Tuesday afternoon, two fifteen, an angel appears late into tutorial (The Sienese School: Simone Martini's "Annunciation". How appropriate!). The door gives its signal whine. I look at my watch in standard reproof, but instantly drop it so entire is my fascination. She's skinny, all limbs; a new born foal whose elegance is just unfurling. She takes her time, slowly infusing the room with her presence as she looks for a seat near the back. I watch her – perhaps my mouth is open – and I think how love is a gift from nowhere. How little I'd expected it: this appointment with destiny! She looks up and waits for me to restart. I hadn't realised I'd stopped speaking, but the shuffling of feet and shifting of chairs tell me that I have. I ask for her name, tick it off my list, not knowing then, but perhaps suspecting, that Alison Aherne is going to change my life forever.

I spend two terms holding back. This contract they've given me is on a year to year basis and I've another while yet to finish my Ph.D: I can't afford complications. Besides, watching Alison from afar brings its own pleasure. There's something abstract and perfect about my infatuation; I don't expect to act on it. Instead, I allow myself teasers. I watch as her gangly gait is replaced with a sense of poise and self-possession. I wait and, gradually, her clumsy, provocative questioning (why are there no women artists? Why are all women depicted as objects?) develops into a more reflective reasoning and understanding. By the end of Hilary she's holding her ground well in class discussions. She isn't fazed by the academic authority banked up against her simplistic line of arguing. I never for one moment question her mental stability. Not for one millisecond of a moment – at least not then – she's a little edgy perhaps, but that's all, and isn't that half the attraction? When finally, we do become lovers, I begin to have my doubts, but still it doesn't stop me. I'm a goner by then of course.

I'm in the stationery section in Easons. I spot her and my heart does its usual back flip. She's ahead of me in the queue buying folders, switching her weight from foot to foot, obviously impatient. I know straight away something is going to happen; am aware of another energy present besides my own excitement. The girl on checkout tots up the goods, takes the money from Alison and bags the folders. She rises up out of her seat and motions to a security guard over by the escalator.

'They're inside her jacket' she whispers; gleeful and loud enough for all to hear. Alison clutches the bag to her chest but doesn't move.

'Open your jacket please, Miss.' The badge on the security guard's jumper is held on by a safety pin. He looks bored, impossible to impress.

'I will not!' Neither the tone, nor the response strike me as that of an innocent person.

'Let's not make a show, Miss.' He performs the lines without irony, and taking hold of her elbow, he pulls her out of the queue. The girl at the cashier desk continues on with the next customer, a prim smile on her lips. I drop the pile of envelopes I was buying onto a shelf. My heart is pumping hard. After so long keeping a professional distance, this moment feels dangerously intimate, if not a little bizarre.

'Alison?'

'Mr Lorenzoni!'

'Peter. Is everything okay?'

Alison pulls away from the guard. 'Unhand me, fiend!' She slips her arm through mine. 'Just peachy, Peter' The guard, shocked out of complacency, gapes in mock horror. He looks back to the cashier desk for affirmation. The girl nods her head, points to her chest. Alison, meanwhile, is dragging me towards the escalator. 'So, fancy meeting you here!'

'Excuse me – Miss!' The guard is tagging after us now like a dog who has sniffed a bone and it is being taken away from him. 'You have to pay for everything, Miss!'

'You can't touch her! You've no right to touch her!' I glare back at him and he withdraws his outstretched hand.

'I've been dying to talk to you, Peter – what you were saying about Caravaggio yesterday. It was amazing!' I had taken my group to see *The Taking of Christ* at the National Gallery. Alison is smiling like we are still strolling back to Trinity. I remember now how beautiful she looked in a blue scarf that emphasised the gold of her hair.

'Alison, whatever it is, you can't walk out with it. Pay at the checkout at the exit.'

'Relax, Peter. The only thing I'm walking out with is you.'

'Miss! I'm watching you, Miss.'

'So, what do you think Caravaggio would be painting if he were alive today? Or would he be painting at all? Maybe he'd be a film director…you know, like Pedro Almodovar!'

'Alison!' Right there in front of me, the guard and anyone interested, she is casually opening her jacket and taking out two paintbrushes from her inside pocket.

'Lend me a fiver, would you.'

What's a man to do? I take out my wallet, give her some money. Alison saunters over to another cashier desk and waits in line to pay. The security guard stands next to her, arms folded, seething indignity. Alison ignores him. After she pays, she takes my arm again and together we walk out; from the gloom of indoor lighting to the glare of a clear April morning.

'He'd be brilliant of course whatever he'd be doing. Though I wish – for painting's sake – he'd still be painting. But what? Do you think there's anything left to paint?' Her golden hair is suffused with sunlight and she's smiling now; part maiden, part minx – it's hard to say which is more. Either way my heart is taken. 'What do you think he'd be painting, Peter?'

'He'd probably be painting you, Alison.'

'You're different.' She says, her eyes squinting, her head held sideways.

'How?'

'You're more… real. Not like you are in college.' I'm lost actually. I lift my shoulders. 'I can't do that,' she says.

'What?'

'Wear different faces. Be a different person in different situations.

'It's called working. You'll find out soon enough.'
'I'm never going to work like that.'
'No?'
'No. I'm going to be a painter.'

Later, she tells me she knew that I'd been watching her; that my desire for her was like a force-field, pulling her in – she would die and I would die if we did not close the distance. If it was wrong, then it was the world was wrong, not us. We become accomplices in love.

Slowly my world contracts to a mini universe where Alison and I are the only inhabitants. I avoid all outside contact. I turn down invitations for dinner. I ignore messages left on my phone. I'm impatient to get away from my students. It's not that I don't like these people any more; it's just that the moment always comes when I look at them and think: but you're not Alison. And I have to go to her, to reassure myself that she is real – that she is not someone I've dreamed up, because a part of me is always uncertain round Alison. I tell her that I love her and she says,

'Why do you love me, Peter?'
'Because you're you.'
'And who is that?'
'You – Alison Aherne!'
'Never heard of her.' And then she laughs, and lets me kiss her.

She comes with me to Italy. She wants to get away from her family she says. I tell her she doesn't need an excuse to go to Italy. I've arranged to meet Professor Gentile before he leaves for his summer house in the Maremma. For over a year now, I've been trying to gain access to documentation in the Bellini family archives. Obviously my creaking Italian isn't hitting the correct level of charm to insinuate myself into the Marchesa's favour. Not one reply to over twenty written requests! Gentile has aristocratic connections of his own; has the necessary *conoscenze* as they say over there. We are to meet at the institute in Florence in June, and meanwhile he will oil some wheels. Alison is debating whether or not to continue with her Degree in Art History. She's painting all the time now; hardly ever opens her course books. When she asks me what I think, I tell her she has the skill of a true artist.

'Yes, but do I have the soul?' her eyes wide, almost fearful, challenge my presumptions. I tell her it is up to her whether or not to switch to Art College, but from having been so certain when we first met, now she needs constant guidance.

'How can you not know these things yourself, Alison?' I've known from day one my path would be an academic one.

'How can you always be so sure of yourself, Peter?' She does that a lot: pits my inability to understand her against her inability to understand me. Is it this constant wondering that makes us stare at one another with such particular intensity? A lot of the time that's what our love feels like; like wonder, or fascination: not understanding who the other is. When she tells her family she wants to drop out of university, they go crazy; give her a really hard time about it. Italy will be the perfect antidote I tell her. She can paint all she likes there. No one will cast a shadow over her dreams. We plan to go just as soon as I finish correcting exam papers.

The night before we leave, we have our first argument. We go out for a meal and as we are leaving the restaurant, we bump into the Dean of Arts and his wife. When I stop to chat to them, Alison completely ignores them; starts tapping her foot.

'You were such a phoney,' she says to me afterwards. I honestly don't know what she's talking about. I had merely made some polite small talk and then parted company from them.

'For Heaven's sake, Alison! This is my job – I have to get on with these people.' It amazes me how blind she is to some things. Our situation is still a little delicate as far as work is concerned.

'Well, I don't like him. His eyes are cruel and his wife looks servile. Probably spends her whole life washing his clothes and cooking his dinners.'

'Oh, Alison, why do you have to be so absolutely yourself all the time?' Then she starts ranting: saying that if I don't love her, I should just leave her. I'm astounded she should say this, also how hysterical she's getting; so much so, I decide to drop the argument. I put my arms around her and hold her till she forgives me. It's a little strange but there's no time to analyse things; the next day we leave for Italy.

My mother phones around the relatives, gets me this amazing farmhouse up in the mountains outside Florence. Some second cousin once removed owns it. Alison can't believe I have relations dotted around Tuscany; that there are other people connected to me here, that I could be walking past them in the street and wouldn't even know it. Perhaps it's something to do with her being adopted she says, but it seems to fascinate her – the easy way I take my place in the world. That's the way she puts it: 'You can take your place for granted. I have to make it up.'

For a while, things are perfect. We have the farmhouse to ourselves and the only other houses around are derelict, their occupants long since departed for work in the cities. We have everything we need and nothing more: bed, sink, cooker, running water. A little shop in the village sells bread, cheese, cold meats and wine. Saturdays, we go to the market to buy fresh fruit and vegetables. There's a primal simplicity to our set-up and we spend those early weeks like children; free from worry and responsibility.

The lushness of the hills is a surprise to Alison; she had expected some sort of scorched earth wasteland. There's a small lake nearby and, when the heat becomes intense, we walk down to it and go for a swim. A cat starts to pay us court; a pathetic looking creature who is slowly lured in by Alison's persistent persuasion and his own growing state of starvation. I'm worried the hunters will get him but I don't say this to Alison. Some lessons I decide to leave to chance.

Most mornings we set off down the track to the village two miles away – Alison with her sketchpad and pencils, me with my books and notes. We sit in the bar drinking coffee, and listen to the locals starting up their day. The bus comes at half past eight or thereabouts. The good Professor Gentile has spoken to some colleagues and has lined up work for me teaching English in this private school near the Piazza Repubblica. It's all basic level stuff after teaching in Trinity but the money is handy. After a couple of weeks I manage to get a few hours teaching for Alison as well. She's nervous at first but the Italians love her of course, for all her oddities, or perhaps because of them. She doesn't bother with grammar or vocabulary work though. Instead, she talks to them. Whenever I go to meet her, she is still chatting to them a good twenty minutes after classes should have ended.

We spend the afternoons visiting galleries, studying close-up those paintings we discussed back in class. Trinity seems so far away now. Seeing her sheer delight, her gathering awe, is as much a pleasure for me as it is for her.

'I can't believe it!' she keeps saying. 'Pinch me – this isn't real!' The extravagance of beauty is almost too much for her to bear. It needs containing – balancing by contrast. She wants to know where all the poor people live. Where is the graffiti? The litter? The crime? It's probably there, but we don't find it.

'Truth, not beauty! Remember Caravaggio!' she says one day, staring those dark eyes back at mine and I'm not sure if she's talking about Art or life.

Maybe that's why she decides to create something ugly herself. She goes into these black moods where I feel her drifting away from me –as though there were some cliff edge towards which she is pathologically drawn. I have to be there, making sure she keeps inside the path. Talking about it gets me nowhere. I anchor her with practical details. I discuss plans for dinner, daytrips out of the city, English lessons, anything as long as it's real and present. Sometimes this brings her out of it. Sometimes I have to leave her to it. I notice she has a problem being on her own out in public. I lose her once in the Bargello and when I find her again she is pale and trembling, rooted to the spot. She hasn't moved from where I'd lost her – like a child too afraid to speak her fear. When I ask her why she's so frightened on her own, she says it's not being alone that's the problem; she just can't deal with people leaving her. Just as she herself used to do, I begin to wonder who Alison Aherne is sometimes. I ask myself where that sassy girl went; the one who breezed her way past the security guard in Easons.

I bring her up to the Palazzo Bellini. There are some tenebrist paintings in the loggia I think she should see. Now that we have a mutual friend in Professor Gentile, the Marchesa has adopted me into the magic circle. I'm the same age apparently as her grandson, Roberto, a little like him too in looks. He'd been shot dead five years ago. Some intruder on their grounds had blasted a rifle shot right through his heart. Every time I call round, the Marchesa tells me the same story, always repeating this "right through his heart" line. She's a very sad old lady. I feel guilty for having hounded her before.

When I tell her I want to bring Alison up to see the paintings, she insists on us coming for lunch. Melanie won't mind cooking for two extra. Melanie is a plain-looking English girl with a fondness for Vick's nasal spray. She's some sort of paid companion to the Marchesa (though I'm surprised such arrangements still exist).

The Marchesa takes an instant shine to Alison, whisks her off to do a tour of the photographs. There's a string of them along the corridors downstairs: the Marchesa with Princess Grace, the Marchesa with Jacqueline Onassis on some yacht.

'Christ! There's even one of her with Edward and Mrs Simpson!' Alison whispers fiercely in my ear once they return. We are hustled into a banqueting hall. Melanie has been waiting to serve lunch for half an hour now and her cheeks have turned the colour of raw liver.

The shutters are closed to keep the room cool and the paintings protected. A wrought-iron chandelier with dim electric bulbs makes a feeble attempt to light up the family portraits. Dark oak roof-beams cast an air of solemnity over the long table. It's hard to remember the sunlight still blazing outside. Alison has her head craned back, taking it all in.

'Sit here, Alison.' The Marchesa, at the head of the table, pats the chair to her right. Melanie dishes out pasta onto plates the size of satellite dishes. Earlier that week, I had found some interesting notes written on one of the bills of sale for a Perugini. I wonder if the Marchesa could enlighten me on its meaning, but she's having none of it. There are days when she plays ball and days when she does not. Obviously this is a no ball day.

'Peter! Why are you always talking about work? We are at the table – let us talk of food, or of love! My mother always told my father, "Leave your work at the garden gate!"' She turns to Alison and grips her arm, 'Men are nothing without their work. Every so often you must remind them there is a life beyond.' Alison smiles. She's a bit intimidated I think. She's said very little since arriving but that doesn't stop the Marchesa from being charmed by her. I must admit looking at her, in that red silk dress and her golden hair, falling over her shoulders, that she's a swathe of brilliant colour in this penumbra of gloom. Melanie pours some wine, offers us parmesan cheese and freshly ground pepper. We wait until she sits down before lifting our cutlery. The Marchesa ignores the food though, lights a cigarette instead, picks up her wineglass and sighs.

'Look at us! All these women and only one man! We should be boy, girl, boy, girl!' and she stabs a bony finger at the empty chairs around us. Her eyes are glistening and I can tell where this is leading, but Alison cannot.

'What's wrong?' she asks and the Marchesa starts to whimper. Melanie looks at me and rolls her eyes to heaven. And so again we listen to the story of Roberto lying dead in the garden with a rifle shot "right through his heart". I'd really like to taste this pasta but to eat would be inappropriate of course. Alison is entranced however. She encourages the Marchesa to continue.

'Really? He was out there on his own?' and she points to the grounds outside. The Marchesa nods her head.

'Over by the apricot trees.'

'Alone…and it was dark?'

'Yes. He lay on the ground dying, with only the stars for company.'

'…that's just the saddest story I've ever heard.' Alison seems genuinely upset for her. She knocks back her glass of wine, pours herself another. Melanie, I notice, has started to eat. Obviously she's heard the details a few more times than I have. I decide to follow suit. Alison persists with the questions: Who found him? Was Roberto her only grandson? Did they ever capture the man who shot him? I'm amazed she can think of these things. Perhaps it's a lack in me – an inability to truly empathise. I remember feeling so uncomfortable when the Marchesa first told me about her grandson. And I know it's ridiculous, but a part of me feels strangely jealous of this Roberto – he's eliciting such sympathy from the woman I love. My silence becomes loaded and though I am angry at myself for being such a fool, I'm angrier still at Alison who continues on: 'What was he like?' 'Where is he buried?' Her lunch is cold when finally she stops talking and starts to eat. She sees my empty plate and it's like a personal insult. She takes a gulp of her wine, glowers at me across the table.

'Did you know about this, Peter?' This feels dangerous. I know the ferocity of Alison's anger, also its brevity. I decide to play it calm. Hopefully I can ride it out.

'Yes. The Marchesa told me the first day I came up here.' I nod my deference to the top of the table.

'How could you not have told me about it?' Alison's voice is rising. I see she isn't going to let a little company distract her from her outrage.

'For God's sake, Alison!' Doesn't she realise how dependent I am still on the Marchesa's good favour?

'I mean, what's wrong with you? Any normal person would've said! But you – you're so wrapped up with your work here – you say nothing!' I can tell she's about to cry. She really shouldn't have drunk all that wine on an empty stomach. The Italians don't approve of drunkenness.

'Stop it!' I hiss back at her. Melanie, I notice is smiling. It's a change for her I suppose, a little drunken Irish scrapping to interrupt the dullness of her life. 'Enjoying this?' I ask her, and then the Marchesa stands up.

'Children! Children – enough! Alison, don't get so upset! And Peter – don't be so angry!' She tuts loudly and sits back down. 'Melanie, be a good girl and open the shutters. We need to let out all this bad feeling from the room.' Melanie pushes back her chair, a little vigorously for my benefit no doubt; leaves behind a waft of wintergreen. With the light comes a little peace it's true. Alison rubs her face with her hands and I can hear her breathing slowing down and deepening. Her anger has passed, like some door has been shut on a furious gale. I know she'll be feeling embarrassed at the scene she has created but I'm not ready to forgive her just yet.

'I'm sorry.' She directs this at the Marchesa but perhaps it's meant for me also.

'Alison, *hai sbagliato paese!* You were born I think in the wrong country. Your heart is Italian and you cannot contain all that you feel. But men are uncomfortable with feelings – you have to forgive them. It's not that they don't have feelings; it's just they're not very good at dealing with them.'

Well, that's just charming! I'll just sit here and turn invisible so! I have to remind myself why it is I am here, because fuck it – I can have tantrums too if I want! It's Melanie who steers the conversation back to matters mundane. There's dessert apparently: ice-cream and strawberries. We can have it with our coffee out on the veranda if we prefer. I make my excuses and head for the bathroom. Once there, I put my head under the cold tap and try to calm down. When I return, the others are underneath the pergola, discussing the plants in the garden. There's a delicious chill running down my back. Alison is stretched out on a lounger in the semi-shade, her arm trailing over the edge. She's rubbing some lavender flowers between her fingers. I kneel down beside her and kiss her hand.

'Let's move here forever, Peter!' she murmurs. It's such a pretty hand, though her nails are chipped and there's a line of ingrained paint under the cuticles.

Later that night, she starts to cry when we're making love. When I ask her what's the matter, she shakes her head and doesn't answer. It's then that I realise: what she said to me before, about not being able to wear different faces – it's true. She can't. I had misunderstood her, had dismissed it as something borne of her immaturity. But Alison can't help but be herself all the time, no matter what situation she's in. A part of me enjoys it – how open and honest she is with her feelings. But I've been coming at it all wrong. I realise that now. It's not that she doesn't know the rules of the game yet; the fact is Alison gets so totally into one mood that she cannot mask it with another. It's as if her emotions haemorrhage inside her, and her mind cannot clot them. I know she went to counselling a few years ago. She told me that on one of our very first dates. I remember thinking at the time that it can't have been anything serious. Now I suspect that it was, and with my doubts a distance opens up between us.

She still won't tell me why she's crying and, truth is, I'm too tired and frustrated to care now. She's shivering though the night is warm and we had kicked the sheets off earlier. I kiss her eyelids shut, turn over on my side and sink into oblivion despite the taste of her salty tears on my lips.

The next morning she's quiet, though she comes outside with me to the wooden bench in the garden. We have our coffee looking out at the view of Florence in the distant heat-haze. She asks me what time my classes finish today and I don't know why but I find myself lying. I tell her half past two. This way I'll have an hour on my own to take a stroll down by the river. Is it such a terrible betrayal? An hour to myself to think my own thoughts? It shouldn't be, but with

Alison, it feels that way. The little white cat creeps towards us for her morning treat. Alison gets up, goes to the kitchen to get her some meat and so is spared the flush of shame that floods my face.

Things continue much as they have done before: mornings teaching English, visits to galleries most afternoons, a swim perhaps in the evening, provided there aren't too many water snakes about. Ostensibly, nothing changes. Change is invisible – like grit inside my shoe; mostly I'm unaware of it but then my foot touches the ground at a certain angle, and I'm reminded: something is awry.

My research in the Marchesa's archives is going well though, and I have made a few important discoveries. I take a train down to the Maremma and meet up with Professor Gentile to discuss plans for a conference he's organising. Alison comes with me though she spends the day outside, sketching in the grounds of the professor's villa. Perhaps she senses something of my apprehension at her possible behaviour. Perhaps she just likes the garden's aspect. On the train back to Florence, she shows me her drawings, happy and expectant, like a small child waiting for unconditional praise. I find myself feeling less and less sure around her. Her mutability becomes infectious. I want her with me; I don't want her with me.

The temperature begins to soar mid-July. The days when we aren't teaching, we stay inside the farmhouse from eleven in the morning till five in the evening. The thought of getting a bus into Florence is unbearable. Alison paints. I work at my thesis. We have dinner at eight and get drunk on the local red wine. When we make love, we don't talk afterwards like we used to; but the need to fuck one another hard is still very strong. Only when she is pinned beneath me on the bed, do I feel I have her close to me. She bores that dark stare into my eyes and my heart swells once more with desire and fascination.

Time skids towards Ferragosto; everything shuts down for the holiday period. The school where we teach English organises a meal on the last day of term. Alison and I are late getting to the restaurant because of the bus timetable. Nearly everyone is finished their main course by the time we arrive. A group of her students crowd round her, pull over a chair they've been keeping for her. I let her go and take my seat next to the school director. For once, the Italians are drinking hard. There have been a lot of exams recently and the need to vent tension is being satisfied heartily, by the students at least. One of them, Gianluca, stands up and proposes a toast to, '*…la nostra gentilissima, bellissima* Alison!' She doesn't fully understand but gets the gist all the same. She stands up and takes a little bow. Her students all cheer and the director, Santoro, nudges me and tells me I'm a lucky man. What did I do to deserve such a woman?

'Not enough.' I tell him. 'Not nearly enough.'

The restaurant owner has to flash the lights on and off to get the last of the students to leave. Most of the staff have long since left to go home to their beds, but Alison and the students are ready for more. There's a club over near Santa Trinitá and Alison wants to go to it. I draw her aside and try to talk her out of it, but she's lost to me; too drunk and too intent on doing her own thing to listen. She throws her arms around my neck.

'Come on, Peter! We never have fun anymore!' She pouts out her lower lip and it's hard then not to smile and give in. Perhaps I have been a bit of a bore.

The moment we enter the nightclub I regret it. I hate these places. They're bad enough back home, but the Italians should have stopped making music after 1850. They're blaring out some crap that sounds suspiciously like the Birdy Song in pidgin English. It's too dark and there's nowhere to sit. We sip our drinks leaning against the wall beside the toilets. The music changes and Gianluca comes over and makes this imploring gesture to me, his hands pressed together as though in prayer, as he nods towards Alison. Well, she's a free agent; it's up to her really whether or not she wants to dance. All the same, I nod my assent slowly, but actually I'd like to knock his head off this wall. Gianluca is one of those Italians, tall and wiry, with a lupine hungriness about him that gives me the creeps. I watch them dancing for a while – Alison's body swaying to the music, her eyes closed; Gianluca's gyrating hips, his eyes feasting avidly. He's an ugly little git – I think I can trust her. I need a cigarette but I've run out. There was a bar we passed on the way here. Maybe they'll have a vending machine. I get my coat and leave without telling Alison. The bar is only a five minute walk away and she probably won't even notice I'm missing.

The guy behind the bar shrugs his shoulders, apologises but they don't sell cigarettes here. I'd have to go to a *tabaccheria* but they're all closed at this hour. I must look a little crestfallen because he gestures to me to sit down, relax. He takes out his pack of cigarettes and offers me one. He lights it and another for himself, asks do I want anything to drink. I decide why not and order a gin and tonic. We chat a little about this and that. He tells me his name is Luciano. He asks me where I'm staying and when I tell him, he says his mother comes from just a few miles away. This is enough to cement a bond and when finally I get up to leave, two gins later, he pats me on the back and puts his half full pack of cigarettes into my top pocket. I feel a little drunk myself when I step back out onto the pavement. The bell at the Duomo sounds out the hour: two o'clock. A fine rain starts to fall. The air feels thick and heavy like a storm is ready to break any moment now. I have a little trouble remembering where the night club is, but eventually I happen upon it, recognising the neon rooster that hangs outside.

It's a little emptier now, though the music is thumping and the dance floor is still full. I look around but can't see Alison. I spot some of the students sitting over in the corner. When I approach them, someone coughs as though to send out an alert signal and my question as to where Alison can be found, is met with an embarrassed silence, and then some mutterings about her having left not ten minutes ago. Gianluca, I notice, is missing also. Instantly, I'm sober. I try to salvage a little of my professional authority and thank them for their help. It's hopeless of course, and I can hear them sniggering behind me as I leave.

I look up and down the street but she is nowhere to be seen. My brain feels swollen; I cannot think the thoughts that are swarming round my head. The rain is getting heavy now. The shit! The absolute little shit! I know the others will know where Gianluca lives but there's no way I'm going back to ask them. Probably though, he's still living with his parents. Probably has a little room still to himself, with his little single bed and his posters of Juve and Madonna on the wall, and right now he is fucking my girlfriend, slobbering those girly lips all over her skin, winding those sinewy arms around her body, telling her to shush – keep quiet! She might wake Mamma! I want to kill him. If I met him now, I would surely kill him. This is what I want and nothing else.

I pace the streets, looking up and down, lifting my head and listening hard whenever there's a light on in one of the apartments overhead. It's completely futile I know, but I have to walk off this anger. Eventually, my breathing calms down and I get a little clarity. I could spend the entire night walking these streets, looking for Alison, or I could walk back to the Piazza Reppublica and get a taxi home; wait and see what morning brings. The rain is sending the last of the city's stragglers fleeing down the side alleys to their cheap hotels. A group of German tourists wearing Bayern Munich tee-shirts are ahead of me at the taxi rank singing football anthems. I listen to them, seething with envy. I'm not sure why. For the certainty of their allegiances perhaps? Or for the sheer abandon with which they're singing?

Instead of going to bed, I open a bottle of wine and sit down at the kitchen table to drink. I smoke Luciano's cigarettes, my heart heavy with hatred and anger, until eventually my head sinks and I fall asleep.

The sun is starting to leak through the cracks of the shutters when I hear Alison lifting the latch of the front door. Between my slow drag up into consciousness and Alison's banging and knocking around in the hall, several minutes seem to pass. I rub my face with my hands and try to clear my mind for this confrontation. I don't know what I'm going to say to her, but I know I don't want to hear any of her crap. I look at my watch: 6.00. Gianluca must have kicked her out before Mamma came in to wake him. I stand up, go to the sink and pour myself a glass of water. As I drink it, I realise all is silent out in the hall. What is Alison doing? The least she can do is come in and face me. I wait another minute. Silence still. I sit down again. This is ridiculous. Then I hear her: whimpering like an injured dog. I push my chair back and go out to the hall.

Alison is sitting on the stone floor, her back against the wall, her knees raised and her head down on her folded arms. I can't see her face but her shoulders are shaking. When I go close, she contracts herself into an even tighter ball and shakes her head from left to right. I slide down the wall opposite; mirroring her sitting position but with my head held up. I want to see her face when she explains to me where she's been all this time.

'How could you?' she says and then she lifts her face and I must admit I'm shocked. Her hair is tangled and stuck to her face with blood and mucus. She must have been crying for a hell of a long time for her eyes to swell up like that.

'How could *I*?' but I'm wrong-footed – unsure now what I should be feeling, how I should be acting. She looks like she's been attacked. What if I've gotten it terribly wrong?

'Yes! How could you? How could you have left me like that?' She's wailing now.

'What's happened, Alison? Has something happened?' I grasp her hand, swivel myself over beside her. I notice that her bare feet are muddy and bleeding. 'Fuck! What's going on?' Alison buries her head against my chest.

'You left me, Peter. You left me and I had no choice.'

'I came back! I came back after ten minutes!'

'I waited half an hour for you! I looked for you everywhere. Why did you leave me?'

'Fucking hell! I only went out to get some cigarettes. I got talking…ah, shit! Shit!'

'You don't love me any more, Peter.'

'What? What are you saying? What about Gianluca? What were you doing with him?'

'Nothing happened. He pretended he was helping me look for you – but as soon as he got me outside, he was all over me … there was a fight…I don't know, oh God!' She collapses again into my arms. Her skin is cold and her clothes damp. Anger swells inside me till my chest is tight with hatred.

'What did he do to you? Did he touch you, Alison?'

She knows what I mean but my question shocks her and, for a moment, she stops crying.

'No! Christ, no! He was holding onto me…I fell and I think I must have blacked out because I don't know… I remember coming round and it was raining. I think that's what woke me up; I was so cold.' She sits up straight again, tries to get a handle on her breathing, but it keeps catching, and all the air in the room isn't enough for her to inhale. I reach out to touch the blood on her feet.

'How did you get home?'

'I walked.'

I say nothing. What can I say? She's walked fifteen miles in the dark to get back to me; I'm a bastard, an absolute bastard.

'You can't leave me, Peter. I have to leave you.' This leaks out in gulps and gasps. She looks so sad. I put my finger to her lips and tell her to hush, none of that talk now. I carry her upstairs and place her onto the bed. I kiss her forehead, pull up the sheet to her chin, tell her to sleep. I'm aware of doing these things, but I'm lost as to what to say. She's hyperventilating, though gradually a little slower; a sudden hiccup at the end of each breath stalls the process. I go downstairs, boil up some water and pour it into a basin. Alone again in the kitchen, my mind races in panic, because I'm realising something – and I must have known it all along. I left her in that night-club and some deep, dark thought was tunnelling through my subconscious: what if she goes off with him? Where will that put us? And I know now what I wanted. I wanted to be rid of her. I wanted Gianluca to take her off my hands. It wasn't jealousy alone that made me pace those streets looking for them. It was another feeling too; black and angry and capable of violence. I think it was hatred. Because although I love Alison (I would die for her, I really would), there is a part of me that hates her, and I can't tell the difference any more, between loving her and hating her.

Christ, what sort of person have I become?

Alison is still awake when I return. She looks at me but says nothing. The air is too charged for me to meet her stare. Instead, I turn my gaze to the end of the bed, dip a cloth into the warm water and lift up her feet. I bathe them one at a time, watching as the dirt and blood dissolve together and turn the water a muddy brown.

White Hunter

by

Peter Caunt

This was his favourite time. Hunting in the day had become too easy, too sanitised. Nocturnal creatures were a different matter. Just as noiseless and cunning as any daytime predator, but so much more of a challenge when the hunter loses one of his senses. He lifted his left arm and took a sip of the gin and tonic. He shuffled in his seat to ease the pain in his legs and adjusted the rifle in his right hand. A large firefly flew though the veranda, directly across his line of vision, cutting a tear in the blackness. He cursed the loss of night vision, but in the after image he drifted back to the time of his first hunt, in North America.

*

His father had been promising him the trip for years, and there he was, hundreds of miles from the nearest town. Sleeping under the stars had been an experience that would live with him forever. He and his mother lived in London, so the night sky was an amalgam of streetlights and pollution, with only the moon sufficiently powerful to elbow its way into sight. The noises of the London streets never stopped; even in the centre of a park the urban wildlife had to compete with the persistent rumble of wheel on tarmac and the clatter of a population constantly on the move. There in the woods he relished the silence.

'What are you smiling about young man?'

'It's so quiet. At home it's always noisy.'

'There's plenty of noise here,' his father said, 'Just let your ears relax, stop expecting to hear the city. The woods are full of different sounds; sounds of all the animals of the night.'

He lay back, emptied his mind and let his hearing drift off into the night. For a while he could hear only the soft pounding of his own heart, then gradually he became accustomed to the soft stirrings within the unseen depths of the woods. He lay awake all night, his eyes tight shut, with his ears following every movement. This was a skill which he would perfect over many years.

In the morning he learnt to stalk his prey. Moving silently through the undergrowth, keeping always downwind. After a couple of hours, his father stopped and pointed. He saw the stag in the clearing. They both stood still, then his father motioned him down onto one knee and indicated that he should fire. He held the rifle to his shoulder. He breathed steadily and took careful aim as he had done so often in practice.

'Stand firm and just squeeze the trigger gently. Don't pull it.'

'Yes Daddy.'

He felt the kick on his shoulder and momentarily lost sight of his prey. Refocusing, he saw the stag still waiting in the clearing. Then, as he watched, it collapsed on the ground. He felt his father's hand on his back.

'Bloody good shot. Well done.'

He looked at the crumpled heap of the creature that had so recently stood proud and tall in the woods. He felt the weight of the rifle in his hand, and he felt the surge of power through his body. That adrenaline rush was something that he had never lost; it had become an addiction.

*

He closed his eyes and the night vision returned. He flexed his left hand and picked up his drink. The pain in his legs had gone but his lower back now ached. Another mosquito landed on his arm to feed. He had spent so long in this type of climate that he had learned to ignore these minor discomforts as he concentrated on his prey. So what if he had minor bouts of malaria. At least the tonic helped. He'd learned that in his first spell in Africa.

*

The lions had been easy. He had been surprised how docile they could be. To get the thrill he often had to provoke them. Still the trophies looked just as good hanging on the wall. The elephants had been different. Most people see an elephant in a zoo as something docile and friendly. They had never met a rogue male. His first encounter with one had given him his closest call. He had been hunting lions for too long and had become soft. His first shot had seemed to be good enough, but the bull had not gone down. He had to hide, but the native bearers tried to run; two of them were trampled. He knew he had to finish it off, but this had become a matter of personal pride rather than duty. It took him the rest of the day to track it down. He saw it turn and face him. It seemed to recognise him from the earlier encounter. He had learned to read the emotions of some animals, but with this bull he knew that the only emotion was pure hatred. It was seven tons at least, doing over twenty miles an hour and still gaining speed. He could feel the adrenaline.

'Stand firm and just squeeze the trigger gently. Don't pull it.' His father's words rang in his ears.

He would have time for only one shot. He waited as long as he could and then fired. He could see the wound from his first attempt and watched as the second bullet hit its target and the beast crashed to the ground a few feet in front of him. He stood for a full ten minutes as his heart gradually slowed. The native bearers emerged from hiding as he calmly measured the length of the tusks. In the distance he could see a group of Masai shimmering in the heat haze, their bright red costumes fluttering in the wind. They never interfered, that was their way; but he could feel their disapproval. The Masai lived at one with the land. They hunted lions to protect their cattle, but they coexisted with the elephant and all other creatures on the plain. His native bearers were different; they were farmers who hated the elephants for the pests they were. Once, in a fit of spite after an unsuccessful elephant hunt, he had shot one of the watching Masai. The others had remained in place, still staring. He could still remember the icy feeling in his spine.

*

He heard a movement, put down his glass and picked up his torch. It was the sound he had been waiting for. The beam caught the eyes, shining back at him in the darkness, and just the hint of a slick black coat; but by the time he had raised his rifle, it was gone. He stretched his aching shoulders. He could wait. He had a little time left; he would have to be patient.

*

He had learned patience in India on a tiger hunt. Tigers were worthy adversaries. They weren't like the lion, lying in the afternoon sun like some tourist on a grand tour, the male waiting for the females to bring in the food. Tigers were loners, much like himself. They stalked their prey. They were true hunters.

Two weeks in a howdah had left him sore and frustrated. Tigers roamed over many kilometres and their camouflage was well suited to the terrain. Finally he received a report from one of the trackers that a tiger had been spotted in thick undergrowth near a temple. They had approached, but the mahout had been reluctant to enter the undergrowth for fear of the elephant panicking if the tiger suddenly emerged. Fires were set to flush it out, despite the protestations of the temple priest. As the fires were dying out and the sun was near setting, he had felt his desperation at another day lost. Suddenly the tiger emerged. His elephant panicked and fled, but not before he got off a shot. The mahout struggled to halt the frightened elephant and he had to hang on with one hand. He turned to see the tiger, bleeding profusely, but gaining on them fast. With only one hand free, he knew his aim would not be good until it was closer. He could not help but feel great respect for the beast. It had used stealth and concealment but now was in full flow, attacking something many times its size, despite the wound in its side. He needed only one shot. By the time the mahout had turned the elephant, the trackers had surrounded the dead tiger. He had been waiting for this trophy to take pride of place in his home and it would be a shame if it was damaged. He examined the body carefully then smiled and signalled the bearers to prepare it for transport. As they were leaving he heard the priest shouting. He turned to the mahout for a translation.

'He is an ignorant peasant of the country. Do not take any notice.'

There was something in the priest's manner that had disturbed him, so he pressed the mahout.

'He is a Hindi, sire. He believes in reincarnation. He says what you do is bad Karma. He says that it will all come back.'

He cared nothing for any of the local religions or superstitions. He had given the tiger a good death. That was all that anyone could want.

*

He swatted at another firefly then put the torch down on the table. His glass was nearly empty. He searched the blackness with his ears. If the panther was out there it was not moving, but he could feel it watching him. The ache had spread well into his chest. Perhaps he had less time than he thought. His tablets were beside the gin bottle, both just out of reach. He tried to flex the muscles in his leg, but they still refused to respond.

He looked down at his thigh. The spider was still there looking back at him, the blood still dripping from its fangs. He had been concentrating on the movements of the panther in the night; just another mosquito bite he had thought. By the time he had noticed, the toxins had spread into his body. Spider bites were rarely fatal, he told himself, but with his heart condition he was not so sure. He could feel the stiffness creeping into his neck, making his head swim. The spider seemed to smile, a miniature assassin watching the last gasps of its victim. The moon came out for a moment and in the night he focused on the eyes watching him. No, not just eyes, he could see the outlines of different animals. There were so many of them, mixing in with his memories from the past. They were all waiting. Waiting for the assassin to finish its work.

He stretched for the tablets to his left. His fingertips just held the bottle when he felt the pain shoot down his arm. His hand went into spasm and the tablets spilled over the porch. He deserved something better than this. He had thought that one day his aim would be less than perfect and he would be trampled by a rhino or mauled by some large feline after an heroic chase. He had given all his victims a noble death; he didn't want to die like this.

He looked from the spider to the outlines in the moonlight, but there was no response.

With a great effort he swung his rifle into position. As he bit down on the barrel he heard his father.

'Stand firm and just squeeze the trigger gently. Don't pull it.'

'Yes Daddy.'

Hostage

by

Sarah Evans

'Ben, this is Rebecca,' Karen says. 'Remember I told you she'd be here. From Amnesty.'

Rebecca is smiling broadly at him as she holds out her hand. She has glossy brown hair swept forward over her shoulders.

'Hi.' He stands, scraping the orange chair across the wooden floor. Her hand is small and soft, and the readiness of her smile makes Ben want to echo it back. 'I'm not sure how much I can add to what Karen's told you, but fire away.'

He's not sorry for the excuse to turn away from the task of stuffing quarterly campaign updates into envelopes. Karen picks up the remainder of his pile. 'I can deal with these,' she says, moving away, leaving them to talk above the background chatter of the other volunteers scattered on tables round the hall.

'So as Julia's partner…' Rebecca starts.

'Friend,' he corrects. She must have known he would say this.

'Okay. As Julia's *friend…*'

She proceeds to ask the routine questions. The answers are ones he's given before. She's less assured than the professional journalists he's dealt with, she twiddles with the ends of her hair, glances anxiously at the tape recorder.

'Well,' she says eventually. 'Thanks for your time.'

'No problem. What will you do with the interview?'

'It's for the web-site. We highlight a hostage a month.' She grimaces, as if realising it sounds like a supermarket promotion. 'I should be going.'

His heart thuds uncomfortably; the intention and voicing it present themselves simultaneously.

'How about going for a coffee?'

She looks at him appraisingly. All he's done is suggest coffee.

'Sure. Why not.'

She waits at the doorway while he seeks out Karen.

'I'm heading off. See you Saturday.' He imagines Karen watching as he joins Rebecca. That's just paranoia. Besides, he isn't answerable to her.

The freshness of the early evening air clears the dust and wax smell of the hall.

'So,' he says, 'coffee or something stronger?'

'Let's stick to coffee. Don't you think?'

'Fine.' His lips twitch upwards. He's having coffee with an attractive woman. That's all.

In Starbucks she orders a Strawberry Frappuccino. They always look sickly to him, but he likes the way she chooses something without hesitation, immediately knowing what she wants. The fact she doesn't insist on paying for hers is somehow reassuring.

'So,' she leans over the table towards him. 'Tell me off the record. What does this stuff about *only a friend* mean?'

The directness takes him aback. But it's good she asked.

'I knew Julia for about a year. She's been gone for two. That's not a great ratio. Of course I care about her. But I can't think of myself as her partner any more.' The term never fitted anyway. He doesn't want to remember back, to the stop-start of knowing her, the weeks when she'd be off on one of her trips – the danger never felt quite real, 'I have a charmed life,' she'd say – the times she'd return, when she'd want to pack everything in: friends, art, theatre; hot, dense intimacy. He doesn't want to bring back the early days of missing her, the sleepless nights, when every muscle ached her loss. 'It would be more interesting to talk about you.'

It feels like the first day skiing when he hasn't done it for a year. It takes him a while to find his rhythm, to ease into his balance. His social skills have rusted; he's spent too long hanging out with Julia's sister, Julia's friends. Too long doing nothing but think of Julia. Sitting here is pleasant, seeking to be entertaining, responding to Rebecca's lively account of herself. He takes her in more fully. She isn't beautiful – not like Julia – but her features are growing on him as they become more familiar, as he notices the olive skin, the eyes that are a greeny-blue, as he watches the rise and fall of her breasts when she laughs.

'I really should go,' she says.

'Where are you heading for?'

'I have one of those flats at the Barbican. Small, but convenient.'

'I could walk with you.'

Her eyes narrow at him.

'I don't think so. Not this time.' His heart thuds again. *Not this time*, sounds promising.

'So do I get to get your number?'

'Why don't you give me yours?'

The whole of him sinks down within. He doesn't have the heart for playing games.

'Because…' He pauses, looking at her directly. This is a gamble. 'You might not ring.'

Her eyes maintain a grip on his. He waits for her to weigh him up, figure out what to do.

'Okay,' she says eventually. 'What are you doing Saturday?'

'Nothing I can't rearrange.' He'll figure out some excuse for Karen.

'I'm supposed to go to this private gallery thing.' She twists her lips amusingly. 'An old college friend of mine. I never really get her stuff. But I feel I ought to go and offer support. Why don't you come with me? I always feel an idiot going on my own. We could grab dinner afterwards.'

'Sounds good.'

She fumbles in her bag produces a small card.

'The details are on here. Shall we say about six? I still need your number. In case something comes up.'

He laughs.

'Definitely not then.'

She laughs too, her face lighting up, warm and vibrant.

As they go in different directions there's a lightness to his step. A woman looks at him somewhat oddly, and he realises he's grinning. His fingers twist the small card.

It's only when he glimpses Westminster that he realises the route he's taking. It means passing beneath Julia's flat, with its glass and chrome sparseness, and wide view out over the river. He turns around, though going to Victoria is further, and means changing trains. This has to stop. He clenches his hands, feels a hardening within, the half formation of a plan.

He's tired by the time he gets home. He'd like just to pour a drink and snack on comfort food, before flaking out and flicking channels. But that would just postpone things.

A selection of postcards are still pinned to his kitchen notice-board. As he takes them down he holds back from turning them over to re-read the illegible scrawl. The messages were never particularly personal anyway.

In the living room he picks up the photo frame. Julia never liked him taking pictures of her. This one was in Paris. She's laughing with her head flung back. 'I don't see why you need a picture,' she'd said. 'It feels morbid. As if you're stacking up things to remember me by.'

'You're away such a lot.'

'And will having a picture compensate?' Her laughter was teasing. Julia always had complicated objections to things no-one else would question. He'd taken the snap anyway. She never had a photo of him.

His fingers struggle with the catch at the back of the frame. He gives up, places the whole thing with the postcards. The image is stored electronically of course. He can think about deleting it later.

The birthday card she gave him is in his bedroom. 'This is from me,' the cartoon figure still says. 'Go ahead be thrilled.' Of course he had been, even though it was hopelessly late. He adds it to his pile.

The bathroom cabinet is full of bottles that accumulated whenever she slept over; they contain her familiar fragrances. What did he ever think he would do with them? They are easily consigned to his kitchen bin. He goes to fetch the rest. Then he stops.

He finds a large brown envelope.

The bottom drawer of his bedside table is stuffed with things he hardly uses: skiing gloves and hiking socks. He shoves the cards and photo into the envelope, slides the package in at the bottom. The next time he opens the drawer he'll decide. He'll chuck it then.

He's ten minutes early. He'll walk round the block before going in. Moving might help damp down the mix of nervousness and excitement. This is not a big deal.

By the time he descends the stone steps to St Martin's crypt, it's still five minutes to. He glances round: the teaming self-serve counter looks incongruous amidst the stone archways and worn flagstones. She's sitting at one of the café tables already waiting, her head turning from left to right. Of course she'd want to be on time for her friend's exhibition.

He half jogs towards her.

'Hi, I'm not late am I?'

He leans down towards her, offering a social kiss on the cheek. She smells of something fresh and citrus-y.

'I was early.'

She's wearing a black gypsy top, with a thick crocheted trim around the scooped neck, gathered together by a string done up in a loose bow.

'You look nice.' Is that too bland? Too personal? God, is he out of practice.

'Thank-you. So do you. Shall we go in?'

She takes a glass of white wine from the proffered tray at the entrance to the gallery at the side, and he does the same.

A woman scoots over in a blazing trail of flowing greens, and kisses her more closely than he'd dared to.

'This is Ben,' Rebecca says, without any attempt at giving him a label, 'and Miranda.' He senses the woman looking at him, flashing a questioning smile back to Rebecca.

'We'll catch up soon,' Miranda promises. 'You can tell me all the gossip.'

They walk slowly round the brightly lit, windowless room stopping to look at each piece in turn. The paintings are of the squiggle variety. He doesn't get how these are better or more interesting than the pictures his nephews would produce.

'There's a kind of flow to them,' he says. 'An energy.' What bollocks! He wishes he'd had the foresight to look this woman up on-line, see what the critics say.

Rebecca laughs.

'You don't really mean that,' she says in a low undertone.

Their eyes meet in a sideways glance.

'Maybe my interests lie elsewhere.'

'Okay, another ten minutes. I reckon we can leave after that.'

'So, where to?' he asks as they emerge outside.

'How about Chinatown? I haven't been there for ages.'

'Sounds good to me.' It sounds heavy for a first date, if that's what this is.

'So what did you really think?' she asks as they push through the crowds up towards Leicester Square.

'I'm a complete philistine when it comes to modern art. Sorry, I just don't see where the skill is. I'm obviously missing something.'

'No. I'm the same. Miranda was raving over the new Rothko exhibition, and dragged me along. But I don't get it. All those red rectangles.'

They've reached a busy road. He's grateful for the distraction. The pastel colours of Julia's living room are brightened with a large print: Rothko's red on maroon. He is not going to think about her.

In the restaurant they are tucked into a corner. The circular table pressed close against them hosts a large group; they have to lean in towards each other to hear. They settle quickly on the set menu and the house wine, then find themselves thumbing through the *à la carte* anyway. He gets some easy laughs from picking out the grossest sounding dishes: duck's web and fish lips; jelly fish. They speculate on what dragons' whiskers really are.

He asks her about her work, tries to describe his own amusingly. Researcher for the BBC has it's moments of fun, and a lot of very dull routine. They exchange views on the latest films.

'I love French films,' she says.

'Me too.'

He pictures holding her hand in the dark.

The waitress places small bowls in front of them, and chopsticks.

'I'm lousy with these,' Rebecca admits.

'You can't possibly ask for a fork. Here.' He reaches over to take her hand, bending her fingers so she holds the sticks in the fashion he finds works well enough for him. Julia laughed and told him his method was completely wrong.

Rebecca smiles back knowingly. But she doesn't withdraw her hand.

The waitress returns with dishes that sizzle and smell of garlic.

'My breath will stink,' Rebecca says as she balances a mouthful up to her lips, which glisten in the flicker of the burnt down candle.

'Mine will too.' Their eyes meet.

They talk. They eat. They laugh. This is going well. There are small, but more personal, revelations. His allergy to pomegranate seeds; her aversion to anything fishy. God he's missed this, the undercurrent, the game. She twiddles with the ends of that black string which dangle between her breasts. He pictures reaching over to pull the ends of the bow.

It's still early by the time they've finished.

'A drink somewhere?' he asks.

'We could do.' She doesn't sound convinced. 'Maybe I've already drunk too much.'

'We could get coffee. Or just stroll?'

They start to drift towards Covent Garden. A loud group of women sway towards them, one of them sporting a large L sign. He feels like a learner too. He takes Rebecca's shoulder to save her colliding with the lurching stilettos. When they reach the square they pause to watch the jugglers and laugh at their banter. Pause again to listen to the plaintive strains of Bach played on a violin. A rose seller stops in front of them.

'No, don't,' she says. Julia always meant the things she said. He can't know if it's the case with Rebecca.

They stand awkwardly. He should think of something else to suggest.

'Okay!' She sounds decisive. 'My shoes are beginning to rub. I'm going to head for the tube. You can come back for *coffee* if you want.'

His heart is racing. Is her emphasis to say that's exactly what she means, or to point out the ambiguity of this?

'Great.' It is only coffee she has offered.

Her flat is small, with a vertiginous view over the blue rectangular lake. It is full of candles and trailing scarves. She turns on a lamp in the living room, which casts dim shadows through the woven cloth draped over it.

'Like I said. Small and convenient.'

'Mine's pretty small too. Not quite as convenient. But Wimbledon's quite pleasant.'

'I've never been.'

'You'll have to come over sometime.'

She shrugs, non-committal.

'So. Really coffee? Or something stronger?' He's probably drunk enough, but he hesitates. Would alcohol feel more intimate? 'Definitely coffee for me,' she adds. 'I can't hold alcohol the way I used to.'

'Coffee's great.'

He follows her into the kitchen in which sloping yellow cupboards compete for space with the standard white goods.

She turns away from him to fill the kettle. He watches the soft curves of her profile, the way her hair parts at the back, leaving her neck pale and vulnerable beneath. As she switches the kettle on he steps behind her, places his hands lightly on her shoulders and gently kisses her neck. She is standing very still. He turns her to face him, moves his hands down to trace her arms, before reaching under them and round her back. He bends in to kiss her; she tilts her head up towards him.

He thinks of Julia. Pushing the thoughts away will only make them more persistent. The last time he kissed her was at the airport: last call for the flight to Gaza. Then she shrugged her canvas rucksack over her shoulders and left without a backwards glance. He hasn't kissed a woman since. He can no longer remember what it was about kissing Julia that was so unique. His mouth closes round this woman's lower lip, he steps closer; his hands follow the ridge of her spine, her breasts are pushed against his chest. And now this is all he is thinking of, the rhythmic probing of his tongue against hers, the slow caress of his hands, her fingers reaching into his hair. He's wondering just how soon he can let his hands wander lower still, or move them towards the those hanging ends of string. It isn't just sex he wants. Though he does want that, badly. It's the whole thing. Holding her afterwards. Sleeping beside her. Waking to the slight shyness of new lovers, to the sense of a beginning.

Then she pulls away. She gives him a further pecking kiss, as if to soften her withdrawal.

'The kettle's boiled,' she says, and he releases her. 'Is decaf okay?'

He breathes deeply, tries not to feel disappointed. He wants to step towards her, press his body against hers, move her hair properly out of the way to kiss her neck again. At other times, in other situations, that's exactly what he'd do. But perhaps she's right. They should take things slowly.

Back in the living room, she turns on the light which feels harsh and glaring. He sits on the sofa, but she chooses an upright chair by the table. She won't return his gaze.

'I've enjoyed tonight,' he says. Please may she at least look at him.

When she does so, her face has lost its earlier ease.

'Ben, I'm sorry. I don't think this is going to work.'

'I didn't think my kissing was that bad.'

There's a flicker of a smile, but it fades and dies too quickly.

'It isn't that.'

'What then? I thought we had a nice time.' He sounds too desperate.

'We did. I'm sorry. This is all my fault. Going out tonight was a mistake.'

'*It's not you, it's me.*' He mimics the clichéd brush off. He doesn't mean it to sound harsh or bitter.

'It's Julia.'

'That's not fair.' He thought he'd explained.

'I know it's not.' She raises her eyes to look at him again. 'Ben, tell me, if Julia was released, would you want to see her?'

'Of course.' What else is he supposed to say? 'Of course I'd want to see her. That doesn't mean I expect we'd get back together. Look…' He tries to think what it is he hasn't already told her. 'Maybe if I believed that if – when – Julia is released, we could slip back to what we were, that I could just be that bloke who was in love with her, maybe I'd wait. But I've changed. I've no idea what two years captivity will have done to her, but she'll have changed too. I don't believe there are any happy endings for me and Julia.' He knows with leaden certainty that it's true, that what they had, his infatuation with her beauty and her life, the nights of rapid talk and spiralling laughter, the intensity of physical need, the rarer moments of quiet reflection and revelation, none of this is enough to survive separation and ordeal.

The room is very quiet. It's for her to say something now.

'It's not I don't think you're doing the right thing. There's no reason to sit around waiting. But believing isn't the same as what you hope. I mean look at you. Your friends are her friends. You spend half your free time with her sister.'

'I was planning to back out from the campaign.' He should have done this already. It's not as if he ever believed the candle-lit vigils and the placard bearing marches ever achieved much, beyond giving him and Karen the sense of doing something.

'Maybe I'm wrong. This isn't about Julia. It's about me. I took this job because I care about human rights. I don't want to be saying all the right things while hoping that she's never released, because I couldn't be sure, not really, what you'd feel if you saw her again. Maybe I'm just too selfish. I don't need this kind of baggage.'

'It wouldn't have to be like that. I thought we were getting on well.'

'Maybe that's the problem. I like you. I mean *really* like you. That's what makes it dangerous. I'm sorry. I think you should go.'

'We could at least be friends.'

'Come on. It isn't friendship either of us wants.'

As he closes the door behind him, he feels empty. The plan forms in his mind. He's almost looking forward to getting back to his flat. This time he will be ruthless.

He takes two bin liners from the cupboard under the sink.

In one he places the envelope with those cards and photo. He adds his half used jar of shaving foam, the brand she bought him once and he's never changed it. Just like he never stopped buying her brand of coffee, her whisky. He adds those to his bag too. A T-shirt of hers, and a couple of pairs of those silky shorts she always wore, are thrown in afterwards.

In the other bag he places the deep-pile towels he bought after she complained his were like sandpaper; he's never used them for him. He takes the shirt she said she liked and puts that in too. He can never face wearing it.

He hesitates in front of the open wardrobe door. His hand reaches to the top shelf for the dressing gown she bought him. He tries not to stop and pass his fingers over the roughly woven cotton with its bands of deep red blending into rich orange then brown. He's never worn it, is never going to. Only as he ties the ends of the bags does he realise that he's been biting his lip, it's bleeding.

The streets are quiet. A pile of junk blocks the doorway to Oxfam, underneath the sign asking people not to deposit stuff there. But this can't wait. He leaves one bag. The other he deposits in a public bin. It's only when he's almost home he freezes. He retraces his steps. Anyone watching, would think him a nutter. He takes out the dressing gown, empties the contents of someone else's carrier bag and stuffs in the gown instead. He has to squeeze the Tesco bag into the narrow opening of the bin. He can't afford the risk of those earthy shades staring back at him from the shop display.

It would be stupid to say his flat feels different. Tomorrow, he'll go shopping; he'll enjoy choosing things differently. Perhaps he'll drop by Rebecca's in a couple of months. He turns on his PC, deletes the file with Julia's photo, then clears the recycle bin.

It's as he undresses for bed that he remembers, the thing his mind has been trying to hide away.

He knows exactly where it is.

The book of love poems he bought, and never got to give her, is still sitting on his shelf, tucked into the midst of his untidy piles. It isn't the book he's been keeping from himself. Disposing of that will be relatively easy. Inside it is the small card, the same vibrant colours as the dressing gown it accompanied. He stares at the blocks of red and orange, then turns it over.

Not to be worn too often! Love Julia.

She never said she loved him. The words on the card don't mean anything. Women write *love* to people they hardly know. It didn't mean anything.

He twists the card between his fingers, round and round, so the writing blurs. It was only ever semi-legible.

He could tell himself he can't face going outside again. He could simply place the card in his kitchen bin. But he would only retrieve it tomorrow. From the bottom of his wardrobe he takes out his box-file of essential identifiers. His birth certificate and passport. The scraps of paper with their arrays of *A*s and *B*s that always seemed such flimsy proof of aptitude. The family photo, taken years ago, all four of them beaming for the camera.

He adds the small card, slipping it in at the bottom. One day, soon, he'll break free. He doesn't quite have the strength, not yet.

The Game of World Domination

by

A J Kirby

The homecoming wasn't what I'd expected; there was no crowd-lined High Street, no ticker-tape and no marching band. I remember Grandfather's stories about coming home from the Second World War; the street parties, the heart-felt thanks from local dignitaries and, of course, I remembered his tales of the women queuing up to meet him with almost star-struck, lusty eyes. The boys were back in town, and life could start up again. When I returned home, nobody even noticed that I'd been gone.

Of course, we hadn't come home victorious, had we? We'd struggled like hell out there though, and surely we deserved, at the very least a thank you. But something was wrong. I knew it when the plane first dropped us at that old airstrip out by the lake. All the boys hadn't been able to keep still for the whole flight; we bounced our way through that long journey and constantly ribbed each other. Harvey, the Second Lieutenant, kept joking that now we'd all be able to see if Private Liddell's missus was really as fit as she was on the picture he carried around with him. We all suspected that he'd cut that picture out of a dirty magazine, of course, but there was nothing malicious in our banter. Deep down, we all wanted that blonde with the pouting lips and the curvy figure to be waiting for us, too.

And then we stepped off the plane. There'd been an almighty struggle to be first off, but in the end, Paul Hutchins – Hutch – barrelled his way through the crowd and... and he just stopped. Behind him, everyone was trying to elbow each other out of the way; we all wanted to see, like when we were kids going on holiday and I just had to see the sea before my little sister. I don't know why we had to be first, we'd all get to enjoy it for ourselves later, but I always had a competitive spirit, and the army just built it up for me.

Then the whispers started: 'There's nobody there.'

Instead of our families, our welcoming committee was a rusty old double-decker bus. Some Colonel or Desk Sergeant climbed out and told us that before we were allowed to do anything, we had to go to the barracks and change out of our uniform; we weren't allowed to travel home in it. They'd issue us with travel vouchers and then we could go home. Mutterings of discontent passed around the troops like a cigarette. Most were disappointed that their wives and kids hadn't been allowed to be there to meet them, but there were some – the younger lads in particular – who'd been looking forward to travelling home in full uniform. They'd been hoping for those same star-struck, lusty stares my grandfather told me about, no doubt.

After changing into mufti, most of us headed directly for the station, although a hard-core group of the crazier boys went straight into the first boozer they clapped their eyes on. I was in the first party, of course, and we were left at this tiny little country-village station, like fish out of water. We all had these huge eighty litre rucksacks which made us look as though we were coming home from a pleasant hike in the grassy hills rather than a bloody, sandy war-zone. Most of us could hardly even bring ourselves to speak to each other, but as the first train pulled in, we made quick promises to keep in touch and to meet up for beers at some point in the future. Thing was though, it was all for appearances. Some part of me didn't want to see any of these guys again. I'd already spent more time looking at the face of Mark Birch, for example, than my own nephew.

Only one of the lads got on the same train as me; most of them were heading in the same direction; into the city, but we lived even further out in the sticks. The train was packed full of commuters coming back from what they'd call a hard day's work so we had to sit at different ends of the carriage. I sat around this table, squashed in with three other people. Although I was facing two of them, nobody met each other's eyes; there was something dishonest about it.

I began to feel self-conscious; compared to their pristine clean suits and shoes, my old jeans and T-shirt seemed scruffy. And I probably stunk, too; I'd rushed so much at the barracks, I'd not even had time for a shower, and we'd travelled for the best part of a day. So I stared out of the window and tried to enjoy the view. I'd taken this train journey so many times that I should have delighted at the russet colours of the trees in autumn, or the rolling hills; familiar and comforting like a rumpled old blanket, but it just didn't seem right, somehow.

At the stop before mine, more people poured onto the train. Where were they going to sit; the luggage racks? An old woman hobbled on last, dragging behind her this old tartan trolley with all of her shopping in it. I watched as she tried, politely, to wheel it down the aisle. There were people standing in the aisle now though, and some of these suited men gave her dirty looks as she tried not to run over their polished shoes. I watched her mumbled apologies as she tried to find somewhere to lean and only succeeded in knocking over a man's briefcase. Nobody got up to offer her their seats though, and I started to feel those angry bubbles at the bottom of my stomach.

Finally, I couldn't bear it any longer. I stood up. 'Would you like to sit here?' I shouted across to the old woman.

The man whose briefcase she'd knocked over tapped her on the shoulder and pointed in my direction. She nodded and a grateful look passed over her face. Getting out of my seat was no easy feat though; I virtually had to climb over the table to make room. None of the other people wedging me in even budged an inch to make it easier for me, or for her. I felt like asking the whole carriage who they thought had been fighting for their rights to even take a train, or to wear those bloody stupid suits. But of course, I didn't say anything. I just boiled away inside and wondered what the hell the country was coming to.

The other thing that struck me about that hopeless train journey was the constant electronic buzz which accompanied nearly every passenger as though it was their ghostly twin. They were laden with stuff – mobiles, games consoles, Ipods, laptops. Nobody talked to each other, but everyone was talking. It was deafening; just the old lady and I stood out as different. We weren't part of this bright spanking new electronic Britain. In fact, I didn't feel much a part of anything any more. As the train pulled into New Mills station, I'd almost been expecting my heart to be in my mouth, but I felt nothing. The place wasn't my home any more. I looked at it as it really was; a collection of old, grey buildings, small factories and council houses. Just a place you pass through, not home.

I walked in through the front door feeling really strange. It was though I was in another dimension or something; it was both a recognisable home, and yet it wasn't home any more. Mam and Dad were curled up asleep on the sofa, like cats. They didn't wake at the sound of my key turning in the lock, but when my boots clomped onto the carpet, Mam woke up alright. She hated anyone walking in the house without first taking their shoes off; she must have had a sixth sense about that kind of thing. She woke up groggy, confused. She looked over at me and barely even registered me. Then came the double-take.

'Ian!' she yelled.

Dad woke up with a start. 'Margaret; what is... Ian! You're home!'

I grinned, sheepishly. Mam climbed to her feet, seeming to struggle as she did so – God she looked suddenly old – and then she was on me, slavering kisses on me, hugging me, taking a step back and looking at me and then starting the whole cycle all over again. Dad stood behind her, politely waiting his turn. He had his hands clasped behind his back as though he were surveying an untidy garden and working out just what he could do to rescue it. He too looked old; somehow, he'd shrunken like a prune.

Finally, Mam allowed Dad his go; he didn't know what to do. He reached over and ruffled at my hair, but then something in him gave way and he staggered forward and clasped me in one of his world-famous bear hugs. I thought he'd never let go. And now Mam was crying; mascara streaked her cheeks. She hugged both of us, and all suddenly felt well with the world. But the thing that really topped it off for me was that proud glint in dad's eyes when he finally released me from his grip.

'The army told us we couldn't come and pick you up... We were expecting you tomorrow... Oh, the house is such a mess... Your sister's only coming round tomorrow now, too... Bobby and Jean are at their Dad's house... How are you?' said Mam, becoming her usual, hundred-mile-an-hour self at last.

They were a bit disappointed when I decided that I wanted to go out. Mam kept saying that she wanted me all to herself just for one night, but for some reason, I felt like I had to get out of there. She was starting to stifle me again. She'd already told me off twice for trivial things like putting a tea bag in the kitchen bin instead of the new recycling bin, and for those cigarettes she found in my rucksack. She used to smell my fingers, you know, when I'd been out with my pals. Somehow, she never wondered why I came back from "playing football" every night with hands smelling strongly of fairy liquid from Danny Morris's house.

Anyway, so I had a bath, found some glad rags at the back of my cupboard – probably hopelessly out of fashion by now – and I walked up to the Queens Hotel. That used to be my local, and I was pretty much sure that some of the old faces would be in there. I was absolutely bursting with stories to tell them – stories which, of course, I could never have told Mam and Dad – like when, on my twenty-first birthday, Hutch had spiked my coffees with brandy and I'd fallen asleep on watch. Bloody hell; I'd nearly been Court Marshalled. But my pals liked stories like that; ones about brushes with the law or stupid things we'd done which at the time we thought were the end of the world, but which we could now look back on and laugh.

The Queens was a pretty soulless place, to be honest; dead every night apart from Friday when it was renowned for its lock-ins. When we used to go in there, the only people in there were people who, for some reason, thought they knew better than you, even though they spent their whole days staring into that mirror behind the bar. But we liked it because we could go into the back room – the pool room – and turn it into our own little club-house. Oh, the fights we used to have when some poor sap would try to invade our territory!

I pushed open the door; feeling the warm, tangy air hit me. Straight away, I knew that something was different. Then I remembered what Dad had told me, with a wink, before I left the house; they've only gone and banned smoking in pubs now. What a mistake that was for places like the Queens; now you could smell the old men that had pissed themselves on the bar-stools, the stale beer, and worse, their bloody awful cooking.

I stepped in, hoping to recognise somebody, but even old Cotton-Eye, the perennial gloomy barman of our youth, wasn't there. My heart sunk; despite a day of disappointments, I'd still built myself up for this entry. Somehow, I'd started to think that maybe after everything, there'd be a surprise "Welcome Home" party for me – even if that did mean that we'd have to tuck into Bev's five-day-old sandwiches.

At the corner of the bar, I spotted someone I vaguely remembered. It was the father of one of my old pals, I was sure of it, even though he now looked like some wizened old drunk. I approached him, hoping to get some information out of the man.

'Are you Danny's dad?' I asked, nervously. If it was Danny's dad, I knew all about the reputation the man carried around these parts.

'Who's askin'?' said the man, not even looking up from his pint. His knuckles flexed, perhaps involuntarily.

'Ian… Ian Birtles,' I said. 'I was mates with…'

'I know who you are,' growled Danny's dad. 'Danny told me all about you fannying about joining the army. What you do that for?'

I was taken aback. I thought this hard man would at least have some respect for a fellow fighter. 'Erm… I wanted to serve my country. I wanted to learn a trade… I did mechanics.'

'Ha,' sneered the man. 'Did you kill anyone out there then? You have been away, haven't you, looking at that sandy colour on your skin?'

'I've just finished my tour. I've signed out. Do you know where Danny is? Do you know where any of the boys are?'

'They don't come in here no more. Danny's off in Hazel Grove these days with his slag of a missus and her bastard kid. The other no-marks he used to hang about with are probably all on smack these days. It's a bloody epidermis; all of 'em are on it. Can't get enough of the stuff. Want some?' he said, with a cruel smile on his cracked old face.

'So they don't come in here any more?'

'They don't go anywhere son. Unless it's out buying smack, robbing for smack or taking smack. Bloody smack-heads,' he said, and gulped the rest of his pint down in one. 'Now, you'll be flush if you're just back off tour. Put another in that.'

I walked away from the Queens with a thousand thoughts running through my mind; prime amongst them being self-disgust. Why on earth had I bought that bitter old specimen a drink? Maybe I was still a little scared of men like him, despite the training the army had given me. I wandered the lonely streets, trying to think of somewhere to go, something to do. Again, everything was exactly the same but somehow different, just like the house. I realised that perhaps what had changed was me; the things I'd seen, the people I'd known, the war. Living in small-town New Mills had brutalised my old friends and war had brutalised me. I didn't know which was worse

My only option was to return home, which I did in the kind of tail-between-the-legs shame that the cat uses when she's been out hunting and not caught anything. If this was going to be how life was now, I wasn't sure that I wanted it.

The sight of a small red car – a hairdresser's car, they used to call them in the army – parked on the driveway behind Dad's chunky people carrier, perked me up no end though. Surely it was my sister Rachel's car. I sneaked into the house and surprised them all, bursting in, all-smiles. Rachel nearly dropped the baby – I have a little niece now, as well as a nephew – but then handed her over to Mam and we hugged, a little awkwardly I might add.

Young Bobby backed away from me when I approached him; he was a little wary of me now. Clearly, he hardly even remembered the hours when I used to baby-sit for him and we used to play toy soldiers on the rug in front of the fire.

Rachel tried to cajole him out of his shyness: 'Come on Bob. What was it you wanted to say to your Uncle Ian?'

But Bobby hung his head. He was scared of me.

'Bobby likes playing Risk, Ian; why don't you have a game with him? Show the lad real military tactics,' Dad piped up.

And unbelievably, the little boy obediently trotted off and pulled the box of Risk from the cluttered cupboard under the stairs – the one I used to hide in. We both stretched out across the Ikea rug, just like we used to, and we set up our small armies.

When the game began, Bobby started to cheat; every time he rolled the dice, he'd throw them so hard that they landed underneath the sofa. He'd retrieve them and then make up the score he needed. My armies started to diminish across the board. Young Bobby threatened world domination. Every tiny red triangular game-piece I was forced to remove represented something like five thousand men.

And I asked myself how special I really was. Who was I, amongst the thousands of people that died, to deserve some kind of hero's welcome? And in the ungainly triangular shapes of the armies, I saw failure. How could these pieces ever fit into any of the round holes of everyday life? I knew then that I would sign up again as soon as they'd have me back.

Vintage

by

A K Benedict

On our wedding night, me garter deep in presents, you read out the bottle and waggled your eyebrows. We kept it for our first anniversary but, a year later, opening it didn't seem right. The grapes would be too keen, still bouncing out of their flesh.

The next year you said that it needed more time to grow into itself, let the flavours deepen. We played a game where we guessed what it would taste like.

'Chocolate,' I said.

'Spam,' you said.

'Gold,' I said.

'Bed,' you said.

Ten years in and we thought we'd let it mature some more. Imagine what it would taste like on our ruby wedding, I said.

It's our silver anniversary and I'm here with the bottle. The cork takes some shifting; I nearly break my wrist. I pour it into the last of our wedding glasses and it is so thick, Charlie, and red. I smell cinnamon and cherries but it doesn't taste like them. Can you guess what it tastes like? It tastes of camping gas, my sunburned skin, your sneaky fags and earthy tumour. Most of all, it tastes of the yellow gum in photo albums, laid open on your side of the bed.

A Gangster Smile

by

Chris Callard

The first time I see Archie, waiting in the playground, I hate him. Of course I hate him. He is fat with the weight of regular restaurant dinners. He has tight, dyed blond curls, and a complementary perma-tan. And he smiles, all the time. The joke's on the rest of the world.

Why wouldn't I hate him? I can usually work people out on first impressions, and I don't like my impression of Archie. City boy, almost certainly, and if not, of the type. There he is, with his wife (blonde, you needn't have asked), picking up from school a daughter who wears ridiculously fancy suede boots. She's six, like Lily. Need I say more?

I've never spoken to Archie before, but I know who he is, who they are. Archie and Talia. I'm not going to talk to him now, but I'm watching him. Through the classroom window the children are fetching their coats – I can see his reflection. I'm watching those constant smiles, that's what's really getting to me. What's there to smile about? All we're doing is waiting for our children to come out. So you're the kind of hands-on father who's there to collect his children from school. Big deal.

'Hi,' I say. I've walked over to Archie. 'Which one's yours here then?' I'm a friendly guy, I could have picked anyone to talk to. Archie tells me he's Maxine's father – he uses the word 'father' – and, after a moment's hesitation, deigns to introduce Talia. I shake hands with her as though we haven't already met, though we have.

'Haven't seen you at collecting time before,' I say.

'No, I'm usually working,' Archie replies, moving from one foot to the other. I can only describe this as a swagger.

'I'm here most days,' I say. 'My girlfriend and I, we kind of share the childcare.'

Why am I talking like this?

Archie continues to grin at me, and says nothing. I silently curse myself.

'Why are you so bothered about him?' asks Andrea, when Lily is in bed. She is almost laughing, but making a show of listening so as not to annoy me. I reiterate my distaste for City boys, for suits, for men and women who 'poison society for their selfish career advancement'. My well-worn rant bores even myself, and I trail off into silence. I cannot help being like this. The world doesn't work properly and we all think we know whose fault it is.

'I don't think he works in the City,' says Andrea when I've finished. I can sense a certain satisfaction at this deflation of my argument, as compensation for having to listen to my diatribe again. 'I'm almost sure of it. Talia talks about him often being at home in the day.'

'Works from home, then. Dealing in third world currencies on the internet or something.'

'Or maybe not.'

'Well what does he do then?' I sulk, quietly.

'Talia won't say,' Andrea says, turning from the table to clear her plate.

'Well isn't that odd? Isn't that a bit strange?

Andrea raises her eyebrows. She obviously doesn't think so.

'I'll bet you he's into something dodgy. Some people – you can just tell. It's the way he and his wife smile, it's – sinister. They're looking at you and you can see they have no considerations beyond themselves. No normal empathy for others.'

'And you can tell all this from their smiles, you say?' says Andrea.

'Don't you think he looks like, I don't know, the drug-dealing type?' I counter.

'And you have been known, at times, to be the drug-taking type.'

'I'll bet you he's dodgy. Something just tells me. He goes around all high and mighty and I bet it's through something criminal.'

'Do remember you did just make that up,' says Andrea.

'Doesn't mean it's not possible.'

'Or that it is.'

'Low-life criminals still have to send their kids to school, don't they? Why not to Lily's school?'

'Don't you go spreading scurrilous rumours,' warns Andrea, and chucks me on the cheek.

'So what work do you?' I ask Archie, next time I see him, alone, in the playground. I'm being nice as pie. It's a perfectly reasonable question.

The smile stays fixed, but Archie's eyes flit from side to side. He's checking to see who's nearby, that's what he's doing! Is he going to tell me a cagey secret, because I look like the kind of guy who could keep one? I feel a ridiculous moment of pride.

'You know,' he says. 'Buying and selling. Import export.' His eyebrows are slightly raised. He's asking if I'm cool enough, if I can cope with this kind of information. Is that what he's doing? Well actually yes I can, thank you. But don't think that puts me on your level, that doesn't mean we're going to be partners in crime, Mr Drug Dealer. Don't think I'm like you.

'Right,' I say, as though I couldn't care less what he'd said. Archie turns away to look through the classroom window.

'Saw this great band on Saturday,' I say, without even realising I'd started speaking. 'The Moppets, this local band. They're amazing. You should see them if you get a chance.'

'Oh yeah?' says Archie. Children stream out of the classroom door and he looks away, making a show of looking for Maxine. I'm glad not to have to follow up such ridiculous aggrandising.

Archie eyeballs me. His pupils are tiny.

'Go out a lot then, do you?' The smile has cracked open all up one side of his face. He doesn't look away.

'Well, you know,' I mutter. 'Bit more difficult with the kid now. But I still try and keep up with things a bit.'

Where is all this coming from?

'What about you?'

'I only really get to my club.' Now Archie turns away and calls to Maxine. 'Martino's. At the marina. You know the place? I've got friends who come in by boat and we meet up there.'

Friends with a boat. Right. I've got you. Who might be helping out with a bit of import export, eh?

I tell myself to stop being childish. Aren't we just two fathers talking in a playground? No, because you're one of those private club people, aren't you? I hate those places.

'I'm not really into those places. You know, private clubs. Not my thing.'

I'm going to find Lily and go. I can just avoid him in the future.

'Oh?' Archie says. His smile is now a leer.

I'm starting to walk away to grab Lily. 'They're just a bit, you know. Divisive.'

Oh, good idea. Finish up by trying to convince him to what, give up his money with a bit of socialist discourse?

'Each to their own.' Now Archie turns his back, as though he can't be bothered with me any more. 'Having a bit of a do for my birthday next weekend actually. Not interested in coming then?'

'Oh. Well – '

He eyeballs me again. 'Two weekends in a row a bit much for you?'

You cheeky fucker.

'No, sure. I'd love to. We'd love to. I'll check – I'll tell Andrea. We'll be there.'

'Great. Martino's, from nine. Just give my name at the door.'

It's Saturday. We haven't managed to find a babysitter, and Andrea has insisted I go because I was the one who was invited and anyway she can't stand places like that, and now I'm stepping off the bus, on my own, at the marina. I have a suspicion Andrea knows how I got myself into this because she keeps going on about how broadminded it is of me to have made friends with Archie after everything I said.

Inside Martino's Talia sees me first, she pulls me over to her little group, and kisses me on both cheeks. It would be churlish of me not to mention that she is determinedly sexy. She introduces me to her (all female) friends, some of whom look reasonably normal, and not disgustingly expensively dressed, as Talia herself is. The music, playing to an empty dance floor, is surprisingly good.

After a while I see where all the men are – seated in large leather booths around the edge of the room. Archie will be embedded in one of these male cliques, no doubt. I continue talking to Talia and her friends, I make them laugh – I'm the only man amongst the women.

I'm rather enjoying myself. Finally Archie comes over, says nothing to any of the women, and leads me off to a booth I hadn't noticed, hidden further away in the club's shadows. He's chatting to me as we walk, he's saying the usual nervous host things about not knowing how many people are going to turn up. I'm feeling victorious. That I might even enjoy myself. Maybe Archie will even have some drugs going.

The booth in which Archie sits is populated by the meanest bunch of hardnuts I have ever seen in the flesh. Archie indicates the spare chair next to him. I look around and cannot see a single female figure.

Archie introduces me to all seven of them. 'Marco and Juan are over from Spain,' he says of the two men to my right. Theirs are the only names I catch. Why did they leave a spare seat for me? My mind formulates scenarios wildly. Is this a gang? Are they planning something here? Does Archie – does he think I'm in for a cut of whatever they're up to, or something?

Archie introduces me. 'Ed's an editor.'

'Good name then,' says one of them. They all laugh in a low rumble.

'Copy-editor,' I say, to avoid a silence. 'It's – a bit different.'

No one says anything to that. No one says anything much at all. The only social activity appears to be drinking. Everyone has an identical glass of iced golden liquid in front of them. In the middle of the table are two bottles of Scotch and a decanter of soda water, which seems quite moderate until I realise that every time one of the whisky bottles is emptied a waiter suddenly appears, unprompted, and replaces it with a full one.

I sip at my drink, trying to look interested in the scant conversation. Another extra glass appears next to mine and Archie half fills it from one of the bottles.

'Don't you like Scotch, Ed?' he asks. 'I can sort you something else out if you'd like.'

I make a plan to sit this out until midnight, and to foreshadow my exit by looking progressively bored, thus indicating that Archie's parties are generally quite dull. Because this is quite dull, whatever kind of edgy lives these guys might lead, or pretend to lead. I find that I no longer care about Archie, I'd just quite like to be back on the sofa with Andrea and that bottle of wine she opened when I left.

Archie reaches into his pocket and brings out a huge bag of coke.

'Aha,' says the man opposite me, whom I later note is called Stan. 'The goods.'

I look at Archie, who gives no indication of worry that I've heard this.

Right, I think. I'm going to get names, registration numbers, boat numbers the lot, and then I'm going to shop you all before I'm in bed. Even if I do like a bit of coke myself every now and then.

'Got yourself a largish personal supply there, eh Archie?' I say. I've momentarily forgotten that I've drunk quite a lot of Scotch.

'This cool with you, Ed?' asks Archie, and he seems serious for a moment. I cannot tell if he's asking if I'm cool with the drug-taking or that fact that I've cottoned on to the fact that they're drug dealers. It hasn't yet registered that I might be in any personal danger.

Archie snorts a fat line, then pushes a mirror containing two more fat lines over in front of me, and passes me a note. I really don't want to do it. I know how it makes me talk and that I'll end up asking Marco or Juan or whoever to tell me just what it's like being a drug dealer or something.

'Not for me, thanks,' I tell Archie.

'No?'

'Just not my kind of drug.'

You stupid arse. Next thing I know there's a sizeable bag of E's on the table in front of me. I can't refuse.

I casually throw one in my mouth and slip it under my tongue so I can spit it out later.

By now the bag of coke has done the round of the table.

'So what's it like, being an editor?' Marco suddenly turns to me. 'I've done a bit of writing in my time,' he says, without letting me answer. He signals Archie to pass the mirror his way again, and tells me he's got a drawer full of stories but never had any of them published. That figures, I think to myself, seeing as you're a drug dealer, and then immediately reprimand myself for such intellectual snobbery. What's to stop a drug dealer being a writer? Plus, I don't even actually know they're drug dealers for sure. I need to reciprocate Marco's interest in me, so I ask him whereabouts in

Spain he's from, noting it for later, for the police. I tell myself again they're most likely not drug dealers and ask Marco what his stories are about. He describes one of them to me and it's funny, in fact it's very funny. I forget all about the police. I feel around the floor of my mouth with my tongue and find there is nothing there but a few grains of powder.

Later, I'm in a huddle with Archie, and I tell him: 'You know what?' I'm laughing again. 'You know, Archie, earlier I thought, you know, what with that bag of coke and the pills and the boat from Spain I thought for a bit that maybe you were all a bunch of drug dealers.'

And Archie laughs, and it's the laugh that goes with the smile from the school playground, the distant one.

Later still I'm in the middle of the dance floor, dancing with Talia, and really enjoying myself.

And even later we're out the back of the club, the side that opens onto the water, and right there moored by the back door is Marco and Juan's boat, it's this huge motorboat thing, and we get on board and Marco starts the huge engine and then we're out in the open sea. Now there's just Archie and Marco and Juan and me, and these other men seem quite serious, they stare out at the dark horizon without talking, or maybe they couldn't talk over the noise of this enormous engine. And we keep going for what seems like hours, and how I know is that what with the cold air and everything the drugs seem to be wearing off, and now I'm fully aware what we're here for, I know for sure that they're going to dump me overboard in the middle of the English Channel, and no one will ever have any idea what happened to me, and Archie will go to school on Monday same as always and pick up Maxine like nothing has ever happened. I call over to Archie but he doesn't even turn round.

How the hell did I end up like this, I'm thinking.

'Further out,' I hear Archie say to Marco. They look back at the lights on the shore. 'We don't want to see anything.'

And now I'm feeling really ill, though I can't tell from what. 'You all right, Ed?' says Archie, leaning down to where my head's between my knees, and if I look up I can just see that smile again.

'I'm alright,' I say, 'I'm fine,' and then I vomit into the neck of a life jacket. Archie tells Marco to cut the engine.

‘Well, what are we going to do with him?’ I hear Archie say.

‘Do you want to lean over the side, Ed?’ he says to me.

‘What, so you can tip me over? And say I fell out?’ I reply shrilly. ‘No way.’

And I hear Archie tell the others that they’ll have to turn back, and then I’m sick all over Archie’s shoes, and Archie says nothing. And then I’m back on shore and I’m in a cab, and the last thing I remember is Archie leaning over me.

‘Missed out on something special there, Ed,’ he tells me as he shuts the cab door. ‘Floating in silence out on the ocean. Complete blackness. Not even any light pollution. Just you and the stars.’

On Monday, at school, there’s Archie, picking up Maxine.

I go up to him. I have to.

‘Didn’t think you picked her up on Mondays,’ I say, for want of something better.

‘I don’t usually,’ says Archie. ‘Thought I would today.’

I want to punch that smug smile right off his face. I find Lily and go home.

Stepping Stones

by

Christine Reece

Pulling the shiny black door closed behind her, Kelly skipped lightly down the half dozen steps into the small block-paved area that had been, at one time, a front garden. She invariably cycled to Jenny's and always left her bike chained on the inside of the front wrought iron railings. She was reaching for the key to the bike lock, when she spotted that she had a problem, in the shape of a distinctly un-circular front tyre.

'Damn' she said to herself – or so she thought – but she had been overheard by a passer-by who promptly stopped and, leaning on the railing, regarded her with two deep brown eyes and a attractive smile which spread across his face as he spoke.

'Looks like a puncture.'

She tried to look down at the bike, to concentrate on what she was going to do about getting back home and finishing off the coursework which needed to be handed in the next day, but she found her mind – and her eyes – wandering back to the stranger's smiling face.

'Have you got a repair kit in the house?'

'Sorry? Oh, no … and I don't actually live here. I'm in the student village on the other side of town.'

'That's a long push! I could give you a lift if you like. My car's just around the corner and it's a hatch-back, so we'd get the bike in.'

'I couldn't do that … I mean … it's taking you out of your way …'

'Forget it. I'm in town house-hunting for the day so I'm just scouting round anyway. Get it unlocked and I'll be back in a jiffy.'

That was how it had begun, last Saturday. Stephen had dropped her back home and she'd asked him in for a coffee, but he'd been due at another house viewing, so had suggested dinner later that evening.

During the meal they'd talked a great deal about houses, her course, books and films they both liked, and about his work as an Independent Financial Advisor. Kelly could never have imagined herself being quite so fascinated listening to an IFA speak, but she was captivated and was rather disappointed at the end of the evening that he'd made no move on her other than a tender goodnight kiss. He'd explained that he'd be back home in Cheltenham during the week, but would be here house-hunting again on the Friday evening and he'd asked whether he could see her then. As arranged, he'd picked her up from her flat and they'd been for a walk around one of the better areas of the city, ostensibly so he could 'get the feel of it'. He'd taken her hand as soon as they'd left her flat and, later on, he'd slipped his arm around her waist. When it began to get dark, he suggested a drink, pulling her close and kissing her when she agreed. Over the noisy chatter of a trendy wine bar, he'd mentioned another viewing the following day, so she'd asked him where he was staying overnight.

'Actually, I haven't booked anywhere, yet.' They were sitting side by side on a bench seat and he took her hand in his and rested both on her thigh, before asking whether she had any suggestions. She'd been crowing about him to her friends all week, but, somehow, now it had come to this – and she knew exactly what he was after – she hesitated. He was obviously several years older than her – possibly fifteen, or even more – but he seemed so attentive and had, until now, behaved impeccably towards her. The hesitation was only momentary.

'Well, it's a bit cramped, but … you could always stay at mine …if you like?'

'That is what I'd like, Kelly, but are you sure …? I mean, I could easily find a hotel …'

'No, honestly. It's what I'd like, too!'

His love-making was controlled and assured – far above and beyond the frenzied groping and panting efforts of her usual partners, but, as she lay purring in his arms later that night, she told him she'd have to leave early the next morning.

'*Work*, I'm afraid, but it helps keep down the old student debt and Jenny's very good…'

'Jenny?'

'The woman who owns the house I was at last Saturday morning. I do a bit of cleaning for her. She's seriously wealthy, but pretty good to me and it's easy money, really. She's out quite a bit and goes away a lot too, so I can more or less fit the hours in around my uni work.'

'But she'll be there in the morning?'

'She's coming back from one of her trips sometime in the morning, yes. I need to be there around eight, but will be all done by eleven. You could stay here and wait, if you like…or … I could meet you somewhere after – if you're free, that is.'

'Actually, I have a viewing at nine, so what if I drop you at Jenny's, and then pick you up after?'

* * *

By ten o'clock the following morning Kelly had only the guest bedroom and bathroom still to do. Jenny's flight had landed at eight and, when she arrived back at the house, the first thing she wanted was a shower. When the doorbell rang Kelly had started into the hall, but Jenny had called out that she would get it, saying it was probably just the postman wanting a signature for something. Kelly had closed all the internal doors so as not to disturb her employer and was surprised when, turning off the taps in the guest bathroom, she could clearly hear Jenny in the lounge, laughing. She listened for a few moments, wondering whether she was on the phone, but soon heard another voice laughing along with Jenny's, and realised it was Stephen's. She thought she'd made it clear that, just in case Jenny returned before eleven, she'd meet Stephen around the corner in the parking area and she was faintly annoyed and embarrassed that he should have taken it into his head to actually come to the house. She didn't want him to see her as she was – in her work overall, dusters and sponge cloth in her hands – but she also didn't like the way he was chatting and laughing so easily with Jenny. She waited a moment, listening to what was being said and she clearly heard Stephen tell Jenny that, 'for the price of a bar meal and a few drinks', asking a 'local student' to act as a guide to a strange town was 'a better option' than having to 'traipse around after an obsequious estate agent'.

Kelly was stung by his remarks, but, telling herself that Stephen was simply offering Jenny a cover story to explain his arrival at the house where his girlfriend was supposed to be working, she resisted the temptation to burst into the lounge. Instead, she walked calmly past the closed lounge door and into the kitchen. She'd put away the cleaning things, removed her overall, put on her denim jacket and picked up her bag, before the lounge door opened and a smiling Jenny came out of the lounge and met her in the hallway. She had been calmly chatting to Stephen while dressed in a crystal white bathrobe and, quite obviously, very little else!

'Ah here you are, Kelly, all tidied up and ready to go, love? Mr Campbell has been waiting for you.'

Kelly cringed at the way Jenny had managed to make it sound as though she was talking to a child and was glad she'd asked to be paid by direct debit so that she didn't have to suffer the further ignominy of being handed her wages in front of Stephen! Jenny opened the front door and then gave Stephen what appeared to be a very meaningful smile as she shook his hand.

'Goodbye, Stephen, so nice to have met you, and I'll expect a call, then? Goodbye.'

As they walked around the corner to his car Kelly waited for Stephen to take her hand, but he merely toyed with his car keys as he asked her where she wanted to be dropped off.

'But I thought … I mean, aren't you coming back to the flat?'

'No can do, sorry. Hop in and I'll drop you back, but I'm heading off to London straight away. I've a big meeting with an important client who's only in the country for a few hours.' Kelly was disappointed that Stephen found it necessary to brag to her in such a childish way, but even more disappointed that he would not be spending the weekend with her as she had hoped. She was also jealous and annoyed that he'd offered no explanation for his calling at the house, details of his talk with Jenny, or what Jenny had meant when she'd said she would expect a call from him – surely someone as switched on as Jenny wasn't going to discuss her financial matters with a complete stranger she'd only just met by chance?

However, if this was the brush-off it was beginning to look like, Kelly wasn't going to give Stephen the satisfaction of seeing just how upset she was, even though the rest of the journey was excruciatingly embarrassing for her. Stephen appeared to have undergone a complete personality change – all the flattering attentiveness, the tender looks and smiles had disappeared. Even his voice had lost its seductive appeal and he appeared to have adopted the same patronising tone as Jenny had used to her in front of him. It was obvious he wanted her out of his car and out of his life as soon as possible and, when they pulled up at the entrance to the student village, he didn't even get out of the car.

'I'll give you a ring sometime. Must dash, bye!'

So, that was that! Stephen was gone, and he'd left her feeling disappointed, annoyed, used – and *very* stupid for being any one of those, let alone all three!

* * *

After she'd closed the door behind them, Jenny had gone straight to the full-length mirror in her bedroom. She'd checked herself in front of it *before* she'd answered the door, just in case, although she hadn't really been expecting anyone who mattered, but Stephen was a most attractive early visitor and she wanted to check that her impression on him would have been as she would have wanted. Smiling complete satisfaction at her reflected self, she went back to the lounge, took up her diary and wrote, "Stephen ringing" in the empty space that was the following afternoon – Sunday afternoon and evenings were usually a drag, but all of a sudden this week promised to be an exception!

* * *

When Stephen rang early the following afternoon, it was to suggest he pick her up in an hour and they go for a drive out into the country – there were a couple of village properties he wanted to look at, as he hadn't been able to find anything suitable in town. He'd said he was 'really keen' to see her and apologised profusely for 'boring her' with house hunting, but his future home in the area was something he 'simply must resolve' and he would 'greatly value' the input of someone with local knowledge and taste. There was an obvious comparison being made between herself and Kelly and Jenny felt a momentary urge to spring to the defence of the girl. She'd actually become quite fond of her although, deep-down, she saw what Stephen meant and had to admit the efficacy of his comment. He was, presumably, looking to spend hundreds of thousands of pounds and, from the standpoint of someone as sophisticated as Stephen, the input of a more mature and experienced companion would obviously carry more weight than that of a student.

He had said he would 'find a way to thank her' and the barely veiled sexual innuendo in his words reminded her of the appreciative way he had looked at her the previous morning when she had answered the door in her bathrobe. When he hinted at dinner, a thrill of possibilities coursed through her and she hurriedly turned the page in her diary to see what she had arranged for Monday morning – just in case! She had her usual Monday lunch arrangement with Olivia, but Olivia was an old school friend, forty and divorced like herself, so, if need be, she could cancel the lunch and Olivia would fully understand that "potential" such as Stephen just had to come first!

* * *

He arrived spot on time, with a gallant kiss on the cheek and a very tasteful little bouquet of flowers. They toured around three or four villages and he stopped the car in front of several very attractive properties – some of which had an agent's board outside, plus a few of the most impressive which did not – but Jenny knew that all of the houses he showed interest in would have fetched three quarters of a million plus. He'd asked her opinion on architecture, garden layout, local amenities and various other points. He listened attentively to her answers before adding comments of his own, but he hadn't seemed especially interested in any one property, and although she did not comment on the fact, she was rather surprised that he didn't actually appear to have the agents' details on any of the properties concerned.

In a couple of the more promising villages they'd parked up and taken a leisurely walk around, chatting. When she expressed a particular affection for the Georgian period in architecture he had agreed that 'the characteristic allegiance to principals of symmetry and proportion were, indeed, very satisfying' and, within his reply, he had somehow managed to incorporate a compliment not only to her taste, but also to her own physical appearance. Jenny had been well schooled in the art of receiving compliments gracefully and when she'd let him know how much she had appreciated his, he had slipped his arm around her waist and kissed her. She felt there was an unspoken yet mutually acknowledged agreement that the strong physical attraction between them was being strengthened as they discovered mutual tastes and interests.

They'd found a pub with an attractive rustic exterior which had actually lived up to its promise of "Fresh Local Produce and Delicious Home Cooking". The atmosphere was cosy and conducive to the kind of gentle flirting in which they and several other couples were indulging but, by the time they left the pub, the warm and sunny evening had changed into a dark and brooding night. The first splashes of rain caused them to hurry to the car and, by the time they pulled into the parking area for Jenny's mews, it was raining heavily.

'Just sit tight; I've an umbrella in the boot.' Stephen jumped out, and, when he opened the passenger door a few moments later, he was holding a large umbrella open. Laughing, they hurried around the corner and up the front steps, then he took the keys from her and, having opened the door, ushered her in out of the now torrential rain, leaving the folded umbrella out on the doorstep.

Once inside, he dropped her keys on the hall table and then stood smiling at her – apparently waiting for an invitation into her home with that male shyness that every woman finds irresistibly attractive. She took a step forward, put one hand on his shoulder and, with the other, lightly brushed a raindrop from his cheek. His response was immediate. Sliding his hands inside her jacket, he pulled her hungrily into his arms and kissed her with a force that both amazed and delighted her. A few dizzy moments later she lay naked on her bed, watching him hurriedly remove his clothing – her own lay scattered on the floor between the hall and the bed. His eyes held hers as she half raised herself and pulled the quilt from under her, feeling the cool of the satin sheet touch her skin, and then he was with her, his hands exploring every smooth, pampered and perfumed centimetre of her willing body.

* * *

Very early the next morning, Jenny awoke to see Stephen coming back into the bedroom carrying an overnight bag he must have fetched from the car. He sat on the edge of the bed, leaned across and kissed her.

'Good morning, sleepyhead.'

'When do you have to go back home?' She asked, smiling dreamily.

'I'm really sorry about this, but … I'll have to make tracks now. I've a nine-thirty meeting with a potential client in Birmingham.'

'Why so early?' she groaned.

'I'm sorry, but then … I wasn't expecting to be staying last night as well …'

She could see the start of a laugh curling at the corner of his mouth and was so absorbed in his smile and the memory of what had happened between them that she almost let his words slip by. Then something suddenly jolted her brain into action and the question was out before she was even aware she had opened her mouth.

'As well …? So … where did you stay Friday night?'

There was a brief hesitation before he answered.

'Kelly found me somewhere.'

'You mean a hotel?'

She could see he was thinking fast, obviously wondering how far her questioning would go, and a chilling ache began snaking its way through her body. When his answer came, it seemed to her … unsatisfactory.

'No … it was a room in the student village, actually. A mate, who had gone home for the weekend, I believe. Not quite what I've become used to but, well … we were all students once.'

Jenny could clearly see the muscle flinch in his jaw. She didn't really want to hear any more, and yet, out of the protective affection she felt for Kelly, she knew she had to clarify things.

'You … and Kelly … there wasn't anything between you, was there? I mean, you said you paid her as a guide, but…'

'Kelly and I? You're joking, right? She's just a child!'

'She's twenty-one!'

'Exactly, a child!'

He was laughing as he said it, but Jenny clearly saw the muscle in his jaw tighten once more. She forced herself to smile and he kissed her again before going into the bathroom to shower.

Jenny had offered to get up and make breakfast, but he'd insisted she stay in bed. He brought her in a coffee just before six-thirty and kissed her goodbye repeating his promise to phone her that evening. She'd stayed in bed for another hour, but she didn't sleep. She was thinking back over the time they had spent together, expecting to be luxuriating in the warm glow of a new relationship, but instead there was an annoying niggle worming its way into her head and spoiling everything. She'd had enough experience of her husband's infidelity to recognise the guilty flinch when she'd questioned Stephen about Kelly and she was upset to think that she may have inadvertently hurt someone who was not only a conscientious and reliable worker, but also a friend – and young enough to be her daughter, damn it!

The more she pondered Stephen's possible duplicity the more Jenny began to worry about how much she had taken at face value. She remembered the easy way he had chatted to her when he'd first called at the house, and then on the walk and at the pub, but, although they'd seemed to be talking endlessly, she still knew virtually nothing about him. She had a name and he'd told her various things about himself, but she had nothing she could easily confirm – he had given her no address, she hadn't noticed his car registration number and he'd forestalled her when she was about to ask for his phone number by saying he would call her later that day. With a cold dread she suddenly jumped out of bed and raced downstairs, but all seemed to be as it should. Her house and car keys were safely on the ring lying on the hall carpet – Stephen had obviously dropped them back through the door after letting himself out. She then picked up her bag from the hall table and checked her bank and credit cards, but it didn't look as though her purse had been touched.

Taking the bag with her she climbed slowly back upstairs. She felt relief wash over her, followed by a wave of guilt at having doubted him. Sitting on the edge of the bed she fumbled into the side-pocket of the bag for her phone, but there was no phone there, or anywhere in the bag. In the pocket where she always kept her phone she found, instead, her diary which should have been in with her purse. Her phone turned up on the kitchen worktop. She knew she had been quite distracted last night, but she could clearly remember she hadn't even gone into the kitchen when they'd arrived back – Stephen hadn't given her a chance! She knew she'd checked her phone for messages during the drive back from the pub and she'd put it back in the correct pocket – still switched "On" and still functioning, which it wasn't now! Connection to the charger, a frantic pushing of buttons, checking of the battery compartment and the SIM card all failed to produce an answer to the mystery – everything appeared to be in order, but the phone simply would not respond.

Her emotions turned yet another somersault as she tried to rationalise what was happening to her. None of these things seemed very significant on their own and she tried to convince herself she was being paranoid – that it was all the result of some kind of subconscious guilt she obviously felt about her own sexually "loose" and potentially dangerous encouragement of Stephen – but the feeling of unease just wouldn't leave her. She decided that what she needed to do was to talk the whole thing through with Olivia. She and Olivia had shared many secrets over the years including their various misdemeanours at school, sexual exploits at university, details concerning their careers and finances, and, of course, the traumas of marriage and divorce. Each had always proved a good listener to the other, and, when necessary, a source of good advice. So, Jenny would meet Olivia for lunch as planned, and she would tell her all about Stephen. For one thing, she needed to talk through what, if anything, she should say to Kelly ……

* * *

Olivia had had a late night and was unusually tardy in getting out of bed and showering. It was lucky she had nothing on this morning because she really didn't want to hurry. At half-eleven she checked her phone – it was usual for one or other of them to text just to confirm their lunch and today Jenny appeared to have beaten her to it, but scrolling down the message Olivia was amazed to see her friend was suggesting a different venue, across the other side of town and much less convenient for where either of them lived. Presumably this place had come highly recommended by another of Jenny's friends, quite probably the one she referred to when she said, "There's sum1 u MUST meet." Olivia was intrigued and sat in the kitchen with her mug of coffee wondering who this might be – a new lover perhaps, or one of Jenny's "worthy causes" like the tragic young widow she'd given refuge to for a couple of weeks, or the penniless sculptress in need of a decent meal that she'd brought along once before. This really mattered, because she needed to know what to wear – should she dress to impress (always her favourite option), or should she dress more soberly, less ostentatiously? She picked up her mobile and tried to ring, but for some reason the call wouldn't connect and she decided she'd just have to dress to impress and, if necessary, be prepared to do all the commiserating with her words and reactions.

Just before one, Olivia took a table laid for four in the small and dimly-lit bistro. She ordered a bottle of wine and, as she sipped, she wondered about Jenny's choice. It was an area of town neither of them usually visited – the financial sector, full of offices and suited office-workers, but woefully bereft of shopping opportunities!

'Excuse me, but are you Olivia, by any chance?'

She looked up at a tall and extremely good-looking man with a soft smile and the most appealing dark brown eyes. She hesitated and then remembered the "someone" Jenny wanted her to meet.

'Yes, presumably you're … Jenny's friend…?'

'Stephen Campbell.' They shook hands. 'Do you mind…?'

He was indicating the empty seat opposite her and she smiled her agreement.

'Jenny hasn't come with you, then? Typical of her to be running late and her phone's not receiving either!'

'Actually, she rang me half an hour ago and said she'd been held up – some drama with Kelly, I think, but she said for us to go ahead and order.'

'Oh, I see. Well, shall we wait just a bit? Would you like some wine?'

'Allow me.' Stephen topped up Olivia's glass before giving himself just a half-glass. 'I have to drive later. So … you and Jenny meet here often, do you?'

'No, we meet most Mondays for lunch, but we've never been here before. I thought you must have suggested it.'

'No, no. Actually, it's not really my style. I mean … well …'

'I know what you mean – paper table cloths? Formica chairs? I can't imagine what the food will be like! Strange, Jenny's normally so discerning, I wonder why she's brought us to an out-of-the-way place like this?'

'I suppose she'll tell us, if she ever arrives.' He smiled at her once more and, feeling the effect it had on her, Olivia was anxious to know exactly what the relationship was between Jenny and Stephen.

'So, are you and Jenny … um …?'

'Together? Jenny and I?' Olivia felt ridiculously happy to realise that he was laughing at the idea. 'Good Lord, no! I mean, don't get me wrong, Jenny's great but … well, no … we're just friends.'

'So, how long have you known her, I mean … I don't remember her mentioning a Stephen …?'

'Oh, we go back quite a way. I think we met at a concert, originally.'

'A concert?' Olivia almost choked on her wine. 'But Jenny *hates* music, of virtually all kinds!'

'Yes, that's right. I think it was one of these charity things where buying the ticket and saying you were going was the real point to it all, rather than the music.'

'Yeah, that sounds more like Jenny – one of her Causes!'

'Exactly, one of her causes. Actually we met up because we'd both ducked out. We got chatting and shared a drink in a bar somewhere. We swapped numbers and meet up now and again, when I'm in town – which isn't that often and I suppose that's why my name hasn't come up. Although I must say I'm rather offended that she hasn't mentioned me! She's told me all about you.'

'So, what did she tell you about me?'

'She said …' He hesitated, trying to suppress a smile as he continued. 'She said you were attractive, intelligent and charming … and she said … she thought we'd get on well.'

'Really?'

‘Yes, and, if I may say so, I think she was right – on all counts.’ He tipped his wine glass to Olivia as he took another sip and, looking over the top of his glass, he smiled once more.

‘Look, I’m going to give her another ring.’ Olivia dived into her bag and, retrieving her phone she punched in the number. A frown creased her brow.

‘Still no joy? Maybe a different network might work … I’ll go outside in the open and try.’ He stood and walked to the door as Olivia tried to concentrate on what the problem might be between Jen and Kelly, rather than the way Stephen’s hair curled slightly at the nape of his neck and the way his smart-cas trousers fitted so perfectly around his thighs … She pulled herself up and glanced quickly around the room to see whether anyone had noticed her staring after him. When her gaze made its way back to Stephen he was in an animated conversation, waving one arm, and laughing. He raised an eyebrow as he saw her watching, and then he laughed again. Closing the phone, he came back to the table, still smiling broadly, but tried to compose his features as he explained that Jenny wouldn’t be coming after all, but she’d sorted out the problem with Kelly and would ring Olivia later to explain.

‘What was so funny?’

‘Jenny said … she said she was sure we didn’t need her around anyway – that we were both old enough to be able to amuse ourselves without her.’ Once more there was that wonderful smile. Olivia took another sip of wine, aware that she was blushing – at her age! Come on, woman, pull yourself together!

‘So, what do you think?’ Stephen was looking at her enquiringly. ‘Shall we order, or … would you prefer to go somewhere else? I mean, I’d suggest lunch at my hotel, but it might sound a bit forward and, to be honest, the food’s not that good there, anyway.’

Olivia had a feeling she knew what Stephen really wanted and she also knew it was probably a stupid move, but, what the heck!

‘We could go back to my house. I mean we could rustle up something there and my daughter’s coming at three, so I’d have to be back around then, anyway.’

‘But … I mean, that sounds great, but wouldn’t I be in the way …with Jacqueline coming?’

‘Of course not, but how …?’ She stopped herself. It was the correct French pronunciation of her step-daughter’s name that had thrown her, but then Jenny knew the family history and she’d always been careful to say the name correctly.

‘Ah, I probably know more about you than you realise!’ It was accompanied by a playful laugh and Olivia smiled too but, all the same, she was just a little disturbed to think how much Jenny might conceivably have told this man about her past!

They each had their own cars so Olivia wrote down the address while Stephen went to the bar to explain that they wouldn’t be eating after all, and to pay for the wine. When they parted outside the bistro, Stephen took Olivia’s arm lightly and kissed her on the cheek.

‘See you there!’

* * *

They made do with a light salad lunch, Stephen seeming more interested in talking and looking round the garden than eating. They took their coffee outside and sat on the terrace.

‘Did Jenny say your husband built this place for you? Very generous of him, considering you were divorced.’

‘Well, he was actually building it for us to live in together, with Jacqui – he was going to develop the old family estate and make another bundle, but that never went through, so he’s still there, with wife number four. She appeared on the horizon just after work began on this house.’

‘Four wives? Gosh!’

‘Yes, amazing what money can do, isn’t it?’ She hesitated. She didn’t really want to explain the whole complicated saga that was Jonny Brandon, yet she knew she didn’t want to give Stephen the wrong impression.

‘I’m sorry; I don’t mean to sound bitter. I was number three so I went in with my eyes open, but Jonny’s only real love was his first wife, Simone.’

‘Jacqueline’s mother. She was French, wasn’t she?’

‘Yes. She died when Jacqui was a little girl and Jonny has never really recovered from that – I guess he’s still looking for a replacement Simone, except that, in his eyes, no-one is ever going to live up to his idealisation of her, so he's doomed to disappointment, really.'

'You sound almost … sorry for him. I mean, I thought Jenny said …'

'Look, I'm not sure what Jenny has told you exactly, but you have to remember Jenny went through a very messy divorce of her own and she's a friend of *mine*, *so* by her own definition of how these things work, she can't be a friend of Jonny's. I have to say Jonny was hard on his second wife, Sally, but then she couldn't take to Jacqueline and they fought like cat and dog. Jen and I knew Jonny already and we used to call her "Silly Sally"' – she just never grasped the fact that there was no way Jonny was ever going to put anyone else before his daughter. He is very protective towards her – almost to the point of obsession – it doesn't make it easy for her, or anyone around them.'

'But you and Jacqui get on … if she still comes here …?'

'Yes, I think that's why he married me. I soon came to realise that love didn't really come into it on his side, it was simply that, somehow, the three of us managed to be able to share each other. Jacqui was not an easy child, but somehow I managed to keep her at home and out of too much trouble all through those difficult early-teen years. Even though we're now divorced and he's with someone else, Jonny won't ever forget that.'

'You make him sound so human. I … I mean, I thought there were rumours about shady friends and dodgy business deals …' Stephen frowned, realising Olivia was no longer listening to him as her gaze shifted back to the house, but he pasted the smile back on as a tall and attractive young woman swept down the steps to join them.

'Jacqui, darling!' Olivia stood and the two women embraced warmly before kissing on both cheeks, French style. Jacqueline turned to look at Stephen.

'Well, Liv, aren't you going to introduce me to your *friend*?'

'Of course, darling. This is a friend of Jenny's, Stephen Campbell.'

'Pleased to meet you, Jacqueline.'

They chatted away together for a while, Stephen's easy manner charming them both, but when Olivia suggested making a pot of tea he suddenly checked his watch and said he'd love a cup of tea, but he'd have to be going soon.

'Must you, surely not?' They were Olivia's words, but the sentiment was echoed by Jacqui.

'I'm sorry. It's way past three and I'm flying to Geneva this evening.'

'Well, I'll make the tea, then!' Olivia stood and turned towards the kitchen. Inside the house a phone began to ring, but Olivia just heard Stephen ask Jacqui if she'd show him the rest of the garden, down as far as the woods.

'I'd love to. Come on, while Liv makes the tea.' Olivia glanced back at the pair and, as she did so, Stephen appeared to say something to Jacqui then set off at a run down and across the lawn, away from the house, with the eighteen-year old chasing after him, laughing.

When Olivia came off the phone she put the kettle on to boil and mechanically laid the tray. Jenny was on her way over and there was obviously some kind of emergency because she'd said they 'must talk'. Her friend had been driving so had kept the call short, but it sounded as though there must have been some awful mix-up about the restaurant, because Jenny had been waiting at the usual place.

Olivia looked out of the window, but there was no sign of Jacqui so she went to fetch her mobile from her bag. Strangely it was turned off and she wondered how that had happened. Turning it back on, she accessed her records and checked the text message altering the lunch arrangement, but there was no mistake there. It was definitely Jenny's phone – the number had been identified by her own phone as "Jen". Usually Olivia had to differentiate between someone's "Mob" and "Hom", or "Bus", but Jenny only had one phone, her mobile – no home phone and no business number.

When Olivia opened the front door a few moments later it was to a very puzzled and rather angry-looking Jenny who brushed past her and straight through into the kitchen, her heels clicking angrily on the wooden hall floor.

'Liv, where were you, lunchtime?'

'What's going on, Jen?'

'I'm not sure. Where were you?'

'I was at the bistro, like you said, we…'

'What do you mean, "at the bistro like I said"?'

'In your text, this morning, you said …'

'Just a minute, what text?'

Olivia picked her phone up from the worktop and accessed the text before pushing the phone under her friend's nose.

'But … It says it's my number but I never sent this! Anyway, my phone's packed up. Wait a minute, this message was sent at eleven-twenty – my phone has been out of action since before half-seven this morning! Liv, I was at the usual place waiting … for over an hour. In the end I decided you'd probably been trying to reach me to call lunch off, so I went into the Arcade and bought myself a new phone before driving home. As soon as I'd got my address book I tried phoning you, but you were switched off. I was actually really worried something may have happened to you.'

'Oh I'm sorry, Jen, but honestly, I was fine. Stephen came and…'

'Stephen? What's Stephen got to do with all this? How did you meet him? I only met him forty-eight hours ago!'

'What?' Olivia felt a cold shiver run down her spine. 'The text said you had someone you wanted me to meet, and Stephen turned up, but … Jen, he told me he'd known you off and on for years!'

Once more, Olivia looked out of the window, but this time she was almost glad Jacqui and Stephen weren't on their way back. She wanted to sort out this mess with her friend, first.

'Who is he, Jen?'

'We met on Saturday, through Kelly. He was paying her – well, sort of paying her, with an occasional bar meal and that, I think. Anyway, she'd been showing him around a bit – he's house-hunting here, at least, he said he was, but …'

'Oh God, Jen, come on, spit it out! What do you know about him?' The positions had reversed; now it was Olivia who was angry and demanding explanations.

'Not much. He came to the house to pick Kelly up and we got chatting. I mean, he seemed so nice …'

'Yes, yes, I know he's charming, but get on with it!'

'Well, he said he'd ring, which he did, yesterday, and we went out for a drive and a meal and he … well, he stayed the night.'

'You mean …?'

'Well he seemed so, you know … But, after he'd gone I noticed a few strange things and began wondering about him.'

'What strange things?'

Jenny told her friend about the misplaced diary, the malfunctioning phone, the uncertainty over whether he had actually been sleeping with Kelly too, and about the fact he'd not offered any phone number or address. Now, it seemed as though he may have used her phone to arrange a meeting with Olivia – presumably by taking her SIM card and replacing it with a dud.

'But … what's he after, Jen?'

'I'm not sure, but it looks as though he may be working his way through the three of us, doesn't it? If he was with Kelly, then me, then you … You haven't … you know…'

'I may well have done, but Jacqui was here and …' Suddenly she froze. 'Oh my God! Jacqui!' Olivia rushed outside into the garden and stared wildly in all directions. Jenny rushed out after her, demanding to know what was wrong.

'He's with Jacqui! Jen, he's with Jacqui!'

'But where? How long?'

'They went down towards the bottom gate and the … woods. It was as you rang --- ten minutes … fifteen, maybe.'

'Where's his car?'

'Wasn't it out the front? We came here in our separate cars.'

'He must have parked around the corner. He'll have taken her out through the bottom gate and onto the footpath. Quick! You go out the front, I'll go this way!'

Ten minutes later the two women were back in the house, waiting for the Police to arrive. Olivia had phoned Jonny and he was on his way, too.

'You know, I think this may all have something to do with Jonny.'

'Jonny? But how?'

'He was asking about Jonny … he said something about dodgy business deals. He said you'd said things, too…'

'What? I never mentioned Jonny, or even you, I don't think … I'm not sure. But definitely not Jonny, or Jacqui. I think I'd better ring Kelly. Try and get her here, too.'

Jenny went to her bag, made the call and reported back that Kelly was in the city library and would be there in ten minutes.

'What's he going to do to her, Jen? She's eighteen! I know she's not easy, but … she's just a child!' Olivia began to cry and Jenny moved to sit beside her, enfolding the shaking body in her arms, but, all the while, she was thinking about how Stephen had manipulated them all, and how he had denied any relationship with Kelly using the very same words Olivia had used about Jacqui – "She's just a child".

'Come on, sweetie. It'll be alright. They'll get him.'

'How, Jen? How? We know nothing about him! Who he is, what he wants! Nothing! How on earth are they going to find him … in time … before …' A fresh wave of sobs shook them both and they clung each to the other. There were no suitable words, only shame, guilt, and a terrible, numbing fear.

The Police arrived first, closely followed by Jonny and then Kelly who put another link in the chain of events. She was able to confirm that her bicycle tyre had not been punctured the previous Saturday, it had been let down and she admitted she had slept with Stephen, in her Student flat. It looked as though his passing by when Kelly discovered the flat tyre was no coincidence – it had been carefully planned and staged. The Police seemed to think that, from the first, Jacqui was the intended target – or rather, Jonny, through his daughter. The kidnapper must have tracked backwards from Jacqui, possibly watching her, then Olivia, Jenny and finally Kelly, over several weeks, learning their habits and routines. Kelly was the first in a series of "stepping stones" that had given Stephen access to his victim. He had probably seen this staggered path as a safer bet, arousing less suspicion and more likely to succeed than someone of his age making a direct approach to an eighteen-year old girl who was closely protected in her own home and chauffeur-driven nearly everywhere she went. Jonny was assumed to be a very wealthy man, and a ransom demand was expected, but what was clearly of some concern was the fact that Stephen had shown himself to so many people. There were excellent descriptions available detailing his approximate age, height, weight, facial features, accent, manner of speaking – virtually everything about him. This was an unusual display of confidence in a "kidnap for ransom" case and the police were clearly puzzled by this factor.

* * *

For all those concerned, the hours slowly passed, then stretched into days, weeks and months. No ransom note was ever reported to the police, or any trace ever found of either Jacqui or Stephen. Following a chance remark at a press briefing in the early days of the enquiry, the story was dubbed *The Case of the Stepping Stone Stalker*, but even this dreadful example of British journalistic invention did not lead to the solving of the mystery. There were rumours, of course – false leads and misleading falsehoods. Some said "Stephen" was a crossed business associate who had kidnapped and killed Jacqueline out of revenge. Others said a French-Algerian gang had masterminded the snatch to keep Jacqui part of her mother's family. It was also claimed that Jacqui and Stephen had eloped together to some distant shore. Whatever the truth, the case was taken as proof that you could get away with almost anything providing you throw in enough juicy meat to keep the press sharks interested – the ensuing feeding frenzy will spill sufficient new blood to confuse even the most assiduous bloodhound.

Whichever of the printed "truths" you decide to believe, the events together with the ensuing press and public speculation surrounding the Stepping Stone mystery drove apart all those affected by the story. Kelly could not come to terms with her role as the first Stepping Stone and dropped out of university, gave up what she'd seen as her bid for freedom, and went back to live with her mother in rural Devon. Jenny could not live with the prying public interest in – and gross exaggeration of – her "voracious sexual appetite" and left the country, not revealing her intended destination to any of her former friends. Olivia never recovered from the loss of the child she had tried to love for the sake of the father, or from seeing what that loss did to him. She died from an overdose one year to the day after Jacqui went missing. As for Jonny, he was a man already severely damaged by the cruel fates that had taken from him his first and only truly-loved wife. Amid rumours that money was mysteriously "disappearing" from his company, he was eventually arrested for assaulting and seriously injuring wife number four. The newspapers said the argument began when she'd had the temerity to suggest it was high time his first wife's clothing be removed from the house they shared.

Following his death, Jonny Brandon's company and supposed wealth were found to be as withered and depleted as the man himself, but among his personal papers were a series of picture postcards, addressed to him via his second wife, "Silly Sally" at her home in leafy Surrey. There was no message, and the cards were posted in various places all over Europe and beyond. Each depicted a scene in the country of posting. They were all different locations, but each showed a specific tourist attraction – a set of "stepping stones". What Jonny had gone through when each of these postcards was received can only be guessed at, but may go some way to explaining why he died of a stroke at the age of fifty-one – still in prison, a brooding and embittered shell of a man.

End Grain

by

Manus McDaid

Jazz music is much like the sea, with surface tensions failing to corroborate the underlying mutinous vibe – and you can drown in it. Meet Paco Pastorals for example – piccolo jazz-meister extraordinaire and great entrepreneurial genius of late. Late-night drinking sessions of old; way back before the newer, rather ambiguous although legal, 24/7 binge promo's – equally lethal, though!

Enter the valiant-vainglorious: Victor, *in propria persona* ex-naval functionary sea-dog struggling on the dry, dry land whilst, rather shakily trying to balance the log in his cul-de-sac public house: The Chequers. In the nick-of-time, he was approached by familiar, after-hours acquaintance, Pac' - with a view to the establishment of an auxiliary, once-a-month only, Musicians' Club. To be held in the back room, away from the mainstream, c/w entry fee – *virtually* all-night.

In actual fact, the pair of them went way back to '75 when Victor, under the wing of the illustrious Captain Peter Jackson, post [last orders] military career worked as head barman on The QE2; no doubt enjoying The Royal-Connection en route: Mr Pastorals was currently cruising along with one of the resident dance bands, on flute; a free passage to New York. To the famous 'Birdland' night club where he was to further his knack for *improvisation*; Victor's nemesis – JAZZ! Until this little revelation they had enjoyed many a mutinous, after hours boozing session alone/together in splendid isolation.

This was [probably] their finest hour: isolated as journeymen in limbo before Old Victor, the proverbial drunken sailor, jetsam washed-up on the floundering shore of the South Hamptons somewhere; before he came into his bar. Literally: inherited a *last-chance-saloon* - out in the sticks, a bottle-bottom kickback from his dear, late Uncle Romilly. Paco was soon to follow in Victor's wake, though. Accused, on a return booking, of being 'too precious'. Far too 'jazzy' now, as he condescended to the cabaret [my friend] - walking the short pier that was effectively *his* plank to the promenade. He tracked Victor down. It wasn't hard to do as the bullish man left a trail of broken china all over the shop, as if a loose canon off the rails; a runaway train gunning it upcountry – north of Windsor; High Wycombe way.

So, there was Paco – post Cunnard - and his scruffy entourage, to include chairman; treasurer [himself] and vice-president – Victor, of course would be nominally elected as the Main Man presiding over the victuals, he would have to sanction the issue of meal/standard-off-the-roll raffle/tickets (a legal requirement for any late drinking club at that time) on receipt of the *café-culture* entry fee. Such fee to cover the costs of guest musicians ... blah, blah - that was it! A done deal so it seemed: with Victor effectively having to do - **S***weet* **F***anny* **A***dams*.

Strangely, there was a conspicuous lack of any music whatsoever in the pub proper: just the brittle ambience of well-worn bar billiards – *clonk*; the addled grandfather (if time were a river this one would be an eccentric eddy) clock – *whir, clinkety-clank* - set against the contrapuntal, dulcet church bells beyond: *no conflict of interest by juke-box, then*. No loss of disco revenue.

However, round about midnight, just when things were getting nicely mellow; the guest player's swinging and singing and ... it didn't mean a thing. The proprietary 'Old Vic' ran into a sudden squall; bawled them out! Pulled out the proverbial plank – THWACK! A broadside on the bar; first off they all thought he'd decided to join in, liven it up ... have a bit of a go at it himself – post-modern-jazz being as it does (?) Outside the box, he was right there on the down beat, though: the old bugger meant it – Treason!

The rocking boat downscaled on a high 'C' of star-Spangled nonsensical fusion ... stuff as the, much dreaded post-maritime, migraine ensued ...THWACK! THWACK!! 'The Yanks Are Coming' he further declaimed. What musical brouhaha, the planky end-grain staring like loaded barrels, sawn-off menace - straight at them ... Thelonius Monk's classic *Round about Midnite,* on the deviant blowing section, really yanked his ball-and-chain (cut loose from the metaphorical dungeon of p.m. melodies) it seems.

Then the calm, the bottle of rum, the pacifier courtesy of the committee: duly pasteurised, Vic admitted to having a pathological hatred of American [Afro- in particular] jazz music, but as President, conceded to being the proud owner of a somewhat modest [Caucasian] record collection which they were, rather patronizingly invited/pressed up the gangplank of his mind, into the *crows-nest,* to *appreciate*. And, sure enough, next to the gramophone - under a portrait of Regina v. Dredge (**H***er* **R***oyal* **H***ighness,* right up there on the flock-wallpaper) was leaning a stack of old 78r.p.m. EMI/Decca acetate discs containing: *The Complete Speeches of Sir Winston Churchill,* himself. Enough words were uttered from **H***is* **M***asters* **V***oice* to keep them, silently standing-by for most of the night at Victors self-aggrandising, vicarious pleasure. At least until he suddenly went into another spasm and bolted. Down the narrow staircase, over the chessboard tiles, he went; out to the motor and off down the lane – psychologically fugued - toward the opaque horizon, out of his depth as the band played on at the lower deck – mutinous undercurrents prevailing.

He didn't get too far, though as Paco – on the short-straw - soon tracked him down (again) to the outer perimeter, the junction where he had apparently had a go at forking left but didn't quite make … the reverse camber – wall of death. Thus ending up quite compromised at the partition: a telegraph pole. Luckily for him the axles-of-evil balanced-out in his favour as the rack-and-pinion assembly centre-folded neatly up the near-side supporting steel stay … rode it at an angle of 60 degrees north at half-mast. Not that Victor knew that, though. The acrid smell of battery acid, generally toxic stuff … that permeated the interior carcass and the perverse refusal of the ignition switch to engage the starter motor, all duly prompted him to make a break for it – he simply opened the door (against the grain of exponential gravitas) and stepped out.

'Whoosh, wanged-a-wrover on-is gwrassy Noel, Wromilly' - he was last heard to say as Paco observed him rolling down the embankment, into the yawning gullet of the dozy, early morning articulated refuse collection road-train coming round the bend. Snap! Closing time in one brief sound-bite: famous last words it would

seem (oh well, 'Pride goeth before destruction and a haughty spirit before a fall') from the slippery old Vic as he tipped bite-sized into the jaws of defeat – be-bop! More methane to the landfill, beneath the screamingly unprincipled land-gulls, bubbling underground for the final bell – pfttt … Paco Pastorals felt - *the hand of history on his shoulder* - the end of a another gig, tragically cut short as a new sun arose: Victor has been (License Applied For) and gone.

A time to split - from the lubricious lock-in/Davy Jones's Locker crime scene; from the lack of further funding behind *The Chequers masthead* – busted flush [very tight ship]. And, unlike the crooked timber of humanity you can't saw-up a river or walk on it: water falls back down on you in a continuous cadence with neither consequence nor short ends - where the grain should, really stop. So he just went right-on along with it, with the flow - all the way to mainstream land (where you can drive in the *middle*-of-the-road, unambivallently!) *Cool.*

Well, maybe? Even Paco had to admit to it, the slight frisson: he was beginning to feel the heat on his back; Dionysian currents below.

Charity Begins at Home

by

Madeleine Walker

Sophie nosed the car into the queue of traffic, cursing herself for leaving too late and getting caught in the motorway rush hour. Heat shimmied on the tarmac and as she opened the window to let in some air, a hot blast of diesel assaulted her nostrils from the truck idling next to her. The truck driver's tattooed fingers thumped the side of his cab in time to a tune on the radio. A trickle of sweat coursed between Sophie's shoulder blades. She felt uncomfortable and uneasy, but then her sister Harriet had always had that effect upon her.

At the airport Sophie spotted Harriet straight away. A still, exotic figure amongst the bustling travellers pulling their wheelie cases, she was wearing a baggy tee-shirt over a long, African print sarong which had been knotted at the waist. Her hair hung in mossy clumps around her tanned face and an assortment of bags and rucksacks lay strewn at her feet. Sophie ran towards her sister.

'Harriet,' she gasped. 'I'm so sorry I'm late…the traffic was unspeakable.'

Sophie hugged her sister, and smelt a sharp tang of sweat mingled with dust and something else she couldn't identify.

'That's okay. I was rather enjoying myself,' smiled Harriet. 'It's been a long time since I was in an international airport.'

Harriet was on a visit from Tanzania, where she had been working in an orphanage for the last four years. She planned to combine family visits with the celebration of their cousin's wedding.

'Nice dress,' said Harriet as Sophie loaded the luggage into her car. Sophie glanced at her sister to see if she could detect any sarcasm in her voice, but Harriet beamed back at her.

'Yeah, thanks,' said Sophie, pleased that her sister had appreciated the expensive cut of her plain linen dress.

As Sophie eased herself into the driving seat and clipped on the seat belt, she glanced at Harriet's sharp profile next to her, and noticed how much weight her sister had lost since they'd last seen each other – that had been two years ago, at their father's funeral.

'So how are you?' she said. 'How's the work going?'

'We do our best,' said Harriet, 'but there's so much hardship,' she sighed. 'We try to deal with children whose parents have died of aids, children who've been abused. It's an enormous task.'

Sophie had never been close to Harriet. There was five years between them, and when they were growing up Harriet was always the whiny younger sister, trying to muscle in on Sophie's games. Sophie remembered the cruel tricks she played on her sister. On one occasion when Sophie was trying to impress a friend, they had shut Harriet in the cricket pavilion in the local park just as the park keeper was about to lock up for the night. As dusk fell, Sophie felt guilty and they had clambered back over the fence to release the tear-stained Harriet. Sophie had felt sorry enough for Harriet to let her have a drag of her cigarette on the way home – on condition that she didn't tell their mother about the incident.

In her introspective teenage years, Sophie recalled very little of her sister, apart from the fact that she was a dreamy child who always wanted to look after injured birds and abandoned kittens. In the years that followed, the sisters had gone to different universities and then Harriet had gone overseas so their paths had rarely crossed.

Sophie drove Harriet to her new house, of which she was very proud. It was detached and situated in a leafy estate. It had four bedrooms, a good-sized garden, a separate study and a double garage. Sophie and her husband Joe were heavily mortgaged to pay for it and to meet the bills, Sophie had had to return to work after having the children. Now, she was worried about the rumours of a recession. Interest rates had soared and the prices of gas, petrol and food were ever-increasing.

'What a huge house, Sophie,' said Harriet.

Just then, Sophie's children, four-year-old Katie and two-year-old Oliver, barrelled around the corner, closely followed by their father.

‘Hello, I’m Auntie Harriet. You won’t remember me.’ Harriet squatted down to the children’s level, ‘but you might remember Pongo...’ The children took a step closer. ‘…He’s in my pocket. I’ll show you him later.’

Katie hopped around and grinned.

She knows how to talk to children, thought Sophie. I suppose that’s all part of her job.

After a cup of tea and a chat, Sophie drove Harriet to their mother’s house about five miles away, where she was to stay for the duration of her visit.

‘Harriet looks well,’ said Joe later in the evening, after the children had gone to bed.

‘Well, her life is so straightforward. Why wouldn’t she look well?’ Sophie got up and surveyed the garden, noticing with irritation that the hedge was so straggly that they’d be getting complaints from the neighbours if they didn’t cut it back soon.

‘I don’t understand my sister,’ Sophie’s voice quavered. ‘Is she really fulfilled trying to right the wrongs of the world? … I mean it’s all very noble but is she going to do this for the rest of her life?’

‘Well, I don’t know why you’re so cross,’ said Joe, draining his glass of Chardonnay. ‘I think she’s rather endearing. She knows what she wants to do with her life, and she doesn’t care what anyone else thinks of her. I admire that.’

Sophie clattered the dirty plates in the sink. She was peeved because when she had shown Harriet around the house earlier, her sister had made all the right noises until they came to the sitting room where Sophie and Joe had just installed a huge, flat screen, HD, plasma TV. It had been very expensive and Sophie knew that they couldn’t really afford it. Sophie had switched on the television but instead of marvelling at the sharpness of the picture and the intensity of the colour, Harriet had turned to her with a smile and said, ‘Technology is amazing, but is there anything worth watching on the television? When I’m in Tanzania I never give it a second thought.’

It wasn’t the response Sophie had been looking for, and it made her seethe. What right had Harriet to criticise her way of life? After all, she, Harriet, was the outsider, the one with no property, no money and no security.

For the next couple of weeks, Sophie spent a lot of time with her sister. There were picnics with the children, trips to local places of interest, and family get-togethers. Harriet endeared herself to everyone. She was cheerful, wonderful with the children, and helpful around the house. One day, Sophie overheard a conversation between Harriet and her next door neighbour, Rob, during a lunch time barbecue in the garden.

'So what is it that you do in Tanzania?' said Rob, studying Harriet's face.

'At the moment I'm working with teenage mothers to help them care for their babies and children.'

Katie, who was sitting on Harriet's lap, played with her hair.

'You wouldn't believe the responsibilities these young girls have in the rural villages. Sometimes they're the sole breadwinners and if the rains fail they can't feed their families.'

The clatter and chink of cutlery and glasses gradually subsided and a hush descended on the garden as everyone listened to Harriet.

'It is admirable work,' said Rob, 'but don't you ever get discouraged? Africa has so many insurmountable problems.'

Harriet said nothing for a moment, then she replied with a quiet intensity, 'If I can improve the life of just one person in the smallest way, then that's enough for me.' She smiled at Rob.

'Come on Katie,' Harriet said, tickling her niece under the armpits, 'this is boring talk. Let's go and play the horsey game.'

Katie squirmed and shrieked and Sophie felt unaccountably annoyed. Not only was Harriet charming the adults with her selflessness but she was also willing to play the kind of boisterous games with the children that Sophie tried to avoid. Yesterday Harriet had spent over an hour with her head under a tea towel pretending she couldn't find the children. Oliver had laughed so much that fat tears had rolled down his pink cheeks and that night he'd told Sophie that he loved Harriet best of all.

'Just look at her,' said their mother as they watched Harriet charge around the garden neighing and whinnying with Katie on her back. 'She's having such a good time here. What a shame she can't do her good works in this country.'

'I don't think anyone here is needy enough for Harriet,' replied Sophie.

She knew it was a churlish thing to say, especially when everyone was enjoying themselves, but she'd heard nothing but praise for Harriet for two weeks and she was sick of it.

The family wedding was a great success. The best man thanked Harriet for making the hazardous journey to be with them and praised her work in Africa. Sophie was pleased that the occasion had gone well, and that everyone had enjoyed her sister's visit so much. She felt quite indulgent towards her. If Harriet wanted to spend her life in third world squalor then that was up to her. The important thing was that their mother was happy.

That night, after the wedding, Sophie found herself alone in the sitting room with her mother. Harriet was helping Joe put the children to bed.

Her mother placed a blue veined hand on Sophie's arm. 'I wanted the chance to speak to you, Sophie.'

Sophie looked at her mother's face, still lively and attractive at sixty-eight, and she wondered what was coming.

'I've had lots of discussions with your sister since she's been staying with me and I've made a decision that I want you to know about.'

Sophie's heart pumped faster.

'I've decided to put the house into Harriet's name. I worry about her so much. She's got no savings and no home. I feel that the house will give her some security. I do hope you understand, after all, you and Joe have so much.' She encircled the room with her arm and smiled at her.

Sophie felt an icy fist close around her heart.

'Of course, I haven't forgotten the children,' continued her mother. 'I've set up separate trust funds for them, but I feel Harriet's work in Africa is so important, not only to her but for all of us, that I think we should support her in every way we can.' She gazed at Sophie. 'You do agree with me, don't you dear?'

Jumping Off Point

by

Sara Miller

vi.

The cat's saucer upended, water dripping between the slats in the decking, and the cat, old tabby, sitting in a fat slice of sun watching. Zoe tipped the water out, now lifts her bottle and shakes in a little milk, amazed how the colours in the saucer disappear as the milk drips, covering the base. She stirs with a stick and feels the wind catch her curls and then with one pudgy hand grabs white jasmine and flings it in. Her hands smell of jasmine and the saucer is now full of milk and flowers, and she stirs with the stick and calls the cat, but the cat is not stupid and stays safe in the fat sunshine and this, for some reason, makes the baby laugh and she watches the clouds race and stirs the milk and everything is perfect.

v.

Her hands have changed. The lines have moved.

'Zoe, hold the spoon like this,' and it feels strange in her hands as though they have forgotten that they are hands, forgotten that they once knew how to hold a spoon, stir a pot of soup.

'That's it, Zoe. Good girl. What a big girl.' They hold her hand and cheer when she takes a step and she knows she used to walk a straight line but her legs have forgotten, and when she opens her mouth to say, 'I am Kate with a K' only garbage comes out, muffled reminders of far away words, like half glimpsed light through dipped eyelids; but they laugh at that too. She's afraid because this is not her body, and this seems like falling but then that warm woman is holding her again and it's nice there, in the circle of her arms, listening to the thud-thud of hearts echo between them, and Zoe doesn't mind forgetting she was once Kate.

iv.

In one breath the world changes.

iii.

Her name begins with a K and so does mine. There is a sleek cat curling its way around the garden. Cat, cat, Kate. Yes, Kate with a K. Her name is Kate; that woman outside in the rain but dry on the lawn, as I am dry in my chair; she is sitting on the lawn with a man behind her, his hand on her hair. The woman on the lawn and I are nodding in time and tapping her-my fingers on the lawn-table and our eyes meet on the pane, the pane with rain drops that trail focus. She is tired, I am tired, and when my eyes close to blink the rain away it is red and warm; open again brightness flares, then dark and quiet and someone says, 'Time to Jump'. Yes, this is the Jumping Off Point, so I jump and the lady on the lawn falls flat on her face.

ii.

My name is Kate and I have it on this list of things to remember today.

There are tablets, 'you must remember until I can sort things with work.' They are colour coded, he's good at things like that; yellow for morning (sunshine), blue for lunch (jar of decaf), red for evening (sunset). One, two, three, swallowed with water or milk or juice, though today one sticks and then … my throat aches. I eat bread to try and force it down.

This is like love; always around me, in my head and my heart and changing my mind. And love is like this; you begin to forget yourself.

He's been working at my head like a Fabergé egg, pulling out the insides, trying to cut doors and windows, blowing into my ear to clear the brains. I wonder if I hold my hands out could I save any of me, because I've begun to forget things; numbers, reasons, brands of tea.

He wraps me up, 'warm darling against the winter,' and I stand as a statue while he combs my hair, frames my face. His fingers cup behind my head, tilt it left, then right, putting me out to display below the rows of tiny shoes. His mouth is on my forehead; he can't see the jagged crack.

'Where are your keys, the keys?' he shouts and whispers. Something bounces between his chest and mine as he holds me tight, and my shoulder is wet and he is shaking.

We are in our house in London but outside I am walking sandy streets; sand under my feet and in my mouth and I am sure if I turn this way and then that, and pass the chip stand and the promenade, and pass the men peddling cheap t-shirts and go into the dark streets, I will find myself, find her, her, her.

i.

I remember our first weekend away. Four hours from London, trailing my fingers in the wind through rolled down windows. We packed sandwich fillings and chocolate tight against icepacks, then ate slices of deli ham rolled into fingers and melted the chocolate on the bonnet until we could break pieces off. We left the motorway and came down through forests, and he told the craziest stories of horses and dragons. I laughed so hard, laughed like you only can when you are in love and imagine you can see forever. What I saw was the sea, and heard the waves and the seagulls calling; wheeling and swooning through the air. We drove around roads powdered with sand, lines blurring between land and sea. I read the street names aloud and my finger traced the map until we found our rented flat hidden in a back street where the lamps dropped dusty light and the smell of the gardens was still thick with summer.

'Let's go for a walk...'

together

'...and then come home.'

We left the flat with the creeping flowers and wandered giddy with the freedom of it all in the late summer, skirting tourists and ice-cream drips. I held his hand and he walked on the outside, one long leg occasionally kicking down into the gutter to lift the sand.

Down along the promenade, under gulls with white sail wings, there was a car-boot sale, whole lives folded out on melamine tables. We waltzed around the record stalls, jewellery and old annuals, around the car parts and racks of spit thin clothes, and stopped by the woman on a deckchair who had tipped out every drawer from home; one hundred, one thousand memories spread like jetsam.

I ran my fingers over pasted jewels; rough shells from Greece with old whispered wind; an empty wine bottle she'd turned into a lamp.

'Still works love,' she pushed a switch and the bulb lit, light and shadows scattered across the table.

In the corner, under a stack of music scores, well thumbed, there were baby shoes; hand stitched with roses that made my heart beat faster.

'I think they're too small for you,' he said, one finger on my wrist, and I wished that the wind hadn't blown the confetti from my hair. She packaged them in brown paper and I carried them by the string.

We got chips on the pier, chips that crunched like grit between my teeth.

'There's sand in the soil the potatoes are grown in,' the girl said as she scooped into paper cones bright with grease, the smell of vinegar and salt hot in the air.

'Does that mean they don't wash them?' I asked, my cheek against his, but he laughed that low and strong laugh and we turned like a spinning top, my feet on his, to watch the sea for a while.

The lights were on the promenade and leading away in coloured strings from the shore, the sounds of amusements behind us, the streets growing less sandy, and quieter, and stiller, and darker as we left all those people behind and went back to our flat. And in the darkness he laughed low again and spoke against my ear, words like red velvet ribbons, 'Oh Kate', and then deep in his chest, a growl that echoed in my own, and I fell into it.

Later he brought me tea in a cup on a chipped saucer, the tea sloshing into it as he climbed the stairs. That brought a frown but I kept my thumb over the chip and sipped it all from the saucer; to save my bruised lips from the hot tea I smiled, but the truth was my lips were fine; I drank from the saucer because he wanted it to be perfect, and so it was. He left the windows open, in deference to his wife, he said and I asked him to say it again and the heat of it carried us through; the smell of jasmine wrapped around our sleep.

The Big, Bad Wolf

by

Diane Churchill-Evans

'Once upon a time there lived a pretty, little village girl who always wore a red cloak with a hood and so the villagers called her Little Red Riding Hood.'

This is one of Karen's favourite stories. Her mother reads to her every night before she goes to sleep. Karen has been brought up on a mixture of Western and Oriental fairytales. The first Christmas after they had moved to England, Karen's father bought her a colourful picture book of Japanese fairytales that contained a particularly good story about a wise monkey. Really it had been bought as an indirect gesture to her mother, who smiled in tender amusement at her husband's efforts to find the nearest thing he could to her own culture. He confessed he had been unable to find a book of Vietnamese fairytales, or even Chinese fairytales come to that because surely they would have come close to the mark?

Karen has never owned a book of Vietnamese fairytales. Her grandmother, and in turn her mother, are both very good at telling stories. They don't have to rely on the pages of a book to remember what happens and often the best stories they tell are fresh from their imaginations which was a valuable resource in Vietnam where books were harder to come by than in England. Karen's mother had taught at a local school so Karen was more fortunate than most in the number of books she was brought up with but still she was very used to the oral tradition of storytelling in her earlier years.

Karen's favourite Vietnamese fairytale is called *The Fly*. It is about a rich man who lent money to all the poor people in the area at unfairly high rates of interest. One day he visited a poor man to see what possessions he could claim. When he arrived the poor man was out but his young son was playing in the gravel beside their home. When asked where his father was the boy replied, 'My father has gone to cut living trees and plant dead ones, and my mother is at the market selling the wind and buying the moon!'

The rich man was perplexed and asked the boy repeatedly where his parents were. The boy persisted with the same answer until eventually the vexed rich man said, 'Look! If you will tell me what you mean, I will forget the debt your father owes me, as heaven and earth are my witness.'

The wise, young boy observed that heaven and earth couldn't talk and so some living creature should be their witness. The rich man pointed to a fly on the doorframe and said, 'That fly can be our witness!'

This agreed, the young boy explained, 'My father has gone to cut down bamboos and make a fence with them, and my mother has gone to sell fans to buy oil for our lamps.'

A few days later the rich man broke his promise and returned for his money. The case was taken before a local landowner in front of whom the rich man argued he had never seen the boy before let alone made a promise to him. The landowner despaired that it was one man's word against another's and said that they needed a witness. The boy announced, 'There was a fly – a big, fat one, sitting on this gentleman's nose.'

'You liar!' shouted the rich man, 'It wasn't on my nose, it was on the doorframe.'

'Nose or doorframe, it doesn't make any difference,' said the landowner. 'Clearly you *did* make the promise and so the debt is paid.'

When Karen first heard this story she had to have the meaning explained to her because she was still only very young but once she understood she thought it was very clever and so she would ask to hear the tale over and over again. Karen wants to grow up to be as wise as the young boy so that if a rich man ever tries to deceive her she will know how to outwit him.

When Karen came to live in England *The Fly* became more of a favourite than ever before because it reminded her of that far away place that felt decreasingly like home but was increasingly idealised in her mind. Her mother had only just repeated the story of *The Fly* the previous night; 'Oh not again!' she sighs in good humour as

Karen bounces into bed calling *'The Fly, The Fly, The Fly!'* The best bit comes when the young boy describes the big, fat fly sitting on the gentleman's nose. This makes Karen laugh and often, as her mother describes this episode, she gently prods the end of Karen's nose. Karen invariably starts giggling in anticipation long before her mother even gets up to this point.

Tonight though, it is Little Red Riding Hood. Her mother has chosen this on purpose and Karen is shrewd enough to perceive why but she doesn't altogether mind as it is another of her favourite stories. Karen snuggles down under the layers of bed-sheets and blankets that ensconce her. She feels warm and fresh after her bath. The smell of magnolia, her mother's favourite bath salts, waft from her body every time she turns over. Karen is only allowed to use her mother's magnolia when she has been especially good and today her teacher had given her a gold star for comprehension so that awarded her the anointing of magnolia in the bath. The bath salts were of far more use to her than any gold star that had been stuck into her text books by her teacher but even at the age of seven-and-a-quarter Karen can recognise that the stars are a means of earning magnolia baths, and so she works in earnest. The stars always bear a rouge halo that becomes transferred from Miss. Thornton's lips as she licks the adhesive side but in Karen's mother's eyes that does not seem to detract from the fact that her daughter has earned a gold star, and so Karen doesn't mind. Besides, Karen knows the stars aren't real gold, and they aren't even real stars come to that because when did you ever see gold stars in the sky apart from those painted on the charity Christmas cards her mother buys each year?

'One morning, her mother baked some bread and said to her, "Go and see how your poor old grandmother is and take her a loaf and a pot of butter." '

Karen hasn't seen her own grandmother for two-and-a-half-years which, at her tender age, is a very long time indeed. She had wiled away most of her days with her grandmother when she lived in Vietnam. She frequently dreams of being back in her arms and hopes that her Vietnamese name, Doan Vien, which means Happy Reunion, will make it her destiny to fulfil this dream. Her mother named her thus in anticipation of the day when Karen's father would come back to collect them and they could become a real family. That was the day Karen's grandmother cried. Karen had never seen her grandmother cry before. She was one of those women who could cope with anything and Karen liked that. Her mother was not so strong. In those days her mother cried every time a letter arrived from her father. Karen didn't even know what her father looked like at this stage but she suspected he must be very horrible if he could make her mother cry just by something he wrote in a letter. One day Karen's mother tried to explain to her that her sorrow was mixed with tears of joy upon finding that another letter had made it through to them but Karen decided that if you were going to cry every time you felt happy then who would *ever* want to be happy?

Karen is happy living in England. At least she prefers it to the couple of months they had spent living in America when her father first came for them. England is cold but she finds it quieter than America. Karen's grandmother likes quiet. She prefers the solitude of the paddy fields to the bustle of the market and since Karen had spent so much time with her grandmother she likes to think they share identical tastes. Everyone in their village respected her grandmother but there were some whom she overheard criticising her mother. During one of Karen's lessons in which her mother was teaching her English, Karen asked her what she had done wrong. Her mother explained that some of the village people were accusing her of betraying her roots. Karen asked her mother what this meant as she thought only trees and plants had roots. Her mother explained that in the English language people could be said to grow roots too; apparently it was an expression that her father used. Her mother continued to explain that sometimes you had to move home and grow new roots in a different place but that it didn't mean your old roots were bad or that you should ever forget them. When she was next alone Karen examined the soles of her feet to see if she could find any roots. Since there didn't appear to be any there she decided it didn't matter what soil she lived on.

'Walking through the woods she met a wolf. He asked her where she was going, and the poor girl, who did not know that it is

dangerous to stop and chat with wolves, said, "I'm taking this loaf and pot of butter to my grandmother." '

By the time she was living in England Karen knew better than to talk to strangers, especially those who tried to entice her into a car with honeycomb crunch or sherbet, even though they were her favourite sweets. 'But sometimes strangers don't drive cars and what's more', thinks Karen as she tugs on the outer bedcover, encouraging it towards her chin, 'sometimes strangers don't look like wolves at all.' Karen stretches her leg out so that her toes can feel the weight of her mother sitting on the bed. She likes to do this because now, even if she falls asleep, her mother can't leave the room without her knowing.

'The grandmother, who was in bed as she wasn't feeling well, called out, "Lift the latch and let yourself in."

The wolf went into the cottage, leapt upon the poor old woman, and gobbled her up.'

Karen's grandmother was never ill. The only time she ever saw her looking off-colour was when her father showed up to take them both away with him. Her grandmother assured her that it was a good thing but Karen didn't believe her.

'Why doesn't Grandma come with us if the West is such a good place?' Karen challenged her mother.

'Because her roots are long used to Eastern soil,' explained her mother through swollen eyes, 'and she doesn't want to re-plant them anywhere else at her time in life.'

'What time in life was that?' Karen hoped she would know when *she* came to that time in life but seeing as she didn't have any roots yet there was no point in worrying about it. Looking at her feet again, just to make sure, Karen went and fetched a long drink of water to see if that would make any difference.

'The wolf, who was hiding under the bedclothes, shouted, "Put the loaf and butter in the bread bin, and get into bed with me."

So Little Red Riding Hood climbed into bed with the wolf.

"Grandmother! What big arms you have!" she said.

"All the better to hug you with, my dear," came the hoarse reply.'

Karen's mother always puts on a very rough voice when she gets to this passage. The first time she did this Karen thought her mother had got a peppermint stuck in her throat and when she asked if she was alright it seemed to throw her mother off course for a moment. She blushed, said hurriedly, yes she was fine, and carried on with the story in a slightly less husky tone.

'"'Grandmother! What big legs you have!"
"All the better to chase you with, my dear!" '

Karen thought her father had very big legs when she first saw him. Apparently her father had held her as a baby but that is no more than a story to Karen's memory and so since this is her first recollection of her father she always refers to it as being the first time they met.

'It doesn't count if one of you doesn't know about it,' protested Karen to her mother as the strange, large hands swept her up in the air.

Karen had never felt so tall. In fact her father was taller than anyone she had ever seen before but she wasn't afraid because it was her grandmother who had let him in. Her father was big all over. Big arms, big hands, big shoulders and very big legs. Karen looked down at his feet. 'He must have a whole paddy field rooted under those feet,' she thought.

The strangest thing Karen noticed about her father was the way he smelt. It was an unfamiliar, overpowering smell and although it was pleasant enough she had to concentrate hard on not sneezing when he lifted her up to his neck. Most of the time, however, she was too far away from the lofty heights of his neck for the scent to disturb her. Now that Karen has grown to know her father she has become accustomed to his various scents. She can distinguish three in all, depending upon the occasion, and Karen always knows when he is taking her mother out somewhere special because he smells just as he did when he came to fetch them from Vietnam.

Karen wishes she could remember what her grandmother smelt like. Sometimes she struggles to properly remember what she looks like and so she has to go into her parent's bedroom and stare at the portrait her mother has framed on the wall. In truth it is more the portrait that Karen remembers now rather than the actual memory but she can't distinguish where one ends and the other begins. 'If I could only smell her,' thinks Karen who was subconsciously realising the value of the senses in rekindling a memory. Whenever Karen particularly misses her grandmother she asks to go to the Oriental supermarket because some of the smells from here still remind her of her grandmother's cooking and then she doesn't seem so very far away.

Karen's mother sometimes sits staring into the mirror. Then she starts to cry so Karen goes over to hug her.

'I have to keep looking hard into my own face,' she explains more to herself than to Karen. 'It's the closest I can get to seeing her again.'

It will be few years yet before Karen will understand what her mother is doing and by that time she will be looking less and less in the mirror anyway.

' "Grandmother! What big eyes you have!"
"All the better to see you with, my dear!" '

When she was young Karen looked more like her mother but the older she grows the more like her father she becomes. Certainly she will inherit something from his height. It will became strange to her around the age of twelve, thirteen, as she watches her mother getting further and further away from her. By the time Karen is sixteen her mother will come somewhere between her shoulder and her elbow. Her father will still tower above her as always. Her mother says that Karen has her grandmother's eyes when she smiles but Karen notices that her eyes are not as defined as her mother's. Still, they resemble her eyes more than they do her father's which do not seem quite so big and round to her now that she has become accustomed to Westerners.

As for Karen's hair, well that definitely is her mother's colouring, although it's not quite as straight. Her father has mousy hair and at the age of six-and-three-quarters Karen was convinced that he had washed the colour out of it and so her parents had quite a struggle to get her to wash her own hair lest she should loose her pigment too. It was Karen's mother, who loved to make unusual shapes with her hair even though they kept falling out, who taught her what pigment was. At first Karen had pictured cooked pork but when she learned it was something people had, a bit like roots really, she imagined something to do with very short people because she had recently learned that pigmies were in fact people and not pigs as you might expect. Then, however, she could not understand what pigmies would have to do with someone as tall as her father. As usual, the simplest thing to do was to ask her mother who explained pigment as being something entirely different to either cooked pork or short people.

Karen's mother has always had a very good grasp of the English language and from the beginning she has brought Karen up to be bilingual but in spite of her efforts to maintain her daughter's Vietnamese since she has come to the West, it has gradually begun to fall by the wayside. Karen had never heard her grandmother speak anything other than Vietnamese but she had seen her reading a letter from her father one evening, the one that mentioned something about *Visas* and promised her mother she would soon be with him. Her grandmother dabbed her eyes as she read this letter, which Karen decided was not the same as crying like her mother did but her grandmother obviously understood the contents of the letter.

As good as Karen's English was, when she first met her father she still couldn't understand half of what he was saying and she noticed how very differently her mother and father pronounced the same words. It took Karen a while to comprehend her father and she was making good progress in understanding spoken English during her short duration in America but once she arrived in England it was as if she had to start all over again.

' "Grandmother! What sharp teeth you have!" '

Karen's father had big teeth which Karen decided must be very sharp if only on account of their size. She used to think that was why he pronounced things so strangely. Karen was sure she would have spoken strangely had she had to accommodate such a big set of teeth in her mouth but her mother explained that it was owing to the shape of their oriental tongues that they sounded different to Westerners.

She told Karen that some Chinese babies being brought up in the West had the skin underneath their tongue clipped, to help them pronounce English better. Karen thought that sounded hideous and was relieved she hadn't been born on this side of the world. All the same, none of this explained why her father sounded so different to everyone else's father in England, especially as they spoke the same language. She would have to remember to ask her mother about it.

'Karen's daddy's a Yank,' they used to chant at school.

Karen had been puzzled the first time she heard this. There were still a lot of new words to learn and even her classmates had to put in several hours a week at school to learn new words, so Karen wondered what good were they if they couldn't speak their own language? At least she understood half of two languages, which was the same as knowing one whole language, only better.

'Karen and her mummy are boat people,' was another thing they would chant at school. Karen suspected by their derogatory tone that this wasn't a good thing to be but "boat" and "people" were words she understood and she couldn't perceive what was wrong with either of them. It was some time later that Karen's mother explained what the term meant; that it wasn't a bad thing to be after all and that in actual fact she and Karen weren't boat people because her father had pulled some strings and got them a *Visa*. All manner of imagery came into Karen's mind concerning strings and whatever a Visa might be. Prior to asking her mother, Karen had questioned her classmates about 'boat people'. It transpired that none of them knew what it meant either but that they had overheard their parents talking about it at the same time that they were describing her daddy as a 'Yank'. Her classmates didn't know whether it was bad to be called these things or not but they knew that it didn't apply to them so that made Karen different and therefore something to make fun of.

When Karen first came to England and started school the other children seemed only to be aware of her difference on account of these labels but somewhere between the infants and the junior school her classmates suddenly began remarking on physical differences, most notably Karen's eyes and skin. 'Surely they have noticed this before,' thought Karen who had recognised the moment she met her father how different he looked from her uncle. Around the same time at school Karen was having tea at her best friend Fiona Henshaw's house when a neighbour called by and Karen overheard Fiona's mother describe her to the neighbour as being one of the 'boat people'. To her surprise both women broke out into a very sympathetic discourse on the subject. She couldn't grasp what they were saying but there was a lot of cooing going on and as the neighbour was leaving she gave Karen a compassionate squeeze, told her to be a good girl and to look after herself.

' "All the better to eat you with!"

And the wolf leapt upon Little Red Riding Hood and gobbled her up.'

Karen knows what it feels like to be eaten by a wolf. She feels like she was practically devoured just a few hours earlier. You see, Karen had slipped up; she hadn't been taking care of herself as the neighbour had instructed. It had happened while she had been skipping in the road, just outside Fiona's house. Fiona had gone inside to find a tennis racket and Karen had continued skipping. Suddenly, as if out of nowhere, the Wolf was standing beside her. The problem was that he didn't look anything like a wolf at all, far more like the friendly woodcutter and so Karen wasn't on her guard. In truth her thoughts were far away, back in the playground, wondering what Tommy Hughes had meant when he called her a 'half-caste'. 'Not another label,' she thought. Tommy Hughes was in the class above her and so he would surely know what it meant but she was too afraid to ask him. Anyway, too engrossed worrying about the Wolf Cub, Karen failed to recognise the Wolf.

He stood smiling at her with his big, yellow teeth and so instinctively she smiled back.

'They're pretty eyes when they smile,' he complimented.

Looking on the bright side, this episode will save Karen a lot of bother in future years when it comes to being taken in by compliments from wolves. Her puritanical, paternal grandmother refers to wolves as belonging to the collective "opposite sex". When Karen is fourteen years old her paternal grandmother will come over from America to stay with them for three weeks. During one of their conversations at this time she will warn Karen, 'Be on your guard my girl when it comes to the opposite sex.'

It will seem as if the word "men" is too vulgar to use on a young girl but Karen will have long before encountered the Wolf and so she will know well enough the dangers of the opposite sex. All the same, nobody will ever venture to inform her grandmother about this unsavoury incident.

'I bet you can't skip ten times without tripping up,' challenged the Wolf.

'Of course I can,' retorted Karen defiantly. 'I'm seven-and-a-quarter you know.'

'Are you indeed? My, what a big girl!'

Karen liked to be called big because this made her feel strong like her father and nobody ever called him names because he looked so huge and frightening if you didn't know him.

'Well I'll tell you what,' wagered the Wolf as he rubbed his fury chin in contemplation. 'If you can skip ten times without tripping up then I'll give you a piggy-back all the way to the end of the road. How would you like that?'

Wolves like playing games. *'I'd like to meet your grandmother too,'* the wolf had said in the fairytale. *'You take the path on the left, I'll take the path on the right, and we'll see who gets there first.'*

If Karen had only known she was talking to a wolf then she would have realised that his game was a trick. But she didn't know he was a wolf.

'Alright, you're on,' chirped Karen as she got her rope poised for action.

Piggy-backs, pigmies, pigment and pork. Karen knew the difference between all these words now and she loved it when her daddy gave her piggy-backs around the garden or on a long walk. Unfortunately what Karen didn't realise was how much wicked wolves liked little pigs and that what interested the Wolf more than the piggy-back was the pork.

'One, Two,' click, click on the pavement went Karen's shiny shoes.

'Three, Four,' the Wolf was longing for more.

'Five, Six,' he would teach the little pig some tricks.

'Seven, Eight,' he could hardly wait.

'Nine, Ten,' he had won again.

‘Well done! You *are* a clever girl,’ grinned the Wolf.

‘Now for my piggy-back,’ volunteered Karen eagerly.

She ran behind the Wolf and waited for him to crouch down as her daddy did.

‘No, climb up from the front where I can see you and then I'll swing you round. It's far easier that way,’ drooled the greedy Wolf.

This was a new one for Karen but if it was more fun than her usual run and jump she would be sure to tell her daddy next time. So Karen held out her trusting arms and the great, big Wolf swept her up. She later wondered if she should have recognised what he was by his fury chin but her father had grown a fury chin for a short time and he hadn't turned into a wolf. The Wolf's eyes flashed at her and she smiled back. This was too much for the Wolf.

He tried to make some idle conversation but Karen didn't hear because she was too busy thinking about the sharp paw that was clawing its way up her leg. All the while the Wolf was still smiling so Karen thought it must be alright but as the paw persisted searchingly, Karen struggled to understand what he was doing, purely thinking to herself, ‘daddy doesn't do this!' Suddenly, momentarily, it all went dark as the pungently smoky bristles on the Wolf's chin bore down upon her face.

Although you might think you would have recognised a lot sooner the identity of a wolf about to gobble you up, when it actually comes to it…

‘He didn't look bad at all. In fact, he played skipping with me. He didn't offer me any sweets, or tell me mummy was ill, or try to whisk me off in a car. He seemed like an ordinary, friendly man.’

This was how Karen bravely tried to explain it to the kind policewoman who was offering her a barley sugar an hour later. The policewoman was a stranger too but because her mother was there Karen knew it was safe to accept the sweet. No wolf would get past her mother. Karen thought about the young boy with the fly and wished she had been as wise as him.

‘It was lucky you came to the door when you did,’ remarked the policewoman.

‘It was lucky their tea was ready when it was,’ replied Mrs. Henshaw modestly.

'And you say the man was very casual about putting Karen down?'

'That's right. I didn't know what the hell to say in case I scared him off with Karen still in his arms so I hid my panic and nonchalantly called her in for tea as if he wasn't there.'

'He offered no explanation though?'

'No. He simply put her down and said he'd see her around.'

'Well Karen,' smiled the kind policewoman, 'you've been a very brave little girl and have given us a good description of this man. Now just remember, if you ever see him again don't talk to him. Run and find a grown-up straight away. Do you understand?'

People were always asking Karen if she understood things. It was partly because she was… what was that expression? … "half-caste?", and partly because she was a child. Was she still a child though? Karen hopes so as she lies tucked up in bed listening to her bedtime story which, this evening, is being over-emphasised with a moralistic tone. A footnote in her book explains that it was Charles Perrault who first wrote the story of Little Red Riding Hood in 1697. It was an explicit warning to children not to talk to strangers and after writing it he added, '*From this story one learns that children, especially young lasses, pretty, courteous and well-bred, are wrong to listen to any sort of man.*'

From this night on Karen takes Perrault's warning to heart. Karen is unable to put her feelings into words. All she understands is that she has had a terrifying glimpse into an adult world that she had been forced to enter prematurely and at seven-and-a-quarter she wants to be reassured that she is still a child and that she will remain so for a good deal longer.

Listening to her mother read the story Karen savours the soft lamplight that dances friendly shadows over her toys. She laps up her mother's soothing voice that whispers the engaging tale through every scene apart from during the wolf's narration which, Karen decides, is growled particularly fiercely on this occasion. In another of Karen's fairytale books Little Red Riding Hood is rescued by a hunter who kills the wolf. On this particular evening Karen would much prefer to have heard this version. Mrs. Henshaw had saved Karen from the teeth of the Wolf and so surely this would have been more appropriate? Karen's mother has her reasons for choosing the more savage ending. In earlier oral traditions in France, the wolf tricks Little Red Riding Hood into eating some of her dead grandmother. Eventually she escapes by saying she has to go to the toilet which of course in those days was outside the cottage. Karen won't come across this version until she is a grown woman herself and then she will think it is much too gruesome to send any child to sleep on but it will make her reflect upon how there can be different versions to every story, both in books and in life itself.

Still wriggling under the heavy blankets Karen feels warm and safe, as if the events of the past afternoon belong to a late night programme on television that she should never have been watching. She thinks about her gold star and the inviting smell of magnolia and hopes that this will send her to sleep with happy dreams. Karen lets her mother think she has fallen asleep somewhere around the point where Little Red Riding Hood climbs into bed with the wolf. She is afraid that her mother will end the story with some well-meant incrimination on her own experience with a wolf and Karen doesn't want to burst the harmonious bubble of comfort that she is creating in an attempt to rescue herself back into her childhood.

The light clicks out and her mother leaves the room. Even after she has gone Karen can still feel her tender kiss that had tickled her cheek. Although Karen's eyes remain closed she notices how much darker it has gone. She opens her eyes and everywhere is pitch black. She holds out a hand in front of her face and can't see a thing. Presently she is able to make out dim silhouettes around the room. Arnold, her largest teddy-bear, is sitting on the rocking horse. She can trace the outlines of her desk, her doll's house and the easel standing in a far corner. A gentle hue of moonlight filters through a gap in the curtains. Everything is gradually becoming clearer. *Everything*. Karen vows to herself that never again will she be so careless as to allow a wolf to get the better of her. In full and earnest belief of her promise Karen turns over and falls peacefully asleep.

Fools For Love

by

Karen Smith

They walked together along the lighted pier as the sun was beginning to set. They looked for the entire world like two people in love. She stopped suddenly and clung to the side rail and he thought for one moment that she was going to be sick. He kissed her cheek gently, it was cold. She was cold. As they stood by the rail he watched a boat on the horizon, its light signalling to someone, somewhere.

'Let's go back,' he said, taking her hand.

She swallowed hard, and then nodded.

The boat's light had been extinguished and he was surprised to see how far it had moved in such a short space of time.

They walked back together towards the guest house and as they reached the entrance to the pier, he bent to kiss her cheek again, to find that this time it was wet with tears.

Earlier that afternoon

From her window seat in the guest house, she could sit and look out over the sea. It was a beautiful spring afternoon, with a light breeze that licked gently at the waves and the white voiles at the open sash window. The beach was relatively empty, apart from a couple walking arm in arm, their Springer Spaniel bounding at their feet and a woman with a red haired little girl building a sandcastle.

As she looked out at the view, she curled her legs up underneath her and hugged one of the window seat cushions close to her chest. She sighed, bit her lip and smiled to herself. She was happy. She was waiting for her love.

She looked at her watch, it was nearly three. He had thought he could be with her by four at the latest. She wondered how he was, how Miranda had took the news that he was leaving. She felt a wave of guilt tug at her. She liked Miranda and the two boys, she really did. They were nice people. But she loved John. It was that simple.

She took another look out to sea; the sun had now gone behind a cloud and the woman and little girl were making their way back up the beach. Then she turned away and looked at the beautiful brass bed, dressed in white, so virginal and romantic. It seemed a shame to touch it almost, but she moved some of the cushions on to the floor and lay down.

She had been so tired recently and not a little queasy. She looked down at her handbag. Along with a plethora of things she should have cleared out weeks ago was a pregnancy test. She was waiting for John and then they would find out. She looked at her watch again, nearly quarter past. She closed her eyes.

She had met John just over a year ago. She worked with his brother, Daniel, who had invited her to his thirtieth birthday. She wasn't seeing anyone at the time, having just come out of a long term relationship. She certainly didn't go to the party looking for love, but, like an old cliché, love found her. Unfortunately, it was in the form of a married man.

Sometimes when she lay awake at night, she tried to placate her mind by telling herself that she had resisted him for as long as she could, that she had at least thought about the fact that she could potentially be helping to ruin a lot of lives, including those of his two children. But, when he turned up one night out of the blue at her flat, soaking wet from having run all the way there in the rain, resistance proved futile. So their affair began.

Daniel was, understandably, furious with both of them when he found out and he seemed to blame himself, having introduced them in the first place. He came to see her one Sunday afternoon and begged with her to end the relationship. She tried to tell him it was love and that they could do nothing about it, which seemed to enrage him even further. He stormed out, but his last words, spat out over his shoulder, were that John would never leave his wife.

'But Daniel was wrong, wasn't he!' she said to herself as she looked at her watch again. Surely he must be here soon?

Her thoughts were interrupted by a tap at the door. She jumped up, smoothed down her top and her blonde hair, took a quick look at her reflection in the gilt edged mirror, and ran to the door.

'John!' she shouted joyously. But it wasn't John, it was Daniel. And he didn't look happy. Or even angry. Just sad. And sorry.

'Daniel?' Her voice was almost a whisper. 'What are you doing here....where's John?

Daniel fumbled in his jacket pocket and brought out an envelope. A letter.

'He asked me to give you this,' he said, his brown eyes looking straight at her then at the floor.

'He's not coming..... is he?' Her voice escalated at the end.

'Olivia, I think you better sit down.'

She took the letter and sat down on the bed. She didn't ask Daniel to come in, but he did so anyway, sitting on the edge of an armchair just left of the window seat. He was struck by how beautiful the room was, all white, with hints of powder blue, and a gorgeous view over the beach. Just the sort of room for lovers to meet.

Olivia was sitting stock still on the bed, staring at the envelope. He didn't want to force her to open it; she would do so when she was ready. He guessed she already knew what she was about to read and was staving off the moment.

Eventually, she sighed, swallowed and opened the envelope. He watched her face as she read. He saw anger, incredulity and, most vividly, sorrow. Tears fell, streaming down her cheeks. He longed to wipe them away and comfort her, but he didn't know if he would be welcome. It was only went she lifted her blonde head, looked straight at him and began to sob openly that he went to her.

When the wailing stopped and her heaving chest calmed, he gave her a tissue to wipe her face.

'What did he say?' Daniel asked gently.

She regarded him with her pale blue eyes, now red rimmed and swollen, then looked back down at the letter. 'Basically, he's not coming. He loves me, but not enough to leave Miranda and the boys. He's sorry, *sorry*! That's about the gist of it. Oh, and it's over between us.'

'I'm sorry Olivia.' Daniel put his hand over hers.

'Do you think he ever had any intention of leaving her?' she looked at him again.

'Truthfully? No.'

'Then why did he say he would?'

'Because he's a coward. Because he wanted to have his cake and eat it, as they say.'

She sighed. 'Then I've been a fool.'

He stood up and went to the window seat. 'A fool for love,' he laughed. 'You're certainly not the first.'

'That sounds like the voice of experience?' she asked.

'Oh, now's not the time.' He shook his head.

'Why not?' she said resignedly. 'I would like to hear about someone else's pain.'

'Let me make us a cup of tea,' he deflected. 'You look like you could do with one.'

So he made two teas from the things provided on the dresser and they sat silently together, him on the armchair and Olivia curled up again on the window seat. The wind had got up a little, making the waves rougher and the crying of gulls overhead drifted in the window.

'Well?' she asked.

He bit his lip and put a hand through his dark hair.

'Do I know her?' she asked when he didn't answer. 'I do know her, don't I?'

'Olivia, please,' he said. 'You really don't want to know. Not now.'

'Why?' she asked. Then he looked at her and something in that look told her everything. 'Me?'

'Yes,' he said simply.

'Oh Daniel. For how long?'

'Only about five years.'

'Oh my God,' she said. 'And you had to watch me have an affair with your brother.'

'Yes, that wasn't easy,' he smiled ruefully.

'Why didn't you say something, before I met John?'

'When could I? You were in a relationship with Peter. I thought I might make a move at my thirtieth, but then when I introduced you to John, I realised there was no point. There was no one else in the room for you that night.'

Her face crumpled again. 'Oh God,' she said suddenly, 'the pregnancy test!'

'You're pregnant?' Shocked, he stood up.

'I think I might be. I was going to do a test when John got here.' She started to cry. 'With the letter and everything, I forgot.'

She fumbled around in her handbag and pulled out a paper bag. She looked at him. 'I don't know what to do!'

'I guess you have to do it,' he said. 'I'm here with you.'

She left him pacing in front of the window, as if he was the expectant father, while she went in the bathroom. She felt suddenly sick again and her head began to spin. John's letter, Daniel's confession and the possibility of having a baby were too much to take in one afternoon.

'Are you okay in there?' he called, when she'd been silent for several minutes. He was worried about her. He was such a good man. She had chosen the wrong brother.

'I'm fine.' The words came out as a croak. Her mouth was dry and her palms were sweaty. She had to find out, so she did the test. It was positive.

She came out of the bathroom and he took her in his arms. She sobbed into his shoulder.

'It's okay,' he stroked her back. 'I'll look after you, I promise. I love you, I've always loved you.'

The words were nice, but they were not enough. She looked up at him. 'But I love John!'

'I know you do,' he said. 'I know.'

They sat down on the bed and they stayed that way for a long time, Daniel staring at her face, Olivia staring out to sea.

'Are you going to tell him?' Daniel asked.

'No,' she answered. 'And you mustn't either.'

'Not if that's what you want.'

'It is.'

She turned to look at him. He touched her face gently and she leaned into his hand. Then she took his hand in hers, moved forward and kissed him on the cheek. It was a simple act and yet it seemed loaded. Something passed between them and her mouth moved from his cheek to his lips. He knew she was kissing him because she just needed to feel something other than pain, but he didn't care.

A while later when he opened his eyes, she was back at the window seat. She was silent and he wondered if she was crying again, but she turned to him and smiled.

'Are you ok?' he asked, sitting up.

'I think so.' The smile faded. 'I'm sorry Daniel,' she added. 'I care about you very much, but I shouldn't have done that, we shouldn't have done that.'

He got out of bed, pulled on his trousers and went to her. 'It's ok,' he said, kneeling at her feet and taking her hands. 'I love you.'

'Does that make everything all right?' she asked.

'It's a start.'

She sighed.

'I'm hungry,' he said. 'Shall we get something to eat?'

'I don't know. I feel a little sick again.'

'Maybe a walk then, get some fresh air?'

'A walk would be good.'

Together they left the guest house into the cooling early evening and made their way along the front and, as they walked, he offered her his hand. She turned to look at him, almost as if she was weighing up her options – face this on her own, or with someone who so obviously loved her. She smiled, with a hint of resignation, and took his hand.

Breakfast in Alimos

by

Cassandra Passarelli

I rise from my daughter's bed. Shuffling to the bathroom, I shower, then dress in navy trousers, silk blouse and cashmere cardigan. My face returns its mirrored stare, chestnut eyes still resolute, olive skin ravaged to a crêpe. The kitchen is silent, clock hands hover at six thirty, February night clings thickly at the windows. Nothing but Euripides' tail stirs as he dreams in the box by the fridge. As I pour condensed milk into his bowl, he drags himself up and shivers. There has always been a cat, or several, in our house. In the past they were relegated to the verandas, but in my old age I've grown indulgent and let this scrawny scrap sleep in the kitchen. *Ti na kanome*?

First light, filtering through fuchsia curtains, finds my kitchen spotless. The marble double sink and draining board are clear of dishes and scrubbed clean. Through the small window above the scoured oven, bare mountains are growing visible in the dawn. The tall American fridge, a quarter-century old, hums a tune that's crescendoed over time. Family photographs, thumb-tacked to a corkboard have curled at the edges from the steam of uncountable meals. The cicadas' croak, punctuated by bird song, grows more insistent. I prepare half a jug of fresh coffee, set toast, jam and margarine on the table for myself and cook porridge for Vasilli. These days I need to wake him. At least it means I rest. There were years when he woke in the night, crying like a baby but with the might of a grown man. I'd sit, as with a child, night-light on holding his hand... for hours. Not any more; now I'm afraid he'll not wake up. Or do I crave it?

Our old bedroom is stark these days – the hospital bed dwarfs Vasilli, the TV, wheelchair and crane. I place my hand on his forehead to rouse him; he opens his eyes at once. Was he asleep? I wouldn't know. I pull back the covers, pull off underclothes, throw away a sodden nappy and wash his crotch. I ratchet up the backrest, so he seems to sit, and begin to dress him.

‘Come, Vasilli. You haven’t pooped this morning… perhaps later, my dear. How did you sleep? Did you hear that wind? *Po-po po-po po-po*! My goodness, Vasilli, how it blew. But today’s a good laundry day: wind and sun. Let’s put on your grey sweater – we have guests coming for lunch: Antonia and Athenastasia, probably the kids too.’

Bringing the wheelchair as close as I can to the bed, I lower it to the same level, and, with every ounce of strength, slide him onto it. *Po-po po-po po-po!* Thank God he's lost so much weight, else I'd not be able to lift him. Once so proud and handsome in his uniform, now his clothes hang about his wasted body like a shroud. The photographs on the parlour piano remind me who I married – the charismatic sea captain, eyes burning with passion. *Ti na kanome?* His skin is waxen now; pallid with years indoors, smoothed by loving care. I run my fingers through what hair is left on his scalp. Above emaciated cheeks, vacant eyes stare, helplessly. Others say they see anger there, but I don’t. I see love and gratitude. If Vasilli could speak, he’d thank me for years of sacrifice. That’s why he cries; his way of letting me know.

I hear you make your bed and tiptoe to the bathroom not to disturb me. My hearing is so acute… the only one of my senses to have grown sharper. I'm relieved night is done with, but daunted by the day ahead. I listen. With wonder and dread. Do you remember the first time we met, at your father’s house? Our lives lay before us like a cliché… romance, marriage, children. We were too young to know beginnings bear no relationship to ends. You were so beautiful, still are – it's incredible! Aged but not diminished, a woman of poise and radiance. Your steps fade away toward the kitchen, and I hear the odd noise, till you return to prepare me. For what? I no longer ask. There's only death, Olga. I hear the doctors marvel: years ago they predicted in hushed tones I'd not live long. But your care has prolonged my allotted hours into months and years. Devotion takes its toll: unaware, you mirror my decline. When I've gone, how will you fill those empty days? Believe me, agapi moo, it’s harder than it looks.

Wheeling Vasilli into the kitchen, I sit him at the table's head, where he's always sat – except the years at sea. I spent holidays here as a child, the house no more than a cottage then, surrounded by open scrub, with an open view to the sea, the empty beach a skip along a dusty path. At the sight of his porridge, Vasilli makes a guttural cry. He can chew, but dry things get caught in his throat. I spoon in mouthfuls, singing an old *Rubetica* tune, tapping the beat with my free hand on the green tablecloth. He always loved to hear me sing. Between stanzas, I nibble on cold toast smeared with low-cholesterol spread and sugar-free jam. *Ti na kanome*? We grow old together. When he goes, what will I do? I can't imagine: such thought is betrayal.

You have set yourself the task of making me live against all odds. It's selfish: my existence lends yours meaning. You once held me at the heart of your life, keeping the home fires burning while I dropped anchor in ports from the Far East to the Americas. Now I'm dry-docked, you imagine I hold you in mine. All those years at sea... what did we share in common except for a few months here and there? Like some intermittent affair between strangers. How I hungered for the domesticity you took for granted. How you resented my freedom, my indifference. Now you wreak slow revenge.

I'm paying, imprisoned in my carcass. I gouge days out in my mind, each notch a step nearer death, while you keep your banter up, hour after hour. Gamo to Christos! We watch news broadcasts from a world I play no part in, absurd soaps or old Hollywood films. My only escape is sleep – not easy when you have done nothing; neither today, nor yesterday... not for years.

Each morning you dress me like a grotesque doll and wheel me to the kitchen. You feed me bland broths or purées. Ah Olga, I long for good feta and sesame bread we used to start each meal with and your papootsakia, dripping in olive oil. I yearn for wine from our umbelia, the tang of salted pistachios from the yard or sweet Halkitha apricots. But, like my life, my diet has been reduced to a paste without texture or flavour. What I would give to be able to caress your wrinkled cheek! Living's not clock hands dragging around the face: that's not your definition, nor mine.

When he was young and a stranger to me, I made him my icon. Away for months on end, I devised an existence around his absence to keep him alive in our children's hearts. When he came back they were afraid of the stranger at our table. He tried to mask disappointment with harsh words. They were too young to understand. By the time he was fully retired they'd left, got married, had lives of their own. We'd spent just a few years together, when the strokes began destroying the chance of golden years. *Ti na kanome?* The first stroke robbed him of his independence. Followed by the second, third and fourth. Each pilfering a portion: stealing control of his hands, limbs, bowels and finally his voice. Leaving just the burden of his body. Useless, some say, but nevertheless my flesh and blood. I framed my life around him... .

Visitors offer no relief. Most are scared, though they try to hide it. They converse as though I'll respond, ask questions I can't answer, make observations I can't deny. They speculate whether I understand. Some hold my hand, but I feel their shudders of revulsion. I straddle their world and what they dread most. Yet I live, on and on, unable to pass away in peace like other things in nature. A shipwrecked soul condemned to sail in this keeling hull. Some would put me out of my misery, but they've long since realised that I am your reason for living, Olga. It's you they think of when they remain silent. Our grandchildren can't remember how I was. They accept this monstrous, hunched, howling freak, present yet absent, as their Papoo. Gamo to Christos! Some days I swear that, could I just muster a last surge of strength in these impotent hands, it would be your throat they'd reach for, before my own. I'm not angry with God; He doesn't exist. Who'd create such a farce, even as a form of retribution? I could name a dozen sailors who drank, whored and beat their wives yet are still going strong.

Let's switch on the television, wash breakfast things, peel vegetables for lunch. Some potatoes, spinach… yes they'll go well in the chicken broth. Don't worry, dear old Euripides, I've saved some bones for you. Now, let's prepare some *papootsakia* for our visitors.

I feel a certain lightness today, a tingling sensation in the fingers like an excess of electricity. Perhaps a fifth stroke? Well, that would be something – a change of scene: the rush to hospital, bustle of nurses, charts, doctors, tests and visitors. Or dare I hope this one will finish me... a haemorrhage flooding my brain with fluid, suffocating me in my own juice. Please, bastard God, if you exist, let me die today.

'Ah listen, Vasilli, hear what they say? They're getting ready for the Olympics. Soon we will be able to take a tram into the centre of town. *Po-po po-po po-po!* Won't that be wonderful? I'll sit here beside you, my dear, and we'll watch the news. Asleep so soon? Before we've eaten? Well, why not? Siesta... before our guests arrive.'

My Mate Mark Viduka

by

Al McClimens

I was strolling along the main shopping boulevard, enjoying the fresh spring sun, doing no more than glancing in at the shop displays when I noticed them – the shy stalkers of celebrity. They were in a gang of four this time. But one, taller than the rest, more physically present, stood out, literally head and shoulders above the rest. It was Mark Viduka. Some of you may not have heard of this man. I can tell you that he is a footballer, a soccer player. He is an Australian, but like so many of his countrymen he is of European extraction. He feigned interest in a selection of watches, slowing his pace until his companions were some distance away. I had witnessed similar diversionary manoeuvres many times and was not fooled, not for a moment.

I have subsequently developed a tactic to cope with this kind of approach. One upon a time I would have hurried away to escape the attention. But no more. I am now more relaxed with celebrity. I see it as a public role, almost a duty. And like many duties it has its routine aspects, but it has its plus side too. Nowadays I make the first move. It saves emotional effort and embarrassment to all concerned. So I walked over to where the large Ozzie stood, contemplating time.

'Hi, mate,' I offered, calculating that this blokeish sensibility might put the Antipodean at ease in my presence.

His reply was casual to the point of disinterest. So be it. If that was how he wanted to adjust to our social encounter I was not about to upset his equilibrium.

I guessed that he was in town to go about his professional business. I discovered subsequently that he was in fact fulfilling a contractual obligation and would soon be joining his team mates in the north-east of the country where they would entertain foreign opposition that very evening. This demonstrates my ignorance. I do not pay the sports pages much attention. I find them vulgar. The language grates. The photography is lurid. The import of it all is lost on me. But I like to feel that I have some appreciation of the commoner side of life and I seemed to remember a mention of some fixture concerning his team and the local …. I continued in my bonhomie, choosing to close the exchange and simultaneously exhibit my nous.

'Good luck tonight, mate. Give us a wave when you score, yeh?'

I added the rising inflexion so typical of the southern hemisphere and of teenage talk. His whole demeanour lifted immediately.

'Cheers, mate.'

His handshake was firm. I smiled and bade him farewell. He turned and hurried his multi-million pound stride towards his companions who all turned as one and gazed in my direction. They conferred briefly. My new mate Mark cast a salute in my direction. A right arm raised lazily as if to catch the attentions of a passing waiter but then the finger-pointing that was in my direction, for my attention. I tried this manoeuvre myself, hailing a cab with instant success and the meeting was a memory. No doubt it would linger longer in their minds than mine; longer and deeper too, I didn't doubt. And as the taxi pulled away and merged with the traffic I realised that he hadn't even asked for an autograph. He rose considerably in my estimation after that.

I was not always so cosy with fame. Indeed I can recall a moment from some time back when my presence failed to inspire even a modest curiosity from those around me. I was attending a significant sporting occasion, the British Open to be precise, held that year at St. Andrews. The year would have been around 1970, I guess. I wouldn't have gone had it been hosted anywhere else if truth be told. I was watching some Americans on the putting surface of the seventeenth, the par four Road Hole, when I was made aware of a small, tanned, silver haired figure immediately to my left. Our Prime Minister was a small man and he would not have been able to view the contest had it not been for the intervention of his aides who cleared some viewing space.

'Did I hear someone say the Prime Minister would like a Watneys?'

A lackey advanced through the throng bearing his liquid refreshment, already half poured, on a sliver platter. Mr Heath, for it was he, raised the glass to his lips (thin and girlish, as I recall) and with a grin for the press he toasted the company. Our eyes met briefly. He gave no indication of recognition.

I was younger then. More callow. I merely smiled and raised my hip flask and quaffed long and hard. I would have exchanged some pleasantries but he was gone; the glass empty, the caravan already moving on.

I returned my attention to the match. The crowd ooohed as if they were at a pantomime. I blame the media. I made a mental note to give Doug Saunders some putting tips, having noted a minor blemish in his follow-through. And I would have been successful too had not some jobsworth decided that his function was to exclude non-members from the clubhouse. I could have protested and had the man sacked but I would have gained no satisfaction form such a mean riposte. Instead I prevailed upon him to pass on a written note to Mr. Saunders. I included my hotel room and telephone number but no call ever came. The rest is, as the say, history.

I must blame myself for such rebuffs. I simply don't play the fame game, despite holding a hand of aces. I resolutely refuse to employ the trappings of success. No entourage for me; no hangers-on, no PA, no publicist. I eschew such gaudy baubles. They impress no one. They serve no useful function. They attract the wrong kind of attention. No, I live simply. I use public transport. I travel economy. I maintain a modest *pied a terre*, rented. I refuse to give up my paid employment and still draw a salary. Thankfully my employers are unaware of my status and consequently I am not drawn into gossip and tittle-tattle. I do not live in fear of the journalist's pen, phone call or doorstep visit.

It amuses me when names are dropped in an effort to impress. One of my colleagues was regaling an impromptu crowd with a recollection of having met the comedian Mr Alexei Sayle. I say "met" but I believe a more honest and accurate version of events might be that the two gentlemen briefly occupied the same corridor space for a few seconds. My colleague turned to me in the midst of his tale.

'You've met him, haven't you, Al? Alexei Sayle? You must have, man like you.'

Our colleagues hid their amusement behind their hands to spare the fellow's blushes. I ignored his gaffe, dismissing it as a desperate attempt to increase his diminishing status among his co-workers.

'No, I don't believe I've had the pleasure,' I replied, the very model of discretion. Again our colleagues tired to preserve a sense of decorum with stifled agonies.

But of course Alexei and I are old friends. We met at the Empire Theatre in Glasgow some years back and have maintained an on-off correspondence ever since. We met in the bar of said theatre where the portly funny man was performing a series of shows.

'Ello, John,' I said, slipping effortlessly into some well known dialogue as I approached his bar space. He drew a tired hand over his face.

'Got a new motor, then?'

He fixed me with a level gaze.

'Fook off, will ya?'

I continued with the charade. The comedian was clearly trying out some new material. I decided to humour him, even though I was uncertain that this abrasive tone would generate much laughter with an audience. He was, however, an alternative sort of variety act and no doubt his more regular fan base would be highly amused.

'*Chacun a son gout*,' I ventured.

Mr Sayle was clearly impressed and attempted to repeat the phrase but his Merseyside accent was unequal to the task and it came out sounding like 'Cheeky cunt'. I laughed and slapped him on the back.

'Very droll, Alexei, very droll.'

I exchanged some eye contact with the bar staff which suggested that they knew that I knew that Mr Sayle was struggling to maintain the necessary levels of repartee. No matter. I was not in competition. In the intervening years we have corresponded by post, by telephone and more recently by email. Lately though I regret that he has delegated this task to his administrative assistants. Ah well. Their curt tone and veiled threats of legal action do no credit to themselves or their employer. Perhaps this is an acquaintance that has run its course.

Of course there are drawbacks. Only a bumptious fool would deny it. Because I live life on the edge of discovery, never more than an intercepted email away from revelation and the awakening dawn of tabloid headlines inches high I believe I have developed an appreciation of the sanctity of what is, in some quarters, disparagingly remarked on as a 'normal life'. Even so I have never refused a photographer their pay day. I dabble myself. I know of the lengths they must go to, the patience they must endure, the ache of waiting for the perfect shot; the glimpse of opportunity and the chance to shine; all for the short satisfaction of the by-line and a note from the sub-editor.

Even so I prefer to vary my route to work. Consequently I am never bothered, or "papped" as I believe the current phrase has it, as I endure the daily commute. Indeed I quite enjoy playing the photographer myself. My camera, an old style SLR, of course (I cannot abide digital technology) is mounted with a prodigious fixed-focus 500mm lens. I shoot in black and white only. It is the medium of the true photographer. And I print and process my own film, naturally.

My snapshots of local "characters" were rightly praised in the promotional literature accompanying the launch of the Norton Amateur Photographer Annual Award Ceremony. The editorial spoke of the pictures as depicting the underside of city street life in a sympathetic yet accurate style. I should have been pleased, I suppose.

The choice of paper is key. I like to accentuate the grain. I hold back the exposure. I reduce my own involvement as mere photographer to a minimal presence. Good photographs are found, not taken. I have found a lot of good photographs.

I had arrived back at my flat following my earlier meeting with Mr Viduka and was just deciding what outfit would be most suitable for the event. I had several hours to decide. The local press would be likely to turn up and I didn't want to appear over-eager or ostentatious. I settled on a business suit, cotton shirt, no tie and an old pair of brogues. My only indulgence was a pair of silk socks given to me by dear old Stephen Fry. But that's another story.

The event was held in the local church hall and presided over by a councillor with a repulsive Minolta. The photographs were displayed. I smiled and fielded inane questions. I was sharing a glass of a positively revolting Sancerre with some admirers when a photographer from the local rag almost blinded me with his flash gun. The setting was at least two points too high and the result would be hopelessly over-exposed. Amateur. My erstwhile companions, probably less inured to such intrusion, sought company elsewhere in the draughty church hall.

'Got anything more.......' the reporter hesitated, 'got anything more?'

His glance was desperate, his eyes, never still.

'Good money for good pics.'

I asked him for his card and his editor's name.

'You what, mate?'

I repeated my request, fearing perhaps the fellow suffered from some hearing loss.

'Nah, mate. You don't understand. I've done the reporting now. Got the shot. This is just between me and you. Private, like. So, got anything a bit tasty? You must have got some upskirt shots when you was out on the streets then, yeh?'

'Oi, dickead! Take a hike!'

Our conversation was brusquely interrupted by young Tracey, the tattooed teenager and terror of the local tabloids. I believe she may have been from Totley too, come to think of it but perhaps that's just wishful thinking. She was an irregular, if enthusiastic member of the photography group, more inclined to pose than to snap.

'Oh, Jesus..........it's her!'

And with that imprecation my contact in the fourth estate disappeared into the night.

'Let me guess.......he was trying to get you interested in some dirty pictures, yeh?'

I indicated that this had indeed been the case.

'Well, sweetheart, I can show you the originals. Whadya think?'

Tracey opened her large portfolio case and I was confronted by a Rubenesque sight. I had to look, just had to look. She was pictured lying naked on what appeared to be a kitchen table, the remnants of a meal strewn across the wooden surface. The next picture showed her wearing bright yellow domestic gloves. Nothing else. Just the gloves. Clasped in one hand was a toilet brush. Held in that fashion, at that angle, it gave the appearance.......

'You like the Marigolds, then? Nice touch, I thought.'

I uttered what I hoped was an appropriate response and went to visit the toilet. Oh God. Oh my God. I hadn't felt this way since prep school when Miss Bromley gave us the facts of life talk. Miss Bromley. That bosom. Oh my God. Miss Angela Bromely. She of the massive.........On a recent alumni newsletter the revelation had been made that her career in the convent, where she had gone rather swiftly after the 'incident' in the boys' toilets, had been very short lived. She had resurfaced soon after in a much more public place, minus the habit. The url had found its way onto my favourites list. And now Tracey was stirring up these feelings again.

When I returned most of the members had left the building but Tracey had rounded up a small coterie.

'Come on, Al, we're off down the Palace. Got a beer festival on. Move it. Let's go.'

She clapped her hands to add force to her function. Her attitude was infectious.

'Yeh, c'mon, mate,' said Clive. 'Let's go and get a few in and you can tell us about dodging and burning. Anne, you coming too, dear. Come on, make a foursome.'

'Ooooh, you wish,' said Anne. But she was smiling as she said it and grabbed Clive by the arm.

Clive was a turf accountant by day. His collection consisted solely of photographs taken at Owlerton dog track. He was, nevertheless, entertaining company. I believe he even issued "sure thing" tips to accomplices and friends. In the event I relented and let Tracey take my arm for the short walk to the Woodseats Palace.

I had often passed by this establishment. With the increasing laxity of licensing laws the boundaries between public and private have been regularly eroded. Now the design of the front of the building meant that the margins that formerly separated the pavement from the patrons had become increasingly vague. The recent changes to smoking regulations also pushed the patrons onto the public thoroughfare. Because of these blurred edges I didn't immediately understand that we were on licensed premises until Clive pushed a large and cold foaming glass container into my hand. Tracey and Anne were slicing through the throng to colonise a suddenly vacated table by the wall. We all became ensconced and bowed our heads to our libations.

Clive was first to re-surface. The contents of his glass had all but disappeared. He dragged his hand across the back of his mouth and belched deeply. Tracey and Anne followed suit. This behaviour was sadly typical of Tracey; Anne surprised me. A school teacher, a primary school teacher, thirty something, trim to the point of sporty, neatly attired in a sensible jacket and sturdy shoes she banged her glass on the table and slung her jacket across the back of the chair, revealing as she did so, a vast amount of décolletage. Tracey was fulsome in her praise.

'Oooooh, Anne, that's right nice. You get it in Matalan?'

Clive leaned across to me.

'It's like two bald men struggling to climb out of her blouse. Got your camera handy? I want to see them puppies when they escape. Same again, ladies?'

He chuckled and headed off to the bar.

I realised the 'ladies' were looking at me and my still untouched beverage.

Anne indicated the glass.

'You not fond of lager then, chuck?'

Tracey embellished.

'Go for it Al. It's protected by the *Reinheitsgebot*.'

I looked at her.

'The Purity Law. 1516? Barley, hops, water and yeast. Only. Try some.'

I picked the glass up and put it to my mouth. The first thing I noticed was the smell. Pungent and strong. Clear. I swallowed. Good. I sucked more from the glass. Yes. It was good. I gasped and put the glass down on the table, empty.

'Kinell!'

'You needed that then, love,' said Anne.

'Just in time, I see,' said Clive, placing four more foaming measures on the table top.

Ordinarily I drink so rarely. I have a bottle of Armagnac at home in the tantalus which has lasted me five years now. I take a small measure only in extremis. I had imagined it would see out the decade. But this sudden influx of alcohol had altered my brain chemistry. I wanted my colleagues, my friends, the entire clientele, to come and taste this amazing brew.

You alright, chuck?' said Anne, leaning over to touch my leg. I could see the very depths of her cleavage.

'Never better,' I announced, and snatched up the second offering.

'That's a Dortmunder,' said Clive, breathing again after having had his mouth employed in emptying his glass.

'Nice drop too. Strong, pale, clear.'

He paused to savour the brew.

'Ahhhhhhh, yes. Nice drop. Say what you like, they can make a good beer, the Jerries. Cheers!'

'Cheers!' chorused Anne and Tracey.

'Cheers,' I suggested.

I was drunk, once, at prep school, on the eve of my departure. Cider, I recall. I was tricked into this by a chap in the junior year. A Londoner, he was, and something of a "wide boy" as they said at the time. His father was an ex-sportsman of sorts, nouveau riche and incredibly common. Lampard, was it? The boy was called Francis but beat up people who called him by that name and insisted on being addressed as Frank. I have no idea what became of him. He's probably in jail. Anyway, my parents were not amused to find me so ill the next day and my father cancelled the cheque for my final fees. That had been an humiliating experience. In my mind I could still smell the vomit on my blazer. Bu this was different. This was liberating. This was delicious.

Tracey was asking about something called the Oktoberfest.

'Oh, that's a cracking trip,' said Clive. 'A group of us from the greyhound track went there last year. Ferry to Hamburg. Two nights on the Reperbahn. Oh, yes. Smashing.'

Anne had spilled some of her beer on her black silk top and it was dribbling down into her...............

'Ooooooh, Al,' she squealed. 'There's no need to lick it up, honestly. Although I appreciate the thought. Believe me, I do.'

She dabbed at he damp spot. 'Oh, dear.'

Clive just winked at me hugely from behind his tankard. With the curve of the glass creating a lens effect his eye seemed enormous, all-seeing, panoptic.

Tracey suddenly leapt to her feet. I was vaguely aware that she might have been annoyed at my louche behaviour. I was also aware that I would much rather have performed the same service for her. The walls of the pub were by now pulsing in time to the throb of conversation that was building around us.

What's up, Trace?' said Clive.

'What's up? What's up? It's only bleedin' gone ten, innit.'

'The footie!' screeched Anne.

Clive was on his feet immediately. Pints were downed. I was dragged to my feet.

'Sup up, lad,' said Anne. 'We're going over to the Chantrey. No telly in here, is there?'

Out in the street the fresh air had a very salutary effect. I felt cleansed, renewed and thoroughly refreshed. A taxi cab swerved suddenly, its horn blaring and I felt the whoosh of air sweep past my face.

'Steady there, Al,' Clive had me in a very cosy embrace. 'No need to forget the rules, is there? Let's use the pedestrian crossing, shall we? Can't have you getting knocked down? Not till you've got a round in any road. I said, Trace, we can't have 'im getting squashed before he's been to the bar, can we?'

Tracey and Anne found this hilarious and we entered the Chantrey, arms linked, like the front row of a scrum, at least as I remembered it from rugger. The intake of oxygen notwithstanding the atmosphere in the Chantrey was very different. The clientele was very different. This pub was, I was reliably informed, a "proper boozer". I deduced that the word "proper" equated to "full of drunk people". I was also afraid that I counted among their number.

As we gathered around a tiny wooden table the football took place on a small screen bolted to the wall somewhere above our heads. This caused the conversation to become somewhat fractured, our collective attention having been pulled in several directions.

Nevertheless I realised that I had to perform my duty. I approached the bar with something like trepidation.

'Yeh?'

I should have realised that this was an invitation to place an order for beverage but I had missed my window and when Anne arrived at my side some minutes later I was indescribably grateful.

'Did that fucking cow not serve you yet?' she enquired.

'Oi, gorgeous! Cash customers over 'ere!'

I attempted to assist the enterprise by waving my bill in the air.

'Ooooooooooh, watch out. Twenty.'

She had earrings the size of soup plates looped around her ears. Her hair was blonde from a distance but on closer inspection…………….

'Oi, whachoo lookin' at then?'

'Eight bottles of Holsten, please Jools.'

Clive had rescued the situation. He winked and ushered Anne to the table.

'I'll get this, darling', he said, before leaning in to my side as Jools counted the bottles onto the bar.

'Something you ought to know, my son.'

He looked round surreptitiously as I reached for four of the bottles, copying the style of the other customers I could see at the bar.

'Yeh, a word to the wise. Trace likes football, she even likes some footballers, but what really turns her on, if you catch my drift, is people who have met footballers. Play your cards right, you could be a shoo-in. You ever met any footballers, recently then, Al. Premier only, mind. Nothing but the best for our Trace.

'Well………' I began, but a collective groan from the punters suggested that something far more important had just happened on the televised proceedings. We made it back to the table where Anne and Tracey were in a deep embrace. I was momentarily transported back to the boarding school and an image of Miss Bromley and the French assistant at a pantomime surfaced in my brain. But it transpired that the football rather than any emotional entanglement was the cause of their distress.

Anne quickly appraised us of the gravity of the sporting occasion.

'They need to score to go through. There's only ten minutes to go.'

Clive rolled his eyes and sucked at his bottle.

'Got a mate up in Newcastle. He'll be there. Season ticket holder. They pass them on, you know. Through the generations. Father to son. But you were saying, Al, about knowing footballers, yeh......'

He may have meant this as a casual aside but Tracey was upright in her chair.

'You don't, do you?'

'Well, as it happens.................'

At that moment the pub seemed to tilt, the volume to increase and the air was mottled with spilled beer and shrieks of indecipherable noise. It was only the subtitles on the screen of the television that alerted me to the cause of the madness. I admit I had no knowledge of Sparta Prague beyond its probable location in the Czech Republic but their football team now seemed to be on level terms with Newcastle Utd. with the score at 1 – 1. But it was the scorer's name that caught my eye.

I leapt to my feet and screamed at the pitch of my voice.

'That's my mate! My mate, Mark Viduka! Mark, give us a wave.'

I was now the sole centre of attention. Tracey's eyes were wide and staring. Her mouth open. Her beer lopping out of her loosely held bottle. She was apparently in some kind of soccer induced trance.

I turned to my colleagues to explain.

'It's my mate, Mark. He always gives me a wave when he scores.'

By now the attention of the entire pub was focused on the telly, but with many casting doubting glances in my direction. The camera zoomed in on an embracing knot of players in black and white. Then from the centre of the throng emerged a figure I knew. Tall, taller than the rest, more physically present, he stood out, literally head and shoulders above the rest. It seemed as if he was literally carrying the team on his back.

'Mark,' I called, and as if he had heard my call, he turned and with a gaze that bore down directly on the camera he raised his arm and cast a salute in my direction.

The pub shuddered again as a fresh wave of cheers rattled the fittings and I was slapped on the back, fed more beer and congratulated as if had personally intervened. When the final whistle signalled the end of proceedings the Holsten Pilsner flowed like lager. I was awash in bonhomie and alcohol. Tracey clung to my side. I vaguely remember leaving the pub and exchanging phone numbers and kisses and promises with Anne and Clive as they climbed into a taxi. I think Tracey and I were on the corner by HSBC when I keeled over.

'Oh, soft lad, get on yer feet, will you. I can't carry you, y'know. Not in these heels.'

Those were very definitely the last words I remember from that night. And when I woke up the next morning I realised I had been poisoned. My head had swollen to gigantic proportions. My throat constricted. My eyes were unable to focus. I forced them to see and pushed my fingers to where I knew the bedside table to be in search of my glasses. I reached for the alarm clock to confirm the hour of day but the clock was trapped in some mesh of man-made materials. With my other hand I checked to establish the presence of Teddy McJabby, my old mucker from kindergarten who had followed me everywhere. But he was gone. Panic rose in my throat. I raised the alarm clock to my face but found that it was covered in what appeared to be a pair of ladies tights. And it wasn't my alarm clock either. A figure appeared in the doorway to the bedroom. I instinctively shrank beneath the duvet. A duvet! Good God.

'Well now, it's a bit late to be playing the blushing groom, wouldn't you say? Mmmm?'

Tracey, for it was she, was by now kneeling on the bed and looming over me. Her bosoms, unfettered beneath an old T-shirt emblazoned with a character from a kids' cartoon program, swung hypnotically. There was a speech bubble coming from the bald man's face. I began to speak, to protest, to apologise, to explain but Tracey smothered my attempts and all I could muster was 'D'oh.'

After she had pleasured herself she sat back against the pillows in a very matter-of-fact attitude. Her nakedness seemed so natural. I wished for my camera. She exhaled. She spoke…

'You don't recognise me, do you? Well, not like this certainly.' And here she paused to palpate her bosom.

'Last Wednesday, ten thirty or thereabouts? A.M.'

I groaned.

'Knew it was you. Had my eye on you for a while but you never looked my way. Like you were in your own little world. Why d'you do it? Mmm. Why?'

She took my silence for consent and continued.

'Tell you what we'll do. And don't say I'm not good to you. You come down the Jobcentre tomorrow at ten and I'll have details of a job for you. No need to queue, just tell them you've got an appointment with the disability adviser. It's at a lab out on the Parkway. They need a photographer. It's micro something or other, I forget, but it's decent money and there's a strong chance that if they like you they'll make it permanent. You just turn up and give them that big smile and you'll be a shoo-in. Now I'm just jumping in the shower for a bit then I need to pop out so you take your time. Use the kitchen. You'll find stuff. Usual places. .....Oi, what's up?'

I don't think I've cried since Nan died but Tracey had reduced me to tears. She gathered me once again into her ample embonpoint and soothed my sobs.

'Come on, you'll get me started next. I'll do you some breakfast, alright. And when you get your first wage from the lab you can take me out for dinner. Yeh? Eggs alright?'

I nodded.

'Cool. Oh, and one more thing… You don't really know Mark Viduka, do you. I mean I believe you bumped into him that day but……..'

I shook my head.

'Thought not. Cos he's my brother.'

I bushed the deepest shade of crimson.

Tracey collapsed on the floor. For a moment I was afraid she'd had a seizure. But her laughter alerted me to the truth.

'Oh, you should have seen your face. Oh, that would have made a right picture.'

Then she breathed away her laughter and looked out at me from under her fringe.

'But seriously, you shouldn't pretend, you've no need. You can just be yourself. Ok. No more fibs. Try it. You'll see.'

It was approximately three weeks later and I was once again making my way across town having successfully completed my short probationary period with the laboratory. They had engaged me on a temporary contract and given me a modest stipend to cover the initial period of employment. My spirits were high as I was taking Tracey out that very evening to make good on our arrangement. She had also given me to understand that I was to consider myself "on a promise". I had only the very vaguest notion what she was talking about.

I was just contemplating calling in at the florist when a large tour bus pulled in to the space before the Town Hall. Banners advertised "British Sport Week" and "Fitness for All", as government and media came together in a shameless message to the voters ahead of anther round of local elections. The population was being bullied, cajoled and otherwise persuaded that exercise was beneficial. There was apparently some further tie-in with the Olympic bid and this was part of the interminable PR process. Television crews were in place. Lighting rigs had been set up and some familiar faces from regional news programs were chatting by the steps.

A small crowd was gathering and I couldn't resist the impulse to join in. The doors of the luxury coach opened with a hiss and I immediately recognised, though couldn't name, the leggy female athlete who emerged first on to the red carpet that had been hastily rolled to the kerb.

'Over here, Paula!'

The press corps were quite insistent but Ms Radcliffe strolled serenely across the Axminster smiling and waving with a look of considerably less anguish then she normally displays when about her day job. Several others followed whom I did not recognise. As I have said, sporting ephemera is not my forte. Then a man appeared who was immediately surrounded by children of school age, all eagerly thrusting autograph books in his direction. Why are these children not at school was my thought. But this was instantly replaced by recognition. He looked around and met my gaze. He hastily scribbled in a few more books then broke away from his admirers. The ushers seemed nonplussed, unsure and looked to each other for guidance. In a few strides he was before me.

'How ya doin' mate?'

'And then what did you say?' Tracey was as almost girlish in her glee. She pushed her dish of olives aside, swallowed the Frascati then reached over and grasped my lapels.

'What did you say? What did you say then? Tell me or I'll scream.'

I said, 'I'm very sorry, sir, but I think you must have mistaken me for someone else.'

'You never. You didn't…I mean…….you didn't, did you?'

I swirled the dregs of the grappa round before swallowing. I sat back and looked at Trace. She was twenty three, as it turned out. On a fast-track graduate management scheme within Job Centre Plus. And she was my girlfriend. I couldn't believe it.

'Oi, over here! What did you say? Really.'

I contemplated his offered hand and took it. His grip was ferocious.

'Mr Viduka, I'm surprised you remembered. Nice to see you again.'

'No worries, mate. But listen you don't happen know a nice little Italian restaurant round here that I could escape to later. The grub at these official ceremonies… Well, it's okay if you want to look like Paula Radcliffe, no offence, but……..'

Tracey was agog.

'So?'

'So……?'

'So what did you say? Now tell me the full story or I'll cut your balls off instead of sucking them dry.'

A couple at the next table tutted. Well, the woman tutted. The man looked round then couldn't look away.

'So I told him that if he needed to get away from the crowds and didn't want to be pestered by autograph hunters then a short taxi journey would get him to this place and that if he could arrive at approximately 10 pm then we'd be delighted to have his company, what with you being such a big fan and me being his mate, and all.....'

Tracey was suddenly downcast. She laughed, but it was an empty sound.

'But you're not his mate, though, are you? We talked about this, remember? You promised. You said.........'

Her mouth stayed open but no words came out. Her gaze drifted over my shoulder towards the recently opened door and from the small commotion among the waiters I guessed that we were about to have extra company for supper.

Chest Over Ears and Heady

by

Catherine Edmunds

The last of the geraniums shouted in dusty orange as the bus growled by, scattering yellow paper in its wake. Joan felt reckless at the sight of so much colour after a year of darkness. She wanted to pick up the strips and make paper chains to garland the square. It might be more sensible to gather them together and put them in the bin next to the bench, of course, but the bin was spewing out plastic beakers and cigarette stubs, and she didn't think there was room for anything else. She looked around for help (where was Ethan?) willing the shaven-headed steward, who extended from the wall, to turn his legs, if not his head. His white flip flops were a stark contrast to the chestnut trees – the first in the woods to embrace brown this autumn.

Ethan arrived at last in a blue waft of diesel and nicotine and Joan relaxed.

'Did you miss me?' she asked. 'I saw you stood over there by the dolphin, smoking a ciggy and watching the buses go by. Did you notice that pit-bull puppy thing pulling the lady in the smock?'

He remained in profile, not saying anything yet, though the tell-tale crinkle in the corner of his eye gave her hope. His thumb was hooked through his belt loop and he had a torn fingernail. Joan longed to take his finger in her mouth and suck it better.

Two girls sped by on scooters. One wore patent leather shoes and had a creature wrapped round her wrist. She was wider than her shoulders. How did children get so fat these days? The other was fighting a green skirt with a supercilious look. An elderly woman in a striped tee-shirt tried to discuss disability issues, but Joan couldn't listen, not when she knew Ethan would speak of carburettors and manifolds and multi-dimensional modelling, given time.

The shaven-headed steward looked vaguely in Joan's direction over the top of his shades. He was keen to talk to someone, and she felt she should listen.

‘We found a lot of things back in the days when we would rather do a piece of blue paper than stick anything to a shoe. How about this cut-away white vest? I’m trying,’ yes, very, thought Joan, ‘and it’s certainly working. Will it rain, do you think?’

Such thoughts were gently enticing. Ah, the blues, the blues, they beguile those who are prepared to wait.

The bench creaked as Ethan sat down at last. His voice had mellowed over the last year.

‘I love to stare out the windows down a narrow lane, watching for tractors between the trees.’

Joan nodded, not wanting to disturb his train of thought, as he gradually shifted into focus.

‘I’m still here,’ he continued. ‘Always will be. There never was any gentleman from Porlock. That’s an urban myth.’

‘Xanadu – du – du, ripe bananas, plums for tea?’

‘Ha! As if. Nice thought though.’

‘Corduroy trousers and long, long legs?’

‘That’s more like it. For you – always.’

Joan squirmed in anticipation. A fly, steel tined and handsome, landed on her knee beneath the Norman arches, but it didn’t scratch. She listened to the addled saxophonist’s lament and fingered a strip of yellow paper, while the steward ate a pie from Greggs and a drunkard lurched into the bench, mumbling something about movie monster-makers. He strode on, sploshing his beer, and fell against the iron railings, but Joan didn’t have time to nest on anybody’s motorbike – not today. She would move on if Ethan did, but not otherwise, not when she was chest over ears and heady with exhilaration.

A tall young man with a pink carrier bag, one trouser leg slightly longer than the other, sat down on the bench. Joan tried to explain that the seat was taken, but the wording on his tee-shirt ran with sorrow, so she relented.

‘What’s that?’ she asked. It looked like a small pouch of sawdust. The man had very large teeth and cuddled the pouch protectively. A flock of pigeons circled overhead. One feather fell. A boy dressed like Pooh Bear passed by, picked it up and carried it upside-down. His shoulders hunched and his face bent in on itself.

Joan heard the roar of distant buses and saw a vaguely familiar face, but the wrong 'un with the bag had left sharpish, trailing sawdust and falsehoods. She despised his soft arms and bad sunglasses, and the pretence of playing in a band.

She snuggled into Ethan and said, 'We could lie down in the back of a bus – a Sky Express.'

'Yes, I'd like that,' said Ethan, and this time the smile reached all the way to Alcyone and back. 'Very much.'

His eyes shone brown as chestnut leaves. Joan remembered the sadness of well-worn suede shoes, and a cigarette stub rolling over and over a dull yellow car.

A scowling cyclist, round-shouldered and too tall, streamed past in a rush, carrying a Vintners cutlery set. A dark lady smiled. She had a few CDs to sell afterwards, she informed everyone. Joan looked at the church clock. Seven minutes past two. Was that all? Good. Plenty of time.

Beneath the spire, the fallen graves rested uneasily, awaiting a final cadential sequence at dusk.

'Please don't ever play the piano like that,' she said, touching the mass of tattoos up Ethan's arm. She liked the way they both had broken right legs. 'Care to speculate how that happened?' she asked.

'No need to speculate. Lower branches lose their leaves first.'

'You mean the chestnuts?'

'Yes.'

'Time to cross the other leg then. The Rubicon? Lethe?'

He didn't answer, but it wasn't important. She knew.

She heard clapping in the distance.

'So, who am I this time?' she asked.

'A badly fitting boiler-suit?'

'No, silly, stop looking over my shoulder.'

Ethan laughed and a pew ran out from St Cuthbert's church, pulling a small black case to gather the sun's brightness.

Joan's shoes languished at half an inch too long. She favoured old deck chairs and measured the beats until the expected *tierce de Picardy*. The tiger on her shoulder growled, but absconded at last with the steward.

She considered hiding away in a cut-away cycle helmet to avoid the big-bellied women with sad eyes, but there was an orange aphid in her hair, cycling with discernment and too many sequins. She couldn't read the words etched on its leg, and waved it away with the back of her hand.

'Just enjoy it,' said Ethan, 'along with Lenny and his pipe.'

'No Peruvian girlfriend then?'

'No, she's too loud. Look – he's walking with two sticks in parallel motion.'

'How?'

'How string together, you mean? It's easy enough.'

'Darlington 1976, or was it '66?'

'Could be either – or even Paris, I forget – but I've seen that car before. Perhaps it's time to stop observing the others. Gain some perspective. We could always change the number plates.'

His extra arm crept inside Joan's jacket.

'Mmm… good idea,' she said. 'Will it work?'

'Try it on a Wednesday, stuffed along the bench with marmalade.'

'You dear fool.'

'And don't leave your bag unattended.'

'I won't. Ever.'

Ethan turned Joan's hat around and loved her again, quietly and always, throughout the afternoon's dying light.

A flock of pigeons settled and the clock struck six. The pew had returned with sufficient sunshine. It beckoned insistently, and Joan and Ethan drifted back under the Norman arches for another year.

My Holy Brendan

by

Siobhán O'Tierney

I probably spent more time with Brendan than with any one else in my life, ever. I knew each one of his muscles, the width of his palms, the length of each of his fingers, the arch of his back, the power and thrust of his legs. I knew every single movement he could make. And Brendan understood my body better than any of my lovers or husband ever did.

I was five years old the first time I saw him. Mama had caught the 7am train to Dublin, to visit her sister, a nun in St Theresa's Orphanage. My father was as bewildered as me when we met her at the station that evening and saw her hand attached to the hand of a scrawny, scabby, turnip-haired boy.

'Brendan's coming to live with us!' Mama beamed. Speechless, I looked to Da for reason, but he never challenged Mama. 'Hello, Brendan. Welcome,' he smiled.

'Say 'Hello' Aisling,' Mama commanded me.

'Where will he sleep?' I glowered while Brendan studied his frayed shoelaces.

Mama had been all-Ireland dancing Champion four years running before a tractor accident rendered her left leg an inch shorter. She became a dancing teacher, demonstrating every step by standing between two chairs and holding onto the backs of them. At parties she'd do the same, laughing gleefully as her legs flew like pistons beneath her. Some men are supposed to dream of siring a football team but Mama dreamed of bearing her own eight-hand line-up. One eighth of her dream was realised – me. Throughout my gestation she played records of jigs, reels, hornpipes and polkas. I was born feet first, kicking furiously to the strains of the Kilfenora Ceilidh Band. Mama insisted their tape was played, repeatedly, throughout her labour. Poor midwife.

After me there was nothing but miscarriages until eventually the doctor ordered her to stop trying. Next day Mama went to Dublin and got Brendan.

He rarely uttered a sound, not even when Mama washed and creamed and fed and nurtured him like a newborn. If he came near me I sniffed loudly. If he went anywhere near Da I screamed that my legs hurt. The cramps were real, although my growing pains only started the night Brendan moved into our house. But Mama had the patience and persistence of tides. I remember my frustration as time after time she failed to get angry with me. She never smacked me or shouted at me, nor ever missed telling me a bed-time story from Irish legends. I dreamed of Setantas and Oisins and Cuchulains – if she'd brought one of them back from Dublin I'd have welcomed him heartily.

There was only one thing Mama always refused me; a dog. We had no garden and lived over Da's hardware shop in a small flat (he spent every spare moment of Brendan's first month fixing up the loft for him) so Mama always said there was no room even as I reduced my pleas to a rabbit, then a hamster, guinea pig, even a budgie. Mama held firm, she couldn't bear to keep any animal caged.

For two years after Brendan came I stopped dancing (but practised all the steps under my blankets every night after Mama left my room). I'd won my first cup when I was four and loved being on the stage, skimming the boards, my feet flying flawlessly as my yellow hair and fabulously embroidered skirt swirled all around me. Audiences loved me and I loved them. But not enough to share a stage with Brendan, as Mama implicitly intended.

On my seventh birthday I had a party but refused to let Brendan come – he stayed in the shop helping Da. Late that night, long after Mama tucked me up, I heard faint noises by my door. Creeping out of bed, I saw a page under the door. I took it to the window and read under the streetlight; *Happy Birthday Aisling. Please come up to my room. I have a present for you. Brendan.*

The cheek! As if I'd ever go near his bedroom! How dare he! I went back to bed and crossly pulled my blankets over my head. It's a trick. He hasn't got a present. He's teasing. He doesn't even know what I like. Stupid boy. It's probably a marble or something really stupid.

Half an hour later curiosity overcame my pride. I tiptoed across the hallway to the wooden ladder that led to the loft. I could hear the TV in the living room and knew Mama would be stretched out on the sofa with her feet on Da's lap, and he would be massaging them. They wouldn't hear me.

I'm not going to say one word to him, not a single word, I vowed, climbing up the ladder.

He was sat on his bed waiting for me. I looked around, the space was bigger than I expected. Da had painted all the sloping ceilings pale blue, and got a large blue rug at Cullen's Auctions to match. Brendan bent down to get something from under his bed - a shoe-box.

'Look,' he whispered, lifting the lid a fraction. He *was* playing a trick on me, there'd be a filthy hanky in there, or a dead fish – boys at school played tricks like that all the time. Yet I understood, without acknowledging it, that Brendan wasn't like other boys. Rolling my eyes, I edged closer to the box.

'Look,' he whispered, lifting out the tail of a white mouse, which he lowered carefully onto the palm of his other hand. Small as a ping-pong ball, it had shiny pink eyes and a quivering nose.

My pulse rocketed. 'Can I hold it?' I whispered. Brendan gently placed the tiny creature into my cupped hands. It weighed nothing and its feet felt like eider-down tickling my palms. I bit my lips to smother my shrieks of laughter.

'I got it at the pet-shop today. You can keep it up here if you want.'

I understood right away what he was offering; Mama couldn't come up to the loft so the mouse could be our secret. Da might find out but Brendan must have figured, as I knew, that he'd never tell on us. Brendan, who never, ever did anything wayward, was offering to do something he knew Mama forbid outright. He was conning her for me!

I nodded vigorously. He smiled back at me and I saw how he had changed since the night he arrived. His skin was smooth and golden as a new jar of honey and his eyes were the blue of a summer sky. I sat down beside him on his bed and we watched the mouse snuffling round in my hands, laughing every time it tried to run up my pajama sleeves.

'I made a home for it.' Brendan pointed to our old coffee table at the far end of the loft. On it was a large fish tank – our neighbour had called in recently saying she wanted to get rid of it. Her husband, a tropical fish fanatic, had just been committed to St Phelim's.

I remembered Brendan asking could he have it in his room to display a model castle he was building, and remembered thinking, a fish tank to display a model castle: what an eejit!

But the tank was floored with straw and small wooden blocks and thread reels. I grinned my inexpressible gratitude at Brendan.

Next morning I announced I was thinking of dancing again.

'That's grand,' Mama smiled, no more surprised than if I'd asked for my toast to be cut into triangles instead of soldiers. She suggested I join the 8 –10 year olds. I agreed, that meant I'd be in Brendan's class.

Once I asked Mama how she chose Brendan from all the children in the orphanage. 'By his ankles,' she replied. There were nine boys in our dancing class but Brendan was far and away the best, and he was always my partner. In the thousands of hours we danced together, I never once wished he was anyone else.

Often, late at might I spent another hour or so in the loft (Ma ever found out). Brendan would lie on his bed while I sat on his floor playing with a succession of white mice (once there were six babies!) He never said much, trying to find out he was thinking was like playing 20 questions, I'd make guesses and he'd say, 'Yes' or 'No'. People often told him, 'Cheer up, it mightn't happen.' But when it was just me and him, he smiled a lot, a soft wistful smile which used to give me a glowy feeling all inside me.

Near competitions we practiced about four hours daily. Mama loved devising new routines that kept getting faster and more convoluted. Some dances were just for Brendan and me, some for four, six, eight or sixteen of us. Sometimes I imagined we'd the stage bursting into fire from the speed of our feet as we thrilled audiences. Mama mixed in flamenco, tango and ballet and we once started a sixteen hand reel by jumping two feet clear into the air, after Mama met a priest back from his mission with Maasai.

We competed all over Europe, America and Canada, and received standing ovations after sets where Brendan's body flowed and swayed seamlessly with mine. A Boston judge likened us to the two sides of a flag in the wind. For five years running we performed in different New Year spectaculars. Between us, Brendan and I accumulated 72 gold medals, 67 silver, 59 bronze, 83 plaques and 29 cups.

Mama was our manager, muse, coach, adviser, nurse. Wherever we stayed, before bed every night we all trooped to her room to recite two decades of the rosary, one for the Souls of the Faithful Departed and one for the Conversion of Russia. Then we all went back to our rooms, exhausted, and slept like the dead.

But the summer I was nineteen, Mama had to stay at home for an operation that couldn't be deferred any longer. It was the first time we ever left the country without her, but her spirit shadowed us so much that we behaved exactly as always, including the nightly rosaries. I'd have dropped them but Brendan insisted. In New York, we won the sixteen-hand cup and 28 medals between us all. On our last night, the Harlem team invited us to their party. We often got invited to parties but Mama always declined politely.

'We'll celebrate in style when we got home,' she'd promise us, and we always did.

But I told the Harlem dancer; 'We'd love to come!'

Everyone looked delighted except Brendan. 'Aisling,' he shook his head.

'What harm will it do?'

He shook his head again.

Fifteen of us went. Brendan said he'd stay in our hotel in case Mama phoned. I was glad he thought up that excuse, if she called and neither of us was in, it would be disastrous.

I discovered what we'd been missing. Everyone was amazingly friendly, saying our team was their favourite, though maybe they all told each other that. I was thrown every time a girl asked me, 'Where's your partner? Isn't he coming?'

'You want to meet Brendan?' I asked a dozen times with undiminished disbelief. Fools. Didn't they know Brendan was mine? He belonged to my family. We found him.

When a brazen German hussy asked me 'Are you and Brendan lovers?' I glowered at her and she took that as a yes. 'Damn!' she laughed, 'He's so cute!'

I was so bewildered my evening might have been totally ruined if I hadn't so many admirers myself. Toni was of Irish, Italian, Nigerian and other unknown lineage. Looking at his copper skin, mint green eyes and black hair stirred me all up inside. But it was midnight before we got together on a sofa. Toni put his arm round me, 'This is it honey. Nobody's gonna tear us apart now.'

He's so *masterful*; I thought, and felt my bones melting. By now all my team had left but for Clare Carey, on whom Mama had asked me to keep a special eye. She was wrapped round a Kiwi, what was I to do – tap her shoulder and say, 'Clare, back off him'?

Forget it Mama, Clare was well able to look after herself.

So was I.

Inside Toni's mouth was warm, smoky and savoury, much nicer than I ever imagined French kissing could taste. Every few minutes we paused as if as surfacing from a warm sea for air, before kissing again. When his hand touched my breast, excitement somersaulted through me. This was the first night in my life I hadn't said a single prayer.

Clare Carey came over, still groping her Kiwi, and whispered, 'Aisling, we're off now. See you at breakfast?'

'Fine.' I gulped. *Mama will kill me.* My next thought*; so what!*

Toni nibbled my ear, 'Fancy coffee chez moi?'

I never did get the coffee. He led me straight to his bed and undressed me with extravagant endearments. He was bossy, gentle, dramatic and romantic – so exactly like a Hollywood star, I surrendered totally and was thrilled, thrilled again, and more thrilled.

Next morning I woke up to see Toni leaping from the bed, 'Gotta go. Sorry about this, Honey. Hate to leave you but they'll sack me for sure if I'm late one more time. You'll find your way back? It's easy, just turn left and keep walking. Remember your hotel name?'

All the time he was pulling on jeans, shirt, socks and shoes, checking his reflection, brushing his hair. At the door, he looked back at me, 'You still abed? You gotta go, Honey! It's gone eight.'

'Is that it?'

'Honey! Sure that's it. Hell you don't even live round here,' he pleaded as if I'd unjustly accused him of wrongdoing.

'Sure.' I leapt up, smiling to beat the band. But now my *fabulous* body couldn't detain him a second longer.

'You'll be fine, cupcake. Pull the door after you, OK?'

Yet even my abrupt dismissal didn't dampen my satisfaction. All by myself I'd picked up a guy, lost my virginity and had a one-night stand. I had a history!

Everyone was at breakfast, including Clare Carey, so I ran upstairs to wash and change, thinking I'd say I spent the night going from party to party and never went to bed at all.

The only space left was by Brendan.

'Hiya!' But my chirpiness plummeted as he smiled at me so sadly I expected tears to fill his eyes.

'You should've come to the party! It was brilliant, wasn't it?'

I looked to Niamh and Donagh, who nodded back. Brendan look unimpressed. I wanted to have a row with him, but even though I could lie easily to anybody in the world, Mama, Da, Fr Feegan, anybody – I couldn't lie to Brendan, not with him looking at me as if all he could expect from me was grief, even though he was trying so hard to smile.

'Remember the Toronto girls – they invited me onto another party' – so far so true – 'and when I went there, all these fellahs were playing amazing jazz. And then I was invited to *another* party, just down the road and it was *really* jamming.'

Everyone laughed and said I was mad altogether. Except Brendan, whenever I glanced at him the same miserable smile was crumpling his face like a brace he forgot to take off. I wanted to tell him; 'Chill! I'm nineteen and it's 1979! Party time! Relax!'

But the sixties didn't hit Ireland till the eighties and Brendan was in shock because I had stayed out all night.

On our next trip Mama and I rowed constantly because I kept flirting with fellahs from the other teams. I'd catch Brendan watching me talk to them, his face furrowed with unhappiness. But no way was I returning to Mama's rules. She called me a brazen hussy and was horrified when I smiled, the only time I ever saw her really want to strike me. Instead she asked God where she'd gone wrong. But all Mama's disappointment and shame never bothered me, nor even Da's. Like she said, I was cockier than a peacock and talking sense to me was just putting water in a sieve. Only Brendan ever caused me qualms. Not when we danced, that never changed, the music prevailed and our bodies synchronized seamlessly – every other thought forgotten. We never spoke when we were dancing so I didn't have to think what to say to him. But when a dance ended and our bodies separated, it felt like TNT was lurking in our new silences.

I never fancied Brendan; a) I knew him too well, b) he was far, far, far too bloody holy, c) he wasn't remotely my type; tall, dark, handsome, witty, maverick (oh wasn't I original).

But it troubled me that so many girls so obviously found him so attractive.

Had he qualities I couldn't discern?

What if I continued overlooking them?

Shouldn't I have a fling with him, just in case I was missing something?

Another nagging question; did he fancy me?

If so, why didn't he do something about it? He had endless opportunities.

But maybe he didn't fancy me? *How could he not!* He knew all my charms, quirks and foibles; he should have fancied me like mad. Plenty of others did, I often reminded myself.

Sometimes I imagined Brendan confiding to me that he fancied me. Sometimes I imagined telling him that I fancied him - and he was thrilled as often as he was appalled. Sometimes these musings preoccupied me so much I was on the brink of climbing up into the loft to ask/tell him outright, and be done with it.

We had no ambition beyond dancing though. Brendan was so clever, Da wanted him to go to University, but he never wanted to leave home. When he wasn't working in our shop or dancing, he was reading. Before Harlem, I never imagined leaving home either but after that trip, I had to escape - even if it meant no more dancing.

One day Aer Lingus advertised for air-hostesses. Three weeks later I was sharing a flat in Dublin with two other girls and Mama was reciting ten decades nightly for my soul. Brendan took me to the station, and I had imagined he'd shake my hand and mutter a farewell over my head. Instead he hugged me so tightly I gasped. It was even harder than saying good-bye to Da had been. After the train pulled out I started blubbering like a baby.

But I was young and the world was my oyster. I didn't even have time to miss dancing. I loved falling in love and had a fellah in every city, nightly realizing much worse than all Mama's worst fears. Flying around the world you meet no end of tall, dark, handsome, witty mavericks.

Soon after I left, Brendan decided to go to university after all, to study anthropology. I punched the air when Mama said he just couldn't dance with Aoife Kiernan, who'd taken my place.

It took me years to discover that tall, dark, handsome, witty mavericks generally turn out to be creepy, boring, lazy, sneaky, selfish or cruel. Enzo was the most handsome and wittiest of all. We lived on his vine-yard in Tuscany and briefly, I thought I'd cracked paradise. He kept his fondness for violence secret until our baby daughter was twelve weeks old. Hearing about battered women, you think, I'd never put up with that! How could she be so stupid!

Then you find out.

The last time I saw Brendan was Christmas '81. I acted so demure I surprised myself. I often felt him watching me but could never catch his eye. I kept hoping to be alone with him for longer than five minutes – to see if we could chat like we used to, or if I could tell him about the new me that was living so freely, who felt more real than all the other selves I'd ever been (though that too turned out to be a phase). I wanted to know about the girls he met at Uni. Once he surprised us with such a hilarious joke we couldn't stop laughing for several minutes. Mama asked him where he'd heard it and he said, 'Pam, a girl in my class.'

Pam? Who the hell is she? I gulped down my wine.

Brendan did a Ph D and was always away, researching tribes with a total population of 55 or something. It was beyond us all how he ended up doing that. But I never planned not to see him. Whenever

Mama told me he'd be back, I always *intended* to visit home then. But something invariably cropped up, and years passed.

Okay – there was something else. Mama told me over the phone how Brendan came home one week-end with plane tickets already booked for my parents. Him and a Texan girl were tying the knot in Houston 'She's a very sensible girl altogether, with …'

'What does she look like?' I interrupted.

'Pretty enough, I suppose,' Mama faltered, 'A bit horsey.'

I loved her for that. But I felt like half of me had been stolen.

I was on the Rome–Dublin route then, and had been seeing Enzo for nearly a year and he'd already asked me to marry him twice. The next time he asked I said yes. Enzo's villa was perfect for a wedding and we had a brilliant day, with a ceilidh that delighted all his cronies. All of my old dancing team came over – except Brendan. He and his new wife were up the Amazon.

I fled from Enzo one bright spring morning with just Sofie, my little daughter, and one suitcase. I told him we were going to Florence for the day, instead I got a train to Rome, and from there flew to London, then caught a train to Leeds, to Susan, best friend from my Aer Lingus days. I'd been planning my escape for four years. Enzo might trace us to London but after that would be much harder.

Mama took the news like another cross to be borne. Da asked what he could do for me. There was none of the reproaching I expected. But for some years after I wouldn't look anybody in the face. Through contacts, Susan got me an admin job in a theatre. I kept well clear of the tall, dark, handsome ones, and all other men too. Sofie was grave in alarming ways. I never knew how much she'd seen or how much she remembered. But she's very beautiful; chestnut hair, peachy complexion, wide blue eyes.

I was lonely but it was nothing like the loneliness I'd known with Enzo. I longed to return home but couldn't let anybody to see how defeated I'd become – Mama's news was always about engagements, marriages, anniversaries, births and happily growing families. Also, moving back home would make it impossible to avoid Brendan and his wife when they visited and even the thought of seeing him with some woman was unbearable.

Da finally sold the shop and he and Mama moved to a bungalow in Brittas Bay. Sofie and I started spending two weeks there every summer. Da loved his garden and Mama loved reading. I used to think Mama's innocence of the world was pathetic, now I longed for it like something irreplaceable which I'd once had, and squandered. Every night they still cuddled up together on the sofa to watch TV. I'd remind myself I was a woman of the world with a job I enjoyed (theatre manager by then) and total independence. But there was always the gnawing awareness that I'd never enjoy the affection, every night, of someone who loved me, and the absence of such ineffable comfort and solace was crushing.

Every summer holiday Mama taught Sofie how to dance and waxed effusively about my glory days with Brendan. Every time Sofie asked me if she'd ever meet him I told her, 'Next summer hopefully, I not avoiding him, you know.'

Ha.

If Mama or Da ever wondered why I always missed his visits, they never asked. He lived in Texas but came home every other year with his wife and son.

In her final year at high school, Sofie decided she wanted to study History at Cork University. Mama had been planting the idea in her head for years. My infinitely conniving mother also lured Robbie, Brendan's boy, back to Cork University. On her first Christmas holidays, Sofie came back more talkative than I'd ever known her, every other sentence about Robbie – who just happened to be doing the same degree. What a coincidence.

The real shock came at Easter; 'Mum, I'm going to marry Robbie in four years. I've already proposed, and he accepted.' She grinned at my open-mouthed speechlessness; 'He's the one for me, Mum. I know he is.'

'Don't be daft Sophie. You can't *know* that. You're too young. You've got your whole life ahead of you!'

'I knew it after three hours,' she laughed exultantly.

My daughter marrying Brendan's son! That was so unfair! Then guilt assailed me – what mother would be jealous of her own daughter?

But how could I bear that wedding? How could I sit at a table with Brendan and Horseface? No! No! No! Anyway, Sofie was too young. I didn't want her marrying so young. She'd never even had a boyfriend before Robbie. To this she replied, 'Because I never before met anyone worth dating.'

Sofie was never young.

Regular work crises allowed me to keep deferring a meeting with Robbie. But eventually Sofie phoned me from Cork, and announced they were getting married on her 21st birthday, in Reykjavik, just the two of them. But there was to be a party the night before they left, at Mama's house; her new in-laws would be there, and I had to be there too!

Whatever happens, Mama always says it's the Will of God. That makes me laugh or gawp in dismay. Two months before Sophie's twenty first, Robbie's mother picked up some fatal fever in a Bolivian excursion that was meant to be her last. It was.

Now, I know fine well I'm not a nice person. Thoughts cross my mind which should never cross the minds of decent people. Upon hearing of the death of my future son-in-law's mother, I phoned Susan to discuss what I'd wear at Sophie's party. It would be my first time seeing Brendan in 25 years.

I met Susan the following day and after fours hours of searching, we miraculously found the perfect dress – raw black silk, scooped neck, knee-length skirt with side splits. Putting it on, I felt a surge of long forgotten exuberance.

The likeliest outcome – I kept warning myself – was that Brendan and I would avoid one another when possible, otherwise chat awkwardly, then he'd catch his flight home and we wouldn't meet again for another 25 years.

But if Sofie ever had a child, there'd have to be a baptism. At the very least there was that to look forward to.

Alternately I imagined Brendan and me holding hands, walking along the shore into a glorious sunset............... I'd promptly scorn myself; we'd lived more than half our lives apart, he was probably a totally different person to the one I remembered – which was maybe never the real Brendan anyway.

My legs felt skittery as a new born foal's when I stepped into Da's garden. I saw Brendan immediately, he was at the bottom of the garden, talking to Mama's cousin Nora, and was tall and lean as the last time I'd seen him. He saw me, touched Nora's hand, and came striding towards me. I hadn't expected him to hurry to me so quickly, grinning so gladly. My heart jumped into my throat.

'Aisling,' he caught me in his arms and lifted me up until our faces were level and hugged me like he'd never let go. I was laughing but started crying, big shuddering sobs. I couldn't help it. Brendan kept saying my name, and his name was all I could say. I couldn't even utter S*orry about your loss*, which I'd been rehearsing all day.

Then Sofie came over and begged us to dance together. All my excuses – I hadn't danced for years, couldn't remember anything, was totally unfit – were scoffed.

'Of course we will,' Brendan led me across the garden onto the boards Da had laid specially for the party. The moment the Walls Of Limerick finished, Brendan pulled me onto the boards and said something to the musicians.

In memory it feels like a dream, like I imagined it, only I know that how we danced together is still talked about. We started with a waltz, melting together as our bodies rediscovered one another. Then the music quickened and we were doing a foxtrot, then a polka, a mazurka, a tango. Brendan swirled me left, right, forwards, backwards and diagonally, and my feet remembered how they used to have their own life. Everything flooded back to me, how to abandon myself to his imperceptible tips and leads.

Every time the music slowed, our ever-growing audience called for more and the beat quickened again, carrying Brendan and me along with it. I remember our feet tapping, rising and swinging together, our legs and arms embracing and parting and meeting again like one brain controlled them. I felt like I was flying, floating, then flying again, sure, swift and happier than I'd been for decades as joy welled and surged and swelled up inside me.

Eventually – ten, twenty, thirty forty minutes later? I don't know – Brendan twirled me to the edge of the boards and right on through a widening gap as our audience parted and we danced onto the grass, across the garden right down to the back gate, everyone cheering and whooping like we'd just shown them a glimpse of Heaven.

Brendan lifted me and carried me down the wooden steps beyond my parents garden onto the strand below. Then he put me down beside him and took my hand, 'Let's walk.'

'Fine,' I laughed, delighted.

For some moments we walked in silence, then I drew a deep breath; 'Sorry about your loss.'

Brendan looked at me, and I looked away. He knew I couldn't lie. He put his arm round me and we kept on walking. 'Why did we never keep in touch?'

'I don't know,' I shrugged.

'Me neither.'

We started to laugh. I wanted to stop our walk and find a soft hidden spot in the dunes to lie with him. But Brendan kept on walking.

'I love you, Aisling. I always have.'

He was staring straight ahead, not looking at me, but it sounded like he meant it. I opened my mouth to say the same back but what came out was, 'Your wife then? Didn't you love her?'

'Yes. I loved Anna. She was a very good friend to me.'

What did that mean? I pulled away from him. 'So you're still missing her.'

'Yes.'

We continued walking, a gap between us now though he caught my hand and I didn't pull it away. But I was raging. What was he playing at? He loved me, he loved her – what did that mean?

'Did you ever – you know – *fancy* me?' I cried out.

He drew back like I'd hit him.

'Well?' I demanded. 'You must have!' I snapped petulantly, and then – oh, the scorching shame of it, I cried, 'How come you married her!'

'Would you marry me now?' he asked softly.

I gulped, startled. I hadn't expected that – not yet anyway.

'Or if you don't want to live with me, we could live near each other – same road or something. I'd move back here if you like, or Leeds, or anywhere.'

'This is crazy. We've never even kissed. It's all the wrong way round,' I laughed, wanting him to lighten up, he looked so earnest.

I looked at his lips, wishing he'd kiss me. Really, all I'd wanted for now was a snog, not a proposal.

Instead he nudged my back, urging me forward. 'Look how we danced together! What can beat that! It's a beautiful night. Let's keep walking.'

'Brendan!' I laughed spikily. He still hadn't said if he fancied me!

After another few strides something like lightning flashed in my head, stopping me in my tracks as I whispered hoarsely; 'Jesus, Brendan, you're not gay are you?'

He flinched. I slumped onto the sand and drew my knees up and wrapped my arms tightly round them, heedless of my beautiful dress. I stared at the crashing waves with rising panic. Beside me, I heard a sob. I'd never, never seen Brendan cry in my life, not even when, aged ten, a fall from his new bike broke his arm in three places.

'So you've never fancied me.'

I couldn't believe it, and couldn't believe how gutted I felt. A foundation stone of my ego was collapsing. All my life I must have been assuming that he did. 'You used to watch me talking to fellahs. Don't tell me. It was them you fancied. Never me?'

I remembered how trying to get something out of Brendan was like playing 20 questions. He should have cried, 'No!'

But he didn't.

He clutched his head between his elbows and knees.

'Jesus,' I said, repeatedly, and then, 'Tell me! Please, Brendan tell me, what the fuck are you?'

After a harrowing sob, he started, 'I swear to you, Aisling, I have never, ever, ever done anything homosexual.'

The next sob sounded like it was choking him but a minute later he continued, barely audibly; 'I have wanted to. But I couldn't stand the guilt. All my life, Aisling, every night I have prayed not to be what I am.'

I started shivering uncontrollably but not from cold. He touched my shoulder, 'We could be happy. We always got on great and we haven't changed. Can't we try?'

'Did Anna know you're gay?'

He recoiled like I was a viper. But then he said, 'She used to pray with me.'

I started laughing. Hysterically. Cruelly. Heart-brokenly. For the first time it struck me with the force of a door slammed in my face – I had been waiting for this man all my life. Even as I was pledging my marriage my vows to Enzo, I pictured Brendan's face. Tears burned in my eyes but I smirked, 'What, every night before ye slept together ye said ten decades of the rosary?'

He should have said, 'No.'

'And the sex was great!' I taunted, cruel as my five-year old self had ever been.

Brendan grabbed me, pinning my arms against my sides. 'Stop it, Aisling! You've no idea. Stop mocking me and don't mock Anna.'

His hands fell away from me.

I wanted to get up and walk away but my legs were numb. I thought I'd considered every possible outcome, and how to recover from it. But not this.

'Mama and her bloody rosaries!' I cried. 'All that bloody religion! She should never have adopted you!'

'No,' Brendan said vehemently, 'Don't ever say that. Anna and me *were* happy. We'd plenty of other interests we both enjoyed.'

I wanted him to go away.

'Didn't our dancing tonight mean *anything* to you? Can't you remember how happy we used to be, Aisling?'

'Is Robbie your child?'

He shook his head.

'Does Mama know?'

'Of course not,' he looked at me, and even in the moonlight I saw his face whiten.

Somehow, I stood up and started walking. My head felt like there was a cock-fight going on inside it. I wanted to hate him but he was Brendan. I wanted to get back to my hotel, rip off my dress and stand under a hot shower for a long, long time, and get next flight home. But I had to go back to the party and Sofie.

At the garden gate Brendan caught my hand. I tried to pull it back but he wouldn't let me, so we returned to the party like that, and old friends smiled and winked like they were pleased to see us joined.

Sofie and Robbie were alone on the boards, waltzing together. Everyone watching them was going 'aah'. Robbie is tall, broad and blonde, and much more handsome than in the photos I'd seen. Brendan stood beside me and watched them, his face aching with tenderness. I could hear my heart splintering.

Small Beginnings

by

Janet Swinney

When she awoke in the morning with a bumping in her brain that resembled a hangover, she was immediately aware of a creature kicking seven kinds of shite out of a date palm that was not far off. With effort, she propped herself up on one elbow.

'Hey, you!' she shouted.

The creature looked at her morosely.

'You!'

'Adam,' it volunteered grudgingly.

'Leave that tree alone, Adam. Do you think the Creatrix wants somebody vandalising handiwork she's just put the finishing touches to?'

Adam shrugged. 'Humph!' he said, and slouched off down the beach, his arms flailing awkwardly across his body for the want of pockets that were not yet available.

Eve put a hand up to her eyes to shield them against the brightness. She had a strange feeling that somehow she already knew this Adam from way back – a sense that if she were one side of the coin, then he were the other – but she couldn't quite place him. She sank back wearily on the sand and closed her eyes. In the darkness of her head, she tried to recall the Otherwhere she was sure she had been, but the sun flooding through her eyelids, turning everything blood red, rapidly dispelled this impression. Eventually, all she was aware of was the urge to get up and Get On.

After a bit, relations with Adam improved. When he was not stomping about cantankerously, he could be good fun. They lay around for ages delightedly comparing the details of their anatomies. There was, for instance, the squashed fig that nestled in the corner between his legs and his belly. They would watch in admiration as, with an extraordinary independence of spirit, it converted itself into an instrument that wagged about, sensing the environment as though it were taking readings. Eve learned that if she brushed the tip of the instrument with her lips, Adam was translated into a state of dementia in which he could be persuaded to make rash promises. If, on the other hand, Adam dabbled gently in the crevice between Eve's legs, she dissolved like a jellyfish on an incoming tide.

One morning, Eve noticed several spots of liquid spattered on her foot. Alarmed, she bent to examine herself for injury. It was the sort of substance that had sprung up from her skin when she had stabbed herself on plant-thorn. She traced ribbons of rusty stain up along her calf, and then her thighs, until she found more of the stuff welling steadily from a small, dark eyelet between her legs. The edges of this eyelet were carefully finished and neither frayed nor damaged. Mystified, and somewhat frightened, she leaned back against the bole of a tree. Perhaps she was decaying, like some of the small motionless creatures she sometimes encountered on the forest floor. Suddenly, she became aware of a grinding ache at the base of her back. The moment she noticed it, it threaded its way down the backs of her legs and began a jangling ecstasy of pain in the soles of her feet. She stayed for a long time staring wretchedly at her toes. Eventually, though, so much of the scarlet substance had seeped from her that it had blotted the surrounding leaves and she had it smudged all over herself. It was evident that she would have to get up and Get On.

Of all of this, she said nothing to Adam. She felt too depressed. In any case, he was preoccupied with a plan he had for clearing ground next to their small beachside enclave. After some experimentation with the porous fleece lining the pods of dehiscent plants, she was able to fashion something to stop her outflow trickling constantly over her legs. After a few days, she was relieved to find that the flow diminished and eventually stopped. So whatever it was, it wasn't life-threatening.

As her own cycle established itself, their way of life together evolved. Her strength lay in patience and close observation. Day by day, she ventured further into the hinterland where, for long hours, she stood watching the breeze sift through the grasses, listening to the canes rattle and noting how the tree that yesterday bore soft, effervescent blooms today had turned them into parchment spines.

After a while, she began to know the paths of the soft-muzzled beasts that crossed and re-crossed the plain between the forests, and to recognise the pug-mark of the shaggy-bellied cat where it placed it carefully in the mud. When the sun began to sap her strength, she would retreat to the edge of the forest to watch the pulsating allard slowly rotate its brazen scales, or a ragged caw-caw drift evenly around its many nests. Later on, as the air cooled, the distant mountains moved closer, their walls steeped in deepening purple, while their pinnacles and crests still blazed. When, at last, the sky showed cobalt blue, she would make her way back through the forest, where the chickerchack rattled to and fro in the topmost branches and where she might surprise a wide-eyed yambo, burrowing for slugs. On the way home one night, her eye was caught by some broad-bladed leaves shifting about strangely on the ground. Deviating from her path, she moved them aside with her foot. There, in a velvet-lined hollow in the earth, nestled a wary-looking bullifer, with six small bullifers, all in its own image. 'Cute!' she thought, and laughed.

She collected and stored, dismantled and reassembled, recorded and memorised, till she began to understand the principles of construction, of texture and form. Soon she was able to net, to weave, to paste fibres into girdles, straps, and shrouds that could be used in a hundred different ways. Gradually, by watching bird and beast, she learned what the forest and wilderness offered that could be eaten. Steadily her repertoire increased, as she acquired the knack of gathering fruits and berries from their branches at the precise moment before they ruptured or began to rot, and prising nuts and seeds from their kernels the day before they shrivelled and their taste turned to gall. Experimenting systematically, she deduced what could be mashed with what, and what to grind and how, in order to make a palatable treat.

Adam, on the other, hand, was keen on engineering. One day she found him lying on his back at the foot of a tree at the edge of a forest, next to the stream that raced past their encampment. He was watching a lokee leap up and down the trunk. She opened her mouth to speak, but he hushed her with a sign. Eventually…

'Eight spans,' he said. 'If we could get that tree down' – he turned his hand on edge and directed it towards the water – I reckon we could get across.'

Eve raised an eyebrow.

'And?'

'Explore whatever's on the other side.'

'Whatever,' she said, though personally she had never felt short of things to do on this side of the water.

So they set to, scrabbling away at the roots of the tree to weaken its hold on the ground. And eventually, when all its tender writhings were naked, Adam gave the tree a mighty shove. There was a long moment while it teetered, undecided, then, down it came with a crash, its branches bouncing on the opposite bank. It left a gap that let brash sunlight into the private part of the forest, and days later its leaves fell off. But the new arrangement served its purpose. You could cross the stream whenever you wanted, whether it was in spate or not. And there were, indeed, things to be seen and gathered on the other side that were not available nearer home.

While Eve spent much of her time on land, Adam spent much of his in water, either wading the stream with one of her nets, or diving through the salt waves and prising creatures from the ocean floor. Whatever he caught, he sampled, to see if it were edible. Some of the stuff he spat out, shouting 'Pleagh!' and rushed to swill his mouth out with fresh water. Others he recommended enthusiastically. She was having none of it. As the seasons changed, she developed her skills in climbing to the tops of the highest trees to bring down the largest fruit and nuts. These, she was willing to share with him, and he partook.

One day, waking early and suddenly, Eve felt an irresistible urge to go into the long grass behind their shelter and throw up. Her system compelled her to go through wave after wave of unproductive retching. Thereafter, for the first part of every morning, until the sun moved round as far as the headland, it was the same. Eventually, she told Adam. He was as puzzled as she was, but made hopeful noises and tried to divert her attention. At nighttime he made a point of holding her closely, with his knees tucked in behind hers. In this position, with his breath in her ear, it was possible to sink gratefully into oblivion before the next onslaught began.

Then, suddenly, she was eating as voraciously as a shaggy-bellied cat, even sinking her teeth into some of the wall-eyed vermin Adam brought home from his hunting expeditions. Her breasts weighed heavy, and were now covered with writhing blue scrawl. Her belly was beginning to swell and tauten. And as she squatted in the dark at night, marking the moon's passage, she realised that her monthly flow had not been seen for some time. In the midst of fear and unknowing, she decided that she had no alternative each day but to get up and Get On.

One morning, she was standing looking out to sea, wiping the back of her hand grimly across her sour mouth, when she noticed a dark object bobbing in the water some distance out.

'Hey, Adam!'

There was a brief stirring within their shelter, and then a conspicuous lack of movement. She bent under the awning, and knelt over her partner. 'Hey!' she shook him, 'Come and see!' His arm whipped out from among the leaves, caught her round the waist and pulled her over on top of him. As she laughed with surprise, he folded her into the crook of his body, and that was the end of getting up for a while.

Some time later, Adam emerged from their shelter yawning and scratching. He stopped in his tracks. The black object was now stationary on the foreshore where it had been deposited by the waves.

'What the..?'

'See. I told you.' Eve was irked that Adam was intrigued on his own behalf, instead of when she'd wanted him to be.

They padded across the beach, slackening their pace as they neared it.

They began to edge round what was, essentially, a box, never taking their eyes off it. Suddenly a slender shape rose up from behind it.

'Awright?'

They stopped open-mouthed. A very small face with very small eyes looked at them from the end of a very long neck. Unlike their own surface, this creature's was covered in a clever chequered pattern in glistening green, yellow and black: it had no hair.

'Vince. Vincent the Viper.' From somewhere it conjured up a tiny card which both of them stared at then ignored. 'And yous'll be?'

The two of them were speechless.

'Eve an' Adam, I bet.' Vince stretched his lips in something approaching a smile. 'I had a bit of trouble getting this ashore.' He dipped his head in the direction of the box. 'It would have been a pity to find ye werenae hame.'

The viper drew himself up and peered about. 'So, you're settling in then. What with the first time residence, and' - he indicated Eve's stomach – 'the bairn on the way.'

'The bairn?' said Eve sharply, jolted out of her silence. For the first time she was conscious of not wanting to be eyed.

'Aye, the bairn, the babbie.'

Adam held Eve's hand. They looked at the viper blankly.

'Aye, the babbie! Another hand on deck! ' The viper ducked and swayed in an effort to convey hushabye-babyness.

Suddenly Eve remembered the nest of bullifers. 'Ah!' she cried, and she explained the situation hastily to Adam. When he finally got the picture, he seized her beneath her breasts and twirled her around two or three times, so that her feet burned on the sand.

'Whoa, now!' exclaimed the viper. And he explained why this was not the thing to do.

The two of them began to feel a bit less ambivalent about their visitor. They were all beams and smiles. Until, that is, he disappeared momentarily behind the box, reappeared on the ground at its side and worked his way to the front where he raised himself to the upright position again.

'My God!' said Eve in horror. 'You've got no limbs.'

'Yer point bein'?' said the viper, a little testily.

'Nothing. No. Sorry.' said Eve, her eyes downcast.

'No offence taken. Now yous is probably wondering why I'm here.'

Adam and Eve nodded slowly.

'Well, your luck is in. I kid you not. I've got an offer for yous ye won't be able to refuse.'

'Offer?'

‘Aye, it’s a kind of once in a lifetime gift. Say no now, and it’ll never come your way again.

‘What’s the point?’ asked Adam, scraping the edge of his thumb up and down against his temple.

‘It’ll mak a world ae difference to yiz lives.’

‘What’s wrong with our lives?’ asked Eve.

The viper sighed, and wagged his head to and fro. ‘Only five minutes back ye didnae ken ye had a babbie on the way. Ye havnae even begun tae think about what that babbie might need, and how tae tak care of it. Right or wrang?’

Eve and Adam looked at each other. ‘Right,’ they said reluctantly.

‘Come wi me,’ said the viper.

He dropped to his belly, slipped between them and, with a few impressive undulations, made off rapidly in the direction of their shelter. They followed him. Within a few feet of the entrance, he stopped in his track. They stopped too. He began winding himself backwards and forwards, sometimes looking up at the fronded roof, sometimes peering into the shadowy interior. The two of them waited anxiously. At last he turned to them and sighed heavily:

‘As I thought. Looks like a butt without a ben.’

‘Pardon?’

‘Bit of a haughmagandy parlour is it?’ he allowed a lid to slip across his eye knowingly. ‘That about it?’

Adam got his meaning ‘That's about it,’ he said defensively. He felt their love-nest demeaned by that blink.

‘Well man, ye need to give the matter some thought. When the wean gets bigger, where’s it goanae sleep? When it starts tae run aroon, where’s it goanae play?’

‘What's wrong with outside?’ asked Eve.

‘Cactus thorn, red-eye spider, spotted cat!’ said the viper, drawing himself up to his full height and running ripples up and down himself to imply the full menace represented by these creatures.

Eve knew that of these things, only the red-eye spider ever presented itself in the vicinity of their home, and that neither it nor the spotted cat had ever offered them any harm. Still, she didn’t want to run the risk of anything untoward befalling the young one she was about to produce. If there were precautions to be taken, then she would take them.

'And what, might I ask, are your cooking arrangements?' the viper went on.

Adam looked at him bleakly. 'Cooking'?'

The viper turned his gaze on each of them in turn. 'Ah!' he said solemnly, 'You mean yous're still eating stuff raw.'

'What we do is just fine,' said Eve.

'Away tae fuck!' expostulated the viper. 'Fine for a couple of grown-ups with nae aspirations and their taste in their arses.' He explained that after the first few months the baby would need solids that needed to be a damn sight more interesting than mulched grass or pureed twigs, and that as responsible parents and sophisticated adults they ought to be conversant with the refinements of haut cuisine. He introduced them to the principles of cooking over a flame, or in a heated embrasure. He described the joys of braising, baking, boiling, broiling, roasting, frying, grilling, poaching, marinading, stewing, steaming. Then he moved on to sauces: bechamel, bearnaise, hollandaise, soubise, supreme, tartare, vinaigrette and sweet white wine. By the time he'd finished, the two of them were hollow-eyed with hunger.

'See, you're basically roughing it. Which is okay while it's just yous two. But for the wean, and for any future ones, you'll want the best. Right?'

Eve and Adam nodded in avid agreement.

'Then yous've got tae start thinking longer-term. Aspirations, man. Tak yer wee bothy here. As well as en suite bedrooms, ye could have an open-plan living area with dining alcove. A place with downlighters and uplighters where ye can have quality time together. Yous've made a start, nae doubt, but there's a long way tae go.'

The viper spiralled up the post that supported the roof of the shelter and inspected the way it and the branches of the roof had been lashed together.

'Your work?' he asked Adam.

'Yes.'

'Beginner's stuff,' said the viper. He spiralled to the ground again and straightened up. 'Aye, ye could benefit from a few mortice and tenon joints, some coving and a spot of tongue an' grooving.'

Adam was in two minds about whether to tell the viper where to get off. He'd been pretty proud of his handiwork and he was getting tired of the criticism, but those few technical words had an esoteric charm he couldn't resist. 'You mean there are better ways of doing this?' he asked.

'This and a lot mair besides,' said the viper. 'Just pour a bit of water on the sand, will ye.' On the damp surface that Eve made by emptying one of their drinking vessels, and using his tail as a stylus, the viper carefully drew a diagram and explained the workings of the dovetail joint. Adam was truly impressed. 'Could I do that?'

'Is the Pope a Catholic!'

'Eh?'

'I mean, aye. Wi' the right tools and a few basic techniques nae problemo. Extensions, dormer windows, the lot. Same wi' the cooking. But only if yous accept my offer.'

So saying, the viper made off down the beach again extolling the virtues of self-improvement. Adam followed, hanging on his every word. As Eve followed, she could hear the viper ask: 'What aboot making a crib? Nice pitch pine crib wiy ae bit o' fretwork roon the edges.'

Back at the box, the viper eased himself up the side, across the top and hung down the front like a hook 'Now think on,' he said, 'yous'll have one chance. Ready?'

Adam and Eve looked at each other. 'Absolutely', they said in unison.

'Awright then! Let me tell ye: what I have in this chest is all the knowledge that'll exist in the world from now until as far on in as any creature could reasonably foretell.'

Eve's jaw dropped.

'As true as I hang here. Now, just think of what ye could do with that. Not jist your own edication, but think of your wean's. Anybody whae kens how things will turn out in the future, will be able tae mak their way in the world nae bother, and to see off anyone who gets in their way.'

Eve was quick to see the potential. Her eyes narrowed. 'You think there will be people like that?'

'Bound tae be,' said the viper, neglecting to mention Eve's key role in the scenario. 'You've got to gie your own bairns the competitive edge when yous've got the chance. What do ye say, then? Will I open the box?'

'Open it! Open it!' they cried.

The viper dipped his head under the fastener at the front of the chest, and with a bit of fiddling and fuming, tried to prise it open. The other two fidgeted anxiously. At last, the viper retreated to the lid. ' Cannae manage,' he said. ' Adam, man, gie us a hon'.'

The viper dropped to the ground while Adam bent himself to the new-fangled fastening. Eventually, he got it open and threw back the lid. He and Eve looked eagerly inside.

'But,' Eve exclaimed in disappointment, 'It's just rows of blocks.'

The viper ascended the side of the chest, dropped inside and stationed himself on the contents. 'Whit are yous two like!' he declared. 'Go oan, pick one up!'

Adam pulled one of the blocks out from between its neighbours. To his surprise, it fell apart in his hands into a thousand flimsy, fluttering pieces, each of which was yet connected to the others. He juggled with it clumsily.

'It's a book,' the viper explained. 'The harder leaves go on the outside tae protect what's on the inside.'

Eve took one out and looked for herself at the wondrous structure. 'It's beautiful,' she said.

'Aye, but that's only a part of it,' said the viper. What ye've got there is the most recent edition of the *Encyclopaedia Britannica*, the *Reader's Digest Do-It-Yourself Manual* and Auguste Escoffier's *Complete Guide to the Art of Modern Cookery* – definitive authorities on all ye could ever wish to know and more besides. See,' he wagged his head along one row of the blocks. 'Here's volumes thirteen to twenty-wan of the macropaedia, and,' he tapped another row, 'here's volumes twenty-two to twenty-nine. This yin here, with the nifty little handle, is the do-it-yourself book, and the wan with the picture on the ootside, that's the cookery book.'

'I don't see it,' said Adam, seizing on the one with the handle. 'How does it work?'

'Just open it. Take your time.' The viper sat back placidly on his coils. 'Nae scale off Vincent's nose.'

After a moment, 'Ah, yes!' cried Eve. 'I've got it!' She was examining an item beginning with a letter that looked like a wave. '*Sss-Serpentes, snakes in brackets*,' she read. '*Arms and legs gone, no ears, only one functional lung, eyelids missing – a human being in such condition would be institutionalised and under constant care.*' She faltered. Then her eye fell on one of the very small drawings included to further enlighten the reader. 'Hey, that's good, isn't it?' she said, looking up brightly at the viper. 'That's a good likeness, isn't it, Adam?'

But Adam was making progress on his own account. He was flicking through page after page describing wondrous things that could be made and mended, and the arcane ways of making and mending them: grouting and tiling, flaunching a chimney, constructing a load-bearing arch. On each page meticulous illustrations highlighted key moments in specific rituals. These were interspersed by step-by-step accounts of how to carry out the necessary procedures. Adam's eyes moved hungrily from one to another. He was filled with admiration for the ownerless hands shown doing these things.

The viper let them browse for a few more moments. 'Awright then,' he said. 'Let's talk business. I tak it yous're interested?'

'Yes!' they cried, dragging themselves reluctantly away from the pages.

'Congratulations!' proclaimed the viper. 'A kent, as soon as I clapped eyes on yous, ye were a canny pair. Oh aye, there's just one condition.' Somewhere about himself, perhaps his tail, he made a click-click noise suggesting that he'd nearly forgotten.

'What? What?' asked Eve, worried that this much-prized asset might suddenly slip from within their grasp.

'Just a piffling wee thing. In fact you might call it a sort ae bonus.'

The viper dug about inside the chest and finally re-emerged with a short stick in his extended jaw. He dropped the stick at Eve's feet.

'What is it?'

'Wee present. Open it up, eat the contents, gie us the wrapper back.'

'Why?'

‘Company policy. I tak the empty wrapper away wi’ me as a receipt to show the transaction’s taken place. But I have tae see ye eat the contents.’

‘Why me?’

‘Why no?’ countered the viper.

‘I’m not sure. I’ve never had anything we haven’t prepared ourselves.’

‘Ach, ye’re makin’ an awfy fuss. Ye’ll like it, I’m sure.’

Eve picked up the stick and turned it over in her hand. Unusually, it was six-sided with something written along one side. *'Dark Chocolate Pastilles*,’ she read. ‘What do you think?’ she looked at Adam. Adam shrugged and scuffed his feet impatiently on the sand. He was desperate to get on and learn more about digging a drainage ditch.

Eve hesitated a moment then pulled open the cardboard. Inside was a silver sheath.

‘Open it!’ Commanded the viper.

It was tough. Eve burst it open with her teeth, and dark slender discs began to tumble out. She caught as many of the escapees as she could, and trapped the rest by closing finger and thumb over the tear she had made.

‘Now, try one!’ insisted the viper.

Slowly, suspiciously, Eve raised one of the discs to her mouth where she ran it across her lips. It’s smooth surface was more seductive than that of a well-worn pebble. Cautiously, she inserted the disc between her teeth. Its slenderness begged to be broken. She tried with her incisors.

‘Ow!’ she yelped.

‘Try again. Use those teeth at the side. Or suck it.’

This time she succeeded. In an instant or two, on contact with her saliva, the surface melted, and a glorious flavour enveloped her. Her tongue searched out more of its deep, vibrant warmth and was rewarded.

‘Good?’ asked Adam.

‘Mmm!’ she said. Her eyes wandered distractedly. She stuffed another disc into her mouth. This time she let it settle in one piece on her tongue, and moved it around her mouth, so that its pungency curled slowly through her sinuses to coat her brain with velvet. Now there was no stopping her. One after another, the discs disappeared. Adam watched in amazement as she crooned with pleasure. The viper looked at him sidelong. 'Ye'll thank me for this,' he said.

Eventually, reluctantly. Eve handed back the wrapper.

'Well, that'll be us, then,' said the viper. 'I'll leave you folks to enjoy your new treasure.' He rolled to the ground, and rattled off towards the sea. 'Oh, by the way,' he paused: 'There's a packet of Swan Vestas at the bottom of the chest. Ye never can tell when there might be call for them.' And with that he slid into the waves and was gone.

Their lifestyle now changed dramatically. They spent long hours poring over the books. In the encyclopaedia, Eve was particularly taken by the embrace of the letter 'C', so that was where she started. That was how she learned about culture: *Since the infant of the human species enters the world cultureless, his behaviour is powerfully influenced by the culture that surrounds him on all sides.* And how she learned about cities: *The technological developments making it possible for man to live in urban places were, at first, mainly advances in agriculture. Neolithic man's domestication of plants and animals eventually led to improved methods of cultivation and stock breeding and the proliferation of the crafts, which in turn produced a surplus and freed some of the population to work as artisans, craftsmen and service workers.*

So, it was full steam ahead for man, but what struck her was that creatures like herself seemed to have no future in history. They appeared only as adjuncts to man's great endeavours, as in: *Pre-Neolithic man leading a nomadic existence in his never-ending search for food moved largely by foot and carried his essential goods with the help of his wife and children.* Under the heading 'Christianity' she discovered that God was a tripartite being and that none of those parts was female. What cataclysm had occurred to wipe woman so comprehensively from the slate, even from the Divine presence, she wondered, but she could find no clue.

Adam, meantime, thumbed his way steadily through the book with the handle, and was not slow to act upon his researches. He made the crib. Then, growing in confidence, he moved on to construct a barbecue which, thanks to foresight of the viper in providing the Swan Vestas, he was able to have operational almost immediately. So now, in what used to be the still moment before dusk, the air reverberated with the sound of Adam blundering about in the undergrowth, trying to wrest from the forest sufficient timber to keep their barbecue aflame.

Eve now encouraged him to bring home any creature, furry or otherwise, which with a bit of surgery or manipulation could be squeezed into a pot. One of her first culinary successes was *Cotelettes d'Agneau a la Navarraise*. After this, they looked forward to an even more exotic menu.

Some weeks later, Eve's contractions began. She retired into the long grass with a jar of the coolest water, and submitted herself to a process which obliged her to writhe, wrench, heave, strain, laugh and cry until it finally terminated when a small boy-child flopped out into her shaking hands.

To their surprise, the boy-child had no interest in their endeavours. When he wasn't mewling or slavering, he simply latched on to whichever of Eve's breasts was available and clung there like a limpet.

Adam's next major enterprise was a feature fireplace. Using rocks and pebbles, he fashioned a structure which ran the entire length of their dwelling. It had an ingenious funnel at the centre which let the smoke from their fire straight out into the sky. But more than this: there were shelves for cooking pots; alcoves for ornaments; cavities convenient for leaving dishes to ferment; a slab where, on cold nights, you could sit and gently toast yourself, and, unbeknownst to Eve, a narrow crevice where Adam kept the card of Vincent the Viper.

Eve had never quite managed to banish the taste of chocolate from her mind. She had scoured the surroundings to try and discover her own independent source, but to no avail. This was all the more frustrating, as many of her recipes mentioned dribbling chocolate over pastry, or whipping it into a frenzy with double cream. She could only fantasize about the outcome. Adam, however, was somehow in the know. Whenever she was being intransigent about something, he would bring home an Alpini log. Though it couldn't rival that first glorious experience, he could still easily get round her with it, taunting her by holding it above his head, just beyond her reach. In this way, she got pregnant a second time when, actually, she felt far from ready. In this way, he persuaded her to stay at home from dawn till dusk, looking after Cain, their first-born, while he roamed the jungle. She tried everything to prise Adam's secret from him, but he just smiled smugly to himself.

One night they lay by the hearth, relaxing after a five-course meal. Eve was reading from her book; Adam was dozing, and Cain was crawling about their legs. Eve was still on C. '*Canada*,' she pronounced. '*The second largest country in the world in area, but one of the most sparsely populated*'. She flicked idly backwards and forwards for two or three pages. '*British Columbia:*' she resumed, '*The land has a diversity of climate and scenery unparalleled in the nation, from the island-studded and fiord indented coast to the great peaks of the western continental Cordilleras...*' Sounds great, doesn't it?' Adam said nothing. 'And listen to this: *The forest of the Pacific coast, where steep slopes facing rain-bearing winds produce a high rainfall, is Canada's densest tall-timber forest. Abundant moisture, along with the long growing season, is conducive to the growth of evergreens with very hard wood, excellent for construction lumber. Dense stands of immense trees, their trunks rising to considerable heights, their crowns almost touching, give a grandeur to the forest.* Blimey, eh?' Adam merely grunted, but the flame that flickered in the grate kindled something in his half-closed eyes.

Cain continued in his aversion to everything constructed especially for him. Playpens, playrooms – all stayed empty. He preferred quiet spots and solitary coves within easy reach of home. No sooner could he walk, than Adam had him fetching and carrying when he was busy with his construction ventures. Although Cain did his best, he often bodged the business by, for instance, bringing paste instead of filler, or spilling the sealant that had been under preparation for weeks. In this way, he incurred many a tongue-lashing which he bravely bore, blinking away his tears.

Round about the time Eve began to feel heavy with their second child, she became aware that there was some major project under way just within the perimeter of the forest. Adam, and sometimes Cain too, were out there until the light faded. For several weeks the hammering and chopping continued unabated, until at last she could see something with two sloping walls beginning to rise between the trees. Adam preferred to work undisturbed until he had a finished product to show, but this time she didn't even know what he was making. At last her curiosity got the better of her.

'What's that thing you're working on?' she asked one night as he entered their house, the last streaks of orange in the sky behind him.

'It's a loft,' he said gruffly.

'A 'loft'?'

He explained that it was a superstructure for a building which had many diverse uses. You could, for instance, store corn or potatoes in it, or things you no longer had a use for; you could turn it into a hobbies area, or, you could use it as a bedroom for an older child. He pointed out the advantage of the tapering walls which would conduct pouring rain straight to the ground without a drop ever touching the rest of the house.

'Hmm,' said Eve. 'Seems ideal.' At the same time she couldn't help wondering: their home was certainly not the place it had been in the days of the post and a few leafy fronds, yet how would it bear the weight of such an ambitious superstructure. Had Adam got his priorities wrong?

She was standing at the water's edge one morning, watching the foam between her toes, and wishing she could slough off the weight that made her ankles look like marrows, when the chop-chopping that had gone on in the forest behind her since breakfast time suddenly ceased. There was a pause, then two slender trees tumbled to the ground. Another pause, then suddenly the edifice began to emerge from the clearing. In front of it came Adam and Cain, hauling on thick cables. The whole thing rested on tree trunks that served as rollers. Little by little they edged it over the necklet of shells, pebbles and coarse grass that encircled the beach. Steadily they steered it down the slope of the foreshore, halting now and then, with the aid of wedges, to pull the rear rollers round to the front. She held her breath as they approached her and the thing grew bigger. Why weren't they stopping by the house?

Now that they were closer, she could see that the walls of the edifice were subtly shaped and curved in a way she had not anticipated. Her heart swelled in pride at her partner's skill. Now they were down in the tiniest waves. Cain scuttled about while Adam shouted instructions. A different set of cables was brought into play. With a thud and splash, the loft tipped over. Now the two of them put their joint weight behind it, and set to, pushing it further out. To Eve's great surprise, it sat on the swell, like a mature bird feathering its young. Adam jumped aboard, stretched out his arm and pulled Cain up after him. He now drew out from within the vessel a couple of strangely hewn poles which he dug regularly into the water with a sweeping motion. The vessel moved out to the reach where the water deepened to aquamarine and then, beyond that, to azure. Soon, it was beyond the depth at which she could swim. Adam stopped in his efforts briefly and gave her a brusque wave. Cain skipped about him. 'We're going to Canada! We're going to Canada, mummy!' he screamed excitedly, looking vaguely in her direction.

The boat and the figures on board it steadily diminished until man and the boy were no more than small black figures going jerkily about their business. The vessel now showed what she later learned to be a sail. She continued to wave her arm over her head in wide generous sweeps, even though the tears welling in her eyes had turned the glittering water into a dazzling sunburst that obliterated everything. She knew she would never see either of them again. Her heart ached for the little one, who would never be able to fend for himself under any circumstances: she had learned from careful observation that he was so presbyopic he could hardly see his hand in front of his face. At last, when there was nothing, not even a speck, left to see, she turned to go back to the house. On the sandy promontory that rose up towards their former home a clump of brazen gulatchens blared their vulgar scent towards the sea. She knew that from now on she would hate them for their insensitivity.

And so, she went about her silent abode, awaiting the birth of her second child. Basically, there was nothing left to do but Get On, to empty the grate and clean out the pots, to wind and weave wrappings for the expected newcomer. Sometimes, when scraping and scrubbing had worn her fingers so that they bore the patterns of cracked clay and caught on the fibres that she worked, she sat and read listlessly from one of the books. Out of idle curiosity, she continued the passage she had begun so long ago on the subject of *Serpentes*, snakes in brackets. *Fearless, independent and usually solitary, the snake has capitalised upon its apparent deficiencies to become an efficient second- and third-level predator, focussing perhaps 70% of its existence on tracking down, catching and digesting its living prey.*

She widened her repertoire. She ventured into the realms of the bulbous letter 'B', where she encountered *Biblical Literature* and here she began to appreciate the weakness of recorded history and the partiality of those who write it, for Eve was deemed to have sunk the whole human race in exchange for a tree fruit. She laughed bitterly, drubbing her foot against the edge of the hearth until she felt the ache of bruising. What woman would betray herself in return for a couple of pounds of Granny Smith's? Chocolate, on the other hand, that was another matter.

How Little We Know

by

Annette Keen

10.40am. First pick-up of the day. When Terry arrives in the mews they're already waiting out on the pavement, him struggling into the jacket of his city suit, flight bag at his side, her in evening dress. He yanks the door open the minute Terry pulls on the brake, whilst she clicks away down the street in her high heels, in the opposite direction. He doesn't look back, but she does. Terry sees her in his rear view mirror as she stops suddenly, puts a hand to her cheek, turns and waves frantically. His fare is already punching some numbers into his mobile, so it's a wasted gesture on her part. Then they turn the corner.

Terry swings the taxi out into the traffic and joins the stream heading towards the City. As he glances in the mirror he sees his passenger, phone to ear, checking his watch. Should have chucked her out of bed half an hour earlier, mate, Terry thinks. They'll be cutting it fine, to make the flight. He turns off the main road and onto the one-way system, running parallel at first then cutting off right, past the back entrances to shops and restaurants. Turning left at the end, he suddenly hits the brake. Ahead, the road is blocked by a delivery lorry, two cars in front of him. A van pulls up behind him, then another car, cutting off Terry's other option and boxing him in to the queue. He leans out of the window and shouts ahead.

'How long's this gonna take, mate?' he asks.

'Five minutes – less if I'm left to get on with it.'

In the back of the cab Terry's passenger swears.

A young woman appears on their right, rushing along, also in a hurry. She steps off the pavement without looking so as to cross in front of Terry, and a second later a courier motorbike flashes past. The bike just catches the woman's shoulder bag and as it tugs at it the strap breaks. The bag bounces off the cab bonnet and onto the road, where the contents spill out. Things are made even worse when a breeze starts to whoosh everything around - sheet music, papers, and photos.

One of the photos is blown up onto Terry's windscreen, and the image of the girl in the road stares in at him and he back at her, before it slithers to the ground again. She scrambles around gathering everything up, holding her long dark curls off her face with one hand as she does so. She stuffs the whole lot back into the bag then dashes off in front of Terry's cab, disappearing into a dark doorway on the left. Apollo theatre, stage door, Terry thinks absently. He's picked up there plenty of times before.

Up ahead, the lorry driver slams his door and starts up. The queue moves off.

*

April walks on stage and is handed some music. They all have to sing the same song and most of the young girls have to sight-read it because to them it's new. But April's repertoire consists of standards and she knows this one well so she doesn't need to look at the words or the notes. She puts the music down on the top of the piano and tells the pianist her key.

'Up-beat and jazzy,' she adds to him, clicking her fingers and counting in with the tempo *1,2 –1*

Down in the dim light of the auditorium, behind the footlights, the director and his assistant flick through April's CV. She's the seventeenth so far this morning and it's beginning to get tedious. They're ready for a break and a coffee but there are a lot of girls to see in this session and they have to crack on. The pianist swings into the introduction with as much jazz as he can muster at that time on a Thursday morning.

'*How little we know, how much to dis-co-ver...*' April smiles at the darkness and the two dim figures in the stalls as she settles into the song she's sung dozens of times before.

The director uncrosses his long legs, puts April's publicity photos back into their plastic wallet and shifts around in the theatre seat which is starting to feel uncomfortable.

'*How little we understand what touches off a tingle, That sudden explo-sion when two tingles intermingle...*'

'Plenty of projection for chorus,' comments the assistant. 'And she looks good.'

Up on stage, April unhooks the mike and gives the wire a little flick to uncoil it. She's confident with the song, and it shows. The director sits up.

'She's good,' he says. 'Best this morning. We could use some experience in the chorus.'

'Pity she didn't audition yesterday for the supporting roles,' says his assistant. 'And she'd make a better Clarice than Trudy James.'

'You know we need a name up front. Who's ever heard of ...' he flicks the papers over, '...of April Silver? No, unfortunately we've got to have Trudy to bring the punters in. She'll be fine with plenty of make-up and a little tweaking on the sound board.'

'But this girl would be wasted in the chorus.'

The director thinks for a moment as April sings on. Decisions have already been made on leading and supporting roles, but his assistant has a point. He fidgets a bit more.

'See if all the letters have gone out yet,' he says, finally.

'*...and the world around me shat-ters, How little it mat-ters, how little we know.*'

April reaches the end of the song with a flourish and puts the mike back on the stand. In the silence that follows the director taps his pen on the opera glasses locked in the back of the seat in front, and considers. Tap, tap, tap. Perhaps he can manoeuvre a few changes to the casting, if it's not too late. April clears her throat, and waits. The pianist turns the music back to the first page again, ready for the next one.

The director rolls a few possibilities around in his mind, then leans forward.

'Okay April. Stay behind for a while, please.'

*

Terry indicates right and turns the cab away from the slow moving traffic jam ahead of him. Taptaptap. A sudden knocking on the glass partition ensures his attention and he glances over his shoulder at the increasingly irate passenger behind him.

'Is this really helping? Once those lights change...'

Terry pulls in at the kerb and turns to face the passenger.

‘Down there...’ he says, jabbing his finger back the way they've just come, ‘is a line of traffic going nowhere fast. Now I happen to know why that is because...’ he points to the dashboard...’I've got radio contact. Do you want to know what the reason is?’

Without waiting for a reply, Terry goes on.

‘Well I'll tell you. There's a burst water main just around those traffic lights and everything that can avoid the junction is doing just that. Which is why you'll notice a number of other vehicles driving up this little road.’

The passenger looks through the side window to where a procession of cars, vans and taxis is overtaking the stationary cab.

‘Now, you can either leave me to do my job, which is to get you to City Airport in time to catch your flight, or you can get out here owing me only...’ Terry glances back at the blue figures on the clock, ‘... eight pounds forty p.’

*

‘*How lit-tle we know...* oh, sorry...can I start again?’

On stage at the Apollo the eighteenth audition of the morning is underway as the assistant director returns to the gloom of the stalls. His seat squeaks as he flips it down then groans a bit when he sits on it.

‘Letters went out by courier this morning, also Trudy's contract,’ he says.

‘Mmm...pity. Right – let her go, but make sure we keep her details on file.’

The girl on stage struggles with the middle eight of the song and the pianist does his best to keep her on track. She shifts her weight from one foot to the other, concentrating hard on the music, which flutters in her shaking hands. It's a relief when she makes it through to the end.

‘Thanks for coming, Joanne. Let's have the next please.’

There is a pause before another hopeful takes the stage and is handed the music. In the green room, fifteen would-be chorus girls wait nervously for their turn.

*

When Eddy speeds away from the Apollo he is unaware that his courier motorbike has just caused April's publicity material to scatter around in the road - and even if he had realised, his schedule is tight and he wouldn't have wanted to stop just for that. He has three deliveries to make for the Apollo - two west of the city and the third south-east. He plans to head west first, where he knows he has two collections waiting for him. Traffic is bad, but then it always is. Weaving his bike in and out of the other vehicles gives him the advantage and gets up other drivers' noses, which are two good reasons to do it. There is a third, and it has to do with ambition.

Eddy has no intention of being a dispatch rider for longer than is strictly necessary to raise the cash it will take to fulfil his dream, which comes in two parts. First, he will buy a Harley Davidson, and then he will ride it across the USA from New York to Los Angeles. He hasn't ever ridden a Harley Davidson, although he's drooled over a few, nor has he stopped to think through the logistics of the project, but he's unshakeable in his conviction that he'll achieve his goal. In the meantime, Eddy makes his deliveries as quickly as he can, because there is a bonus system in operation that favours speed and encourages the bold.

Some way back from traffic lights at a busy crossroads, he works his way along the nearside of the stationary vehicles, narrowly avoiding scraping their paintwork in the process. Traffic is crawling straight ahead across the junction and barely moving at all on the left turn, which is Eddy's route. He inches nearer the front of the queue, catching someone's wing mirror as he does so and receiving an angry blast on the horn in response. Progress is annoyingly slow and he stands up astride his bike, looking for an opening to squeeze through.

Suddenly, the leading cars creep forward a little and this produces a small gap right in front of Eddy, which he dashes through. Now on the outside of the line of traffic he can make up some of the time he has lost and he steams ahead. A large delivery lorry near the front of the queue releases its air brakes with a sigh and rolls forward just enough for Eddy to dart across in front of the next car in the line. He is now right at the junction and makes his left turn at speed, but because he lacks a taxi driver's early warning system he has no idea about the burst water main Terry was able to avoid. Suddenly, he finds himself driving through what appears to be a lake and into a fountain.

For a moment, Eddy can't see a thing. The bike skids across the road and remarkably, because everything but Eddy is travelling at a snail's pace if at all, nothing hits him. He ends up 50 yards further along the road, in the opposite gutter, still holding the handlebars but with no other part of his body in contact with the machine. A crowd of spectators gathers round him and from their ranks come people who insist he sits down on the kerbside to collect his wits. They help him out of his helmet and stand over him, until the arrival of the water company provides a more interesting diversion, and suddenly Eddy finds himself alone.

He looks around for his motorbike, but can't see it. He gets to his feet unsteadily, and it's at this moment that he spots the bike, complete with his courier-bag of undelivered mail, heading away from him and gathering speed. Anxious to keep on the right side of the law, the thief has also helped himself to Eddy's abandoned crash helmet.

*

A fading star arrives at the mews apartment with a newly topped-up suntan and her roots golden again. Trudy James unlocks the front door and starts to climb the stairs.

'Honey,' she says over her shoulder to Ray, the cab driver, 'Would you be an angel and bring my bags up?'

Ray, unimpressed with her because last week he had Madonna and child in his cab, hauls her bags out of the boot, deposits them on the pavement and glances up the narrow stairs. The fare hasn't been paid yet, so he grudgingly grabs hold of the two suitcases and slowly puffs his way up behind her.

'Hi, baby...surprise! Home already...' Trudy calls as she throws her handbag down on a sofa and moves into the hall again. As he struggles with the bags at the halfway point on the stairs, Ray sees her reading a note on the hall table, which she then slaps back down with a sigh.

Trudy wanders into the bedroom and calls over her shoulder. 'Just bring those bags right in here.'

Feeling suddenly tired after the flight, she sits down and peers at herself in the mirror. Her eyes are drawn to something unfamiliar on the dressing table top. A pair of earrings seems to leap up at her in order to get noticed. She picks one up and turns it over in her hand. A present to welcome her home? She looks more closely. No hallmark, cheap, not her style at all. The earring slips through her fingers and collides with its partner, sending it skidding across the top. She turns to look at the silk cover on the bed. Nicely smoothed - and not, she thinks, by a man's hand. And then in her waste bin she sees a small white tissue with a trace of lipstick on it. She looks at it for several seconds and it seems to grow larger under her gaze.

A wheezy sound behind makes her spin round. The taxi driver deposits her suitcases inside the room and gathers his breath to tell her the fare.

'I'd like you to put those bags back in your cab and take me straight to the airport,' is her frosty greeting to him. 'I won't be staying after all.' Her voice is quieter, but with an edge to it.

Ray would protest if he could get his breath, but in any case the moment is lost because she walks past him into the living room, and starts shrieking into her mobile phone.

'...and when the contract does arrive you can tear it into small pieces, put them in an envelope and post it to the bastard with whom I used to share this flat, with instructions to shove it where the sun don't shine...yes sweetheart, that's exactly right...'

Ray weighs up his options, in monetary terms. Then he picks up the suitcases and sets off downstairs again.

*

1.45am. Last pick up of Terry's day. When he arrives at the entrance to the jazz club there are still plenty of late night revellers milling around. He winds down the window and calls across to the large black guy on the door.

'Cab for Islington?'

While he waits, Terry looks out at the faces on the posters by the club doorway. Musicians, singers, black, white – they gaze back at him, and one is familiar.

After a few moments April comes out, calls goodbye to the doorman and climbs in the back of the taxi. She looks different tonight, more sophisticated – her long curls are pinned up and she's wearing sparkly stuff on her eyes. She looks tired, too. *You and me both*, thinks Terry. He pulls away and re-joins the traffic up on the main road. He glances back in his mirror and catches her eye.

'Did you get the part?'

'Sorry?'

'This morning, at the Apollo – you emptied your bag over the bonnet of my cab.'

April catches on after a few seconds.

'Oh, that was you? No, I didn't...I don't think I was what they were looking for.'

She fishes her mobile phone out of her bag and sees that a couple of messages have been left earlier that evening, both from the same unfamiliar number. Too tired now to bother, she switches the phone off and puts it away again.

'Their loss,' says Terry, and seeing that her eyes are already closed, puts his foot down a bit in order to get them both home as quickly as possible.

~~ The End ~~

More great fiction from Earlyworks Press....

with islands in mind

The girls sit side by side on a bench. They're made of ice for coldness. They're made of steam for shape-shifting. They're in a fish eye lens, pumped up big and stage centre. Their hair is ponytailed, stretched and polished to their skulls. Their clothing is crinkled and huge. Their legs stick out into the path like traps. If you were to walk past them you'd have to banana round them. You'd have to get ready to be not listening in case they said something, something rude, something girl-gang...

from **The Rumour of the Knife** by Jenny Adams

...Annie stood in the centre of her dome and thought about the life-choice she'd made at seven years old. If she'd wanted to be an actress or a pianist, she wouldn't be here now... the remaining original humans lived separately because of the risk of contamination. She should be grateful to be a 'retained elder'. The government kept saying her services were vital – she was one of only a few people who had such a detailed recollection of life before the Big Freeze....

from **The Memory Archivist** by Jude Higgins

Immediately she awoke Hilary could feel the comforting presence of Tildi – a sense of not being alone – someone caring about her. Snuggling under the duvet and savouring a moment of anticipation she knew today was going to be good and the familiar silvery voice confirmed: "Wake up," it said. "I've got plans for you."...

from **Invisible Persuasion** by Pam Eaves

...From the gully far below, Leila heard the dusty gurgle of the river: a man choking on his blood. Two great birds from the plains flapped across the White City, and though no attacks had happened in many years she slid under the shadow of a pillar, tightening her cloak. The birds were giant black fish against the blue stillness of the sky...

from **From The White City** by Philipa Kaori

Survival Guides

An Earlyworks Press Fiction Anthology

This book may not be of much use if you find yourself clinging to debris in mid-Atlantic but if your experience of family, work, love and loss makes you feel as if you are adrift in a storm, consider the characters in these unique and thought-provoking stories – the solutions they find include dieting, murder, a little light creative writing, and disappearing through the hole in a guitar.

Survival Guides 24 stories, 301 pages ISBN 978-0-9553429-29
£8 + £1 p&p to UK addresses

Rogue Symphonies

An Earlyworks Press Fiction Anthology

An attempted coup d'etat fails, but the day of strife is a defining one for a pair of young lovers. In another country, a film-maker stoically guards his reels as one revolution follows another. In quieter climes, a butcher faces his violent past, an author battles with an extremely lively book and a new bakery is watched over by a sapient yeast culture.

In this anthology, lovers, loners and runners forever lead the action, whether their personal stories are played out in 1st 'world War Britain or the 21sr century Middle East.

ISBN 978-0-9553429-6-1 **£6.50** + £1 p&p to UK addresses.